Happy Are Those

A Novel

Dorothy Brown Henderson

Happy Are Those

This book is a work of fiction. Names, characters, the village of Milburn Corners and incidents either are the product of the author's imagination or are used fictitiously. Any resemblance to actual persons, living or dead, events and some of the locales is coincidental. However, the communities and regions mentioned in the novel — Owen Sound, Tara, Keady, Lion's Head, the Bruce Peninsula, Manitoulin Island, Port Elgin, Lake Huron, Kincardine, Boiler Beach, Hamilton and Muskoka — are real places in Ontario, Canada. All are interesting and rewarding to visit.

Editor: Tim Faller
Design and production assistance: Tim Faller Design Inc.
Cover photo: Bonnie Sitter

ISBN 978-0-9938962-1-7

This book is dedicated to women in ministry,
but especially to the Rev. Nettie Wilson Hoffman
who formed my first memory of a minister.
When I was a child and she left our little village church for a new venture,
a male minster arrived as her replacement.
I asked my parents in surprise, "Can men be ministers?"
Nettie is thoughtful, compassionate, musical, God-centred, justice-focused
and will always be appreciated for her
positive spirit, hearty laugh, quick wit and global world view.

Thanks to the Rev. Kathy Fraser
whose real life informs the character of Regina Davis in this story.
Kathy represents the best in ministry
in a manner displayed by so many women (and men):
joie de vivre, creativity, thoughtfulness, compassion,
humour, resilience and deep faith.

Happy Are Those may be read as a stand-alone novel, but the characters and timeline grow from a previous novel, *The Season for Strawberries* (2017).

In *The Season for Strawberries,* Aleda Vastag is established as the first female pastor in Milburn Corners Community Church. She faces challenges when she adopts a cranky old horse as a pet and decides to keep it in the old stone church shed. As she becomes involved in the lives of her parishioners — some charming, some challenging — she struggles with feelings of inadequacy and questions the relevance of her ministry.

What happens when the strawberry social is threatened, and when a tragedy shakes the village to its core?

The Season for Strawberries is a heartwarming and heartbreaking tale brimming with all the joys and sorrows of real life.

True Happiness

Happy are those who know they are spiritually poor;
  the Kingdom of heaven belongs to them!
Happy are those who mourn;
  God will comfort them!
Happy are those who are humble;
  they will receive what God has promised!
Happy are those whose greatest desire is to do what God requires;
  God will satisfy them fully!
Happy are those who are merciful to others;
  God will be merciful to them!
Happy are the pure in heart;
  they will see God!
Happy are those who work for peace;
  God will call them his children!
Happy are those who are persecuted because they do what God requires;
  the Kingdom of heaven belongs to them!
Happy are you when people insult you and persecute you and tell
  all kinds of evil lies against you because you are my followers.
  Be happy and glad, for a great reward is kept for you in heaven.

Teaching of Jesus as found in Matthew 5:3-12a,
Good News Bible, Today's English Version

1

Treasures

July 2002

"Have you something to contribute, Aleda?" one of the women called out as she hurried through the church basement. "Something for the rummage sale?"

The members of the Ladies Guild were hunched over long tables, sorting through piles of donations that grew day by day — faded kitchen curtains, knitted tea cozies, silver tea sets darkened with time, flower vases, goblets and glassware, leftovers from once-cherished sets, cups without saucers and saucers without cups.

"I'll do my best," she called back over her shoulder, wondering if she could bring herself to part with anything in her house. The brown mixing bowl her mother had used for baking but that now sat idle on the top shelf in the kitchen? Her father's outdated atlas of the world, the page for Hungary dog-eared and stained? The seldom-used halter for her old horse, Tracker? I don't use those things, she thought, but it gives me comfort to know they are around me. Perhaps she would find something in her attic, a gem forgotten under the emptiness of the open rafters.

After she had climbed the dusty steep wooden steps, she noticed a cardboard box at the top of the attic stairs, untouched since she had moved in the year before. She sank into a cross-legged position in front of the box, but as she reached out to remove the cardboard lid, she suddenly wondered if mice might have chewed into the box, creating a feathery nest from stationary. She jerked back and, to protect herself from what might be inside, she tucked her hands under her blue T-shirt before flipping off the lid.

It was a useless worry. She smiled at her treasures lying in front of her. Bits and pieces of a former life. She examined a photo of herself as a child. Was she eight? Nine? Standing between her parents in front of the small house where she had grown up. What was the occasion? She couldn't remember.

She picked up a card, still in its envelope, and when she slid it out, the front shone with iridescent blue morpho butterflies, their bright wings edged with black. Opening the card, she recognized the loopy hand-writing of Margie, her long-time school friend from Hamilton.

Science Fact 101: The Blue Morpho Butterfly is so beautiful that everyone notices it. How can you not? So exquisite! But the Blue Morpho has a secret. The undersides of its wings are dull brown, providing camouflage against predators, making it look as if the Morpho is appearing and disappearing as it flies.

Life Fact 101: You are the most beautiful friend I could ever hope for and — what the hell, Aleda — this bad year will pass, and life will bring you much happiness. In the meantime, until the hurt is over, be like the Blue Morpho, appearing when you can, disappearing when things are overwhelming.

Lots of love on your 21st birthday,
Margie

Even after twenty-one years, Aleda's hand trembled as she stared at Margie's message. It *had* been an almost unbearable year. She had just completed her first year at seminary in Toronto. Her father, unable to shake off what everyone assumed was a persistent cold, was diagnosed with terminal cancer and died just days after the school term ended. It was a devastating period for her and her mother. If only, after all the years of struggling to find their way as immigrants to Canada, her parents might have reaped some peace and financial security in their older years.

But that had not been her only heartache. In her first year at seminary she had fallen passionately in love with a classmate. Ben was funny, bright, engaging and they often talked of their future life together. When Ben told her that he had also been dating another classmate and that she had become pregnant and he intended to marry her, Aleda was stunned. Shocked. Devastated.

Not much wonder Margie had written that note, Aleda thought. What a good friend she had been, listening to the outpouring of her grief and confusion through that difficult period.

She and Margie had stayed in touch over the years even though Margie had married and had children while Aleda remained single, circumstances that might have steered friends into different paths and interests. They continued to call each other weekly and it had surprised Aleda when, during their previous week's conversation, Margie had asked, "Are you happy there in Milburn Corners, Aleda?" Had Margie noticed something in her voice? Something hesitant or cautious? Something plaintive?

Happy? Margie once told her that her deepest desire for her own daughters was that they should be happy. But shouldn't life be more than that? Aleda now wondered. Happiness seemed so fleeting, so unattainable at times.

Was she happy? Thinking back over her first year as the minister of Milburn Corners Community Church, she revisited the times when parishioners had shared confidences that she could not disclose — mysterious things that baffled her and continue to confuse her still. On top of that, she had had to deal with some distressing deaths, one of them a heartbreaking teen suicide that rocked their community and still simmered under the surface. People couldn't make sense of this tragedy. To make matters worse, she didn't understand it either. If this is happiness, she thought, sighing, it is flawed and tainted.

She closed the box and stood up. Nothing here for the rummage sale. She would need to look in her kitchen cupboards. As she dusted off the back of her jeans and stretched, she suddenly realized that, on the other hand, there were many things in her life that made her content: she had loyal friends and meaningful work even though, at times, her good neighbour, Roy, had had to remind her of its significance. Surely these were some of the components of happiness!

At mid-morning, wanting to take a break from her work, she stepped out to the corner store. There was always something she needed — cream for her coffee or a fresh loaf of crusty bread. "Where *do* you find this wonderful bread?" she asked Ethel Aylmer, the storekeeper.

"Top secret," Ethel smiled. "If I told you, you might go *there* to buy your bread." It was a logic Aleda could not refute. The bread was probably less expensive at an outlet in Owen Sound, but how would she keep up with local news if she didn't patronize the village store?

Roy was working in his garden as she paused to retrieve her mail from the community box in front of his house. "Roy!" she called out, "there's something on my mind."

"What's that, Aleda?"

"This sale thing. This rummage sale. It seems such a big deal to the women." She stepped closer, then lowered her voice. "The thing is … I can't find anything to contribute and the women keep asking about it. I seem to need all my junk." To her surprise, Roy raised his head and laughed.

"What's so funny?"

"Do what I do," he said. He bent his head in close and said quietly, "I go into the second-hand store in Owen Sound and buy a box of trinkets — old lamps and mugs and cooking pots. I drop them off in the church basement and when I go to the sale, I take the empty box and fill it. I buy old towels or glassware or Christmas ornaments. Whatever will fit in my box."

"Then?"

Roy shrugged. "Simple. Next time I'm out of town I drop the stuff off at a different second-hand shop." She stared at him. "Everybody's happy," he added.

Aleda erupted in laughter. "Roy, you old rascal!" she exclaimed, then wondered if perhaps she was too impertinent with someone who was such a loyal elder in her church. But Roy laughed too, looking pleased that he had amused her. "You've given me the best idea," she said as she tucked the mail into her tote bag and turned toward home. When she had finished her hospital calls in Owen Sound that afternoon she would scout around for a second-hand store.

As she walked into the kitchen, she glanced at the clock. If she called right away, she could catch Margie at her desk before lunch.

"Aleda! So glad to hear from you? Are you all right? You don't usually call me at this time of day."

"I'm fine, Margie. Just wanted to check in with you again about the cottage. Everything still okay for you and the girls to spend a few days with me at the beach on my vacation?"

"Really looking forward to it and so are the girls." There was a pause on the phone line until Margie added, "We can only stay three days … the girls, you know … summer jobs."

"Ah yes, I understand. We'll just make the most of things. But Margie …"

"Yes?"

"About the cottage … it was really cheap to rent."

Margie laughed. "You're warning me that it's not the Taj Mahal?"

"Something like that," Aleda said, then quickly added, "but it's on a nice strip of pure sand, or so the owner told me on the phone."

2
Fire

ON THE MORNING OF THE RUMMAGE SALE, ALEDA RAN DOWN THE CHURCH BASEMENT stairs and called out, "Anything I can do to help?"

"No, it's all organized, but thanks for asking."

"We appreciate the box of donations you left," a woman said.

"Not a problem!" she replied. "Roy helped me out there. Well, if there's nothing I can do, I'll be off."

Perhaps the women thought she had some pressing pastoral duties, but what she had planned was a brisk walk into the countryside. The muscles in her shoulders had never fully relaxed in the past few weeks. I really need a vacation, she thought, as she laced up her running shoes.

Finding the card from Margie with its painful reminder of the death of her father and the devastating breakup with Ben had caused a restless night. She had tossed and turned, thinking about Margie's written message. Would happiness find her? Her mind drifted to Neil Brennan. Would he be part of the mysterious state of happiness she was trying to define? Recently, he just seemed to keep popping up in her life. Was it a coincidence?

A week ago, he had taken her to a Harbour Nights Concert in Owen Sound, but since then she had heard nothing. Why hadn't he called? Had it been a date? The beginning of a friendship? A disappointment? "It is 2002," she grumbled to herself. "Can't a woman call a man after a pleasant evening?" Did she still expect the man to take the initiative? Wasn't it awkward after so many days had passed to call and thank him for the wonderful evening? But how could she call? She knew so little about him and certainly didn't know where he lived.

Walking on the gravelled road shoulder heading out of the village, she suddenly felt hot and tired. Ahead, she knew, was a campground nestled behind a grove of Scotch pine trees. She needed some place to rest. When she spotted a tree trunk, the remains of a once majestic ash, she walked toward it, but at that moment she caught sight of the black and white police cruiser moving slowly out of the village. She inhaled sharply. It was the moment she both anticipated and dreaded.

The cruiser rolled to a stop beside her. "Constable Neil Brennan at your service, ma'am," he called through the open window of the passenger door. "Hop in," he said.

Aleda looked quickly right, then left. Surely there were rules about these things. She hesitated, then pulled open the door and slid in.

"You look like you could use a cold drink," he said, passing her a bottle of water.

"Thank you. It's much warmer than I anticipated."

"You've been okay?"

She took a deep breath, irritated again that he had not followed up after the concert.

A week ago, on the evening of the concert, the first surprise had been the car. When he arrived to pick her up, she had been waiting in the living room. Glancing out, she gasped. In the driveway behind her weather-beaten van was a red convertible. She rushed to the door, breathless.

"Ready?" he asked with a smile. He walked her to the car, his hand under her elbow as she lowered herself into the passenger seat. He pressed the door shut and after settling into the driver's side, he said, "Beauty, isn't she?"

"Um, yes. You could say that. It's just that ..." She struggled to find words. She had not considered that he would own a personal car, having only seen him drive the cruiser. Of course, he couldn't take her to a concert in a police car!

He brushed his hand across the dashboard. "Yup. V8 engine, 260 horsepower. Real fun to drive."

If she had hoped to sneak out of the village unnoticed, to spend an evening with a man, the cherry red convertible was not helping. As Neil backed out of the driveway and shifted into first gear, she felt a blush move up her neck and into her cheeks.

Roy, standing in his driveway holding a watering can, heard the car slide into second gear. "Well, I'll be," he said to no one in particular, although Grace was across the street sweeping her driveway. She leaned on her broom, her mouth open as she and Roy watched the car glide out of the village.

It was, Aleda discovered, a Mustang, though that meant nothing to her at the time. She only knew that it was a car that everyone noticed, and with the wind whipping her hair, she learned that Neil was right: it was a great deal of fun.

Now, sitting in the police cruiser at the side of the road, she wondered again if she should be there. She glanced at mysterious knobs and controls, which she assumed activated sirens and lights. When she detected a pair of handcuffs she shuddered, then stared into a seat organizer at a flashlight, radio, ticket book and what appeared to be a breathalyzer kit. She felt intimidated and uneasy, sitting in a police cruiser with a uniformed man who had a gun in his holster.

He cleared his throat. "I hope you enjoyed the concert last week." Her head swung sharply toward him. Was he toying with her?

"Yes," she said, her irritation and uncertainty rising again.

"I've been away, you see."

When she glanced back at him, he was staring at the steering wheel. "Away?"

"Ireland. I went to Ireland."

"You went to Ireland," she said, her voice flat.

"I had a call from my sister, Carrie. My mother has been sick lately — she has a congestive heart condition." He glanced over at Aleda. "Carrie thought she might not make it this time," he continued. "Mother was asking for me to come home. I got a flight out of Toronto on Sunday." He shook his head slowly. "Sunday night I was in Ireland."

Aleda took a deep breath and waited.

"There were just the three of us growing up," he continued. "My father died when I was four — a motorcycle accident — so we really had to look out for each other. My mother never quite forgave me for leaving," he said, glancing over at her.

"I can imagine that was difficult."

"Carrie and her family are there of course, but my mother always begs me to come home. For years now, she's been asking me the same two questions. 'Neilly,'" Neil shrugged, looking embarrassed, "she still calls me that … 'When are you coming home?'" He glanced across at Aleda, then turned back to stare at the dash board. "She always asks, 'Have you found yourself a nice girl yet? I want to see you settled before I pass on.'"

"Oh, I see." They sat in silence until Aleda heard him sigh. Uncertain as how to bridge the chasm that had opened between them, she said, "This is cute," touching a hand-knit emerald shamrock that hung from the passenger door.

"My friend Mary Bridgette in Ireland made it."

"Just now? When you were home?"

"Yes. The Irish, you know, we're sentimental about our shamrocks."

She felt a tightness constricting her throat and turning toward the door she said slowly, "Well, I must be going."

"Are you not wondering how I answered my mother? When she asked me those questions?"

"Well …"

"I answered her as carefully as I could. 'Mother,' I said, 'As long as I have family in Ireland I'll come back to visit, but Canada has been my home for sixteen years now.' I came over here when I was twenty," he explained to Aleda, "so I do consider Canada home now. I didn't say it quite so plainly to my mother, though. I hadn't realized that Canada feels like home until I said it to my mother." She glanced at him and nodded.

"And the second question, the one my mother always asks next …" Aleda realized that she was holding her breath, while Neil stared straight ahead. "It's just not easy to figure out."

He offered to drop her off at the parsonage, but she politely refused. Feeling confused and unsure of what had happened in their conversation, she swung her legs out of the cruiser, waved goodbye and turned away, walking quickly toward the campground as the police car pulled away and sped into the countryside.

Aleda headed toward a bench under a row of spruce trees in front of the log cabin that served as the camp convenience store. Why had she not remembered to bring money for a cold drink? She wished she had grabbed the water bottle Neil gave her, but in her discomfort, she had left it unopened in the cruiser's passenger seat.

As she passed the cabin's screen door, she heard someone call out, "Hey, Rev!" One of the teens from the village pulled back the door, smiling.

"Michael! What are you doing here? You have a summer job here?"

"Yeah. Cool, huh? It's not too shabby at all. Just have to keep the store stocked and sell stuff. After the store closes, I mow the lawn or do a few repairs here and there."

"Sounds like a great summer job! Good for you."

"Can I get you something from the store?" he asked. "An ice cream bar? Cold drink? My treat."

When he emerged with two ice-cold colas, Michael sank down on the opposite end of the bench. "Yup. A great summer job," he repeated. "Did you know that Savannah was hired as lifeguard?" he said, swinging his hand toward the pool.

"Really? I didn't know that."

"She's great with the kids," he said, shaking his head. "Real strict. Doesn't let them away with anything. But fair. She's a born leader, my mom says."

"Oh, that she is."

"Me … I don't think my dream job would include kids. They come into the store and wander around and sometimes I have to tell them not to touch things. They seem to come in a big mob," he said, tapping the heel of his running shoes in the dirt in front of the bench. "Sometimes I look down the path and say, 'Oh, give me a break. Here comes a whole troop of the little buggers.'"

Aleda laughed. Maybe his job was a little lonely at times. Still, she thought, he doesn't seem to mind hanging out with his minister who is the age of his mother.

"You'll be here all summer? No vacation?"

"Not this year. Trying to save money for university. I got another little job on the side, too."

"Really?"

"Yup. Mowing the lawn for that new lady, Connie, who's moved into the house across from the store."

"Oh, yes. I noticed that house had been sold."

"She's nice. I like her … and she sure pays well. She's pretty too, my dad says, just to make my mom mad. He says he'll gladly cut the lawn if I'm too tired." Michael laughed and they lapsed into silence.

"I love that sound," she said, pointing up to the evergreen boughs. "When I was a kid, I learned a new word while reading a book about a girl named Heidi who lived in the Swiss Alps …" But before she had time to tell Michael about the word she had learned — *soughing*, the sound of wind in the trees — they heard a sound that was neither pleasant nor soothing. It was the shrill, insistent rise and fall of a wailing siren and, in the distance, the echo of a second one.

"What's happening? What's going on?" she exclaimed to Michael, who looked equally baffled and surprised. They rushed down the campground path until they had a clear view of the main street. A fire truck, its red lights flashing, slowed down at the centre of the village, then turned and sped up the hill. Behind came another truck, followed by a water tanker.

A wailing siren came from the opposite direction and they turned to see a black and white police cruiser, its lights flashing, speed past them. They caught a glimpse of Constable Neil Brennan, but he didn't notice them standing on the campground path. His eyes were fixed straight ahead, his face focused and alert. The police car slowed as it entered the village, then ripped up over the hill.

3

Sheep

She hurried home, preoccupied with sirens and the smell of smoke which had begun to drift over the village. The fire must be nearby. Please God, keep everyone safe, she prayed as she hurried through the front door to answer the telephone.

"Aleda, we have a bit of trouble. Are you busy?"

"Not at all, Roy. What's wrong? Is it about the fire?"

"Yes, a fire at the Richardson farm. The barn has gone up in flames and Dorrie has lost all her sheep."

Aleda gasped. "What! I can't believe it! That's horrible! I saw the fire trucks earlier and wondered what was happening." She knew how much the sheep meant to Dorrie. Her first ewe and ram had been a wedding gift from her father. Dorrie grew so fond of them that she couldn't bear to think of them or their lambs being slaughtered for meat, so she began shipping their milk to make cheese.

Roy sighed. "Dorrie just seems in shock. Burt called and wondered if you could go to the farm for a bit of a visit."

"Oh yes, of course. I'll go right away." They were both silent until she blurted out, "What a terrible blow for Dorrie and Burt. What a terrible disaster for the whole community!"

After pulling into the Richardson's barnyard, she sat for a moment in her van taking in the scene, her fist pressed against her mouth and nose, overwhelmed by the devastation and smell. It seemed that the fire had started in the original old wooden frame section that housed the sheep stable and hay loft. Timber posts jutted into the air above the charred beams and the hay loft had crumpled into the centre of the building. A newer section of the barn — a domed steel frame — looked undamaged, yet darkened with smoke and stained with water. The fire trucks and water tanker, now idle, hovered close to the smouldering ruins. Neighbours were gathered nearby, their faces full of sympathy and a morbid curiosity. Neil was holding out his right arm, an indication to the people to stay back.

In spite of the horrifying scene before her, she remembered how that same strong arm, now held out in warning and protection, had lifted her to the top of a three-foot-tall cement piling after the Harbour Nights Concert.

When the last notes from the bluegrass musicians had died away and they had carried their folding lawn chairs back to the car, Neil had suggested a walk along the pier.

"The water makes me a little uneasy. So deep and black," she said. He steered them away from the sharp edge of the harbour wall and stopped in front of a massive flat concrete piling.

"This is where they dock the *Chi-Cheemaun*," he said, pointing. She stared at the piling. "The ferry that connects Manitoulin Island and the Bruce Peninsula," he explained.

"Ah, yes," she said, although she didn't know what he was talking about. He told her that chi-cheemaun was an Ojibwe word for "big canoe."

As they stood together beside the piling, he turned to her and said, "Here, Aleda. Put your left foot here." He crouched down, lacing his hands together, palms up, forming a firm platform. "Put your hands firmly on my shoulders. Hold tight," he said.

Later, she realized how amazing it had been that she followed his instructions. She hadn't hesitated for a moment. She had trusted that what he was asking of her would be both safe and exhilarating. As he stood up, she felt herself being lifted until she was on the same level as the cement piling.

"Step over," he instructed. "Take my hand."

She stepped atop the cement block looking out over the inky cold waters of Owen Sound Harbour, but when she glanced down, her legs begin to tremble. He looked up, grinning, but held her hand steadily and with his other arm he gestured toward the mouth of the harbour. "Look out," he directed. "Don't look down. Look out."

She stood gazing out into the bay. The wind tugged at her clothes as if enticing her to leave, to fly away, but how could she? His hand was holding her so firmly. As she turned toward him, she felt his hands slip around her waist and he lifted her off the piling, easing her down to the boardwalk.

• • •

Sitting now in the Richardson's barnyard staring at that strong arm held out to prevent onlookers from going too close, she realized what she found so intriguing about the man. When she was with him, she felt the thrill of being on the edge of something exciting. But he also made her feel safe. She remembered how she trusted the strong hand holding onto her. She remembered how steady he had been in the past when they faced the shocking teen suicide in Milburn Corners. Yes, she thought now, risk and steadiness, an unusual and exciting combination in a man.

She rubbed the skin between her eyebrows to ease the throb that was mounting toward a headache. Jumping from her van, she hurried toward the side door of the farmhouse and knocked. When Burt Richardson opened the door, she could see that his face was lined, dark and drawn with fatigue and discouragement.

"Come in. Dorrie will be glad to see you." He waved his arm toward the kitchen, then stepped into his boots and pressed shut the screen door, moving out into the yard.

Dorrie was sitting at the kitchen table, looking straight ahead, a cup of cold tea by her elbow. A dry-crusted sandwich curled on a plate in front of her. How different she seemed from the woman Aleda knew from church meetings, her face now drawn, her eyes staring and blank. Aleda approached the table, hesitated, then pulled out a chair and slowly sank into it. She eased her warm hand onto Dorrie's forearm and said her name softly. For a moment there was no response, but then she turned her head to Aleda.

"I'm so very sorry," Aleda said in a quiet voice, gesturing toward the barnyard.

"They were my babies, you know," she said finally, speaking slowly. "My father gave me my first pair. Dorset, they were. My father loved his sheep. He always said that Dorset were the best breeders. Good mothers. Some sheep reject their lambs after they are born, but not my Molly. She was my first."

She had been looking at Aleda, but not really seeing her. Now she turned away, gazing at the stale sandwich as if trying to understand how it had come to be set in front of her. The room was quiet except for the ticking of a clock. Aleda slid her hand down Dorrie's arm and placed it over her cold clenched fist.

They sat in silence until Dorrie said, "I couldn't bear it when the first set of twins were weaned. Everyone said you should take the lambs away from their mother when they are ten weeks old, so I did. But I couldn't stand their crying. They wanted their mother so much." She stared off across the kitchen.

"Yes," Aleda murmured. "It must have been difficult to listen to that."

"That day I said, 'Well, these are my sheep now. They don't belong to Burt. They don't belong to my father anymore. They are my sheep. I can do what I like with them, so I let the lambs back in with their mother. They ran over and started sucking. They were all so happy. I just left them together for almost six months and when Molly came into heat again the lambs were naturally weaned." She stared down into the cup of cold tea. "I couldn't stand the crying," she repeated.

Later, after she had pulled on the oversized T-shirt that she used as a nightgown, Aleda pushed down her bedroom window to shut out the acrid smoke that hovered over the village. People on Main Street had stood outside talking late into the evening. The fire had upset everyone.

As she waited for sleep to claim her, she wondered if she had been of any help or comfort whatsoever to Dorrie. I was about as comforting as that cold tea, she berated herself.

"Would you like me to pray with you, Dorrie?"

"No."

It had been that simple. She just said no.

Surely, I should have done something more, Aleda reflected. Offered to stay the night? Proposed a visit to her sister's farm? Asked if their grown children had been notified? Talked with Burt? Lying in bed, exasperated at what she thought was well-meaning but unhelpful fumbling, she stretched and put her hands behind her head, sighing. Then a familiar voice echoed through her mind. "What you give us, Aleda, is exactly what we need. We need you to remind us that hope is a firm and steady anchor for our souls."

Roy. It was the voice of Roy, her solid, compassionate neighbour, an elder in her church, a man of integrity and wisdom. When, not long ago, she had been going through a private and heart-wrenching time of doubt about the value of her ministry, it was Roy who reminded her that she gave her parishioners much needed hope for their lives.

Did I do that tonight? she demanded of herself. Did I do that for you today, Dorrie Richardson?

4

Shepherd

It seemed to Aleda that the rhythms of people's lives in Milburn Corners revolved around the rising and setting of the sun. So, in the summer, it was often early when she heard her doorbell ring. The morning after the fire was no exception. I should have known, she grumbled as she turned toward the front door, but when she saw who was there, she smiled.

"Good morning, Roy! Join me for a morning coffee?" She swept her hand toward the kitchen.

"Don't want to be a bother," he said, but she noticed that he had already moved into the front porch and stepped out of his rubber boots, a sure sign that he had something on his mind. He shuffled after her, his grey wool socks brushing across the vinyl kitchen floor.

"Please," she said, pointing to a chair at the end of the table. She reached into the cupboard for a tin, then set bran muffins on a plate. Turning to the counter, she picked up an overturned tea cup, revealing a slab of butter. "Ants," she explained. "I have to keep the butter covered. You have problems with ants this year, Roy?"

He shook his head. He sat with his hands folded and resting on the edge of the tabletop, staring at the bran muffins. "No need to bother on my behalf, Aleda. Just had a bowl of oatmeal."

She shrugged. "Bran. They're new at the corner store. Help yourself," she said, slathering butter on her muffin. "You heard that Grace is doing a bit of baking for Ethel at the store?" Aleda stuffed muffin into her mouth and chewed. Roy picked one up and cut it in half.

Even though Grace had been difficult and sharp with her, Aleda found herself rambling on, praising her baking. "She started out with butter tarts. That woman! I've never had a butter tart like that. Just the perfect amount of goo and solid." She laughed. "Now she's into bran muffins. What next? Soon it will be cherry pies with lattice crust. She has become quite the entrepreneur!"

She realized that she was talking too much, stuffing her mouth full of muffin while Roy slowly chewed. She took a sip of coffee, then ran her finger around her plate picking up crumbs. She waited. Whatever was on his mind would eventually become evident.

He set his knife diagonally across his plate and folded his hands together on the edge of the table.

"Well," he said.

"Yes?"

"Grace is a wonderful cook," he nodded. "Took some fresh muffins up to the Richardson's farm this morning ... being neighbourly, after the fire. But she was gone."

"Gone?"

"Dorrie," he continued. "Gone. Burt has no idea where she is. It was real worrisome to Grace," he said, looking down at his plate.

"Well, I can imagine!" Aleda exclaimed, feeling annoyance as she imagined the conversation that the meddlesome Grace must have had with Roy. Then, ashamed that she couldn't seem to let go of her continual resentment toward Grace, she tapped her cheek with her hand in a little chastising gesture. "What's to be done about Dorrie?" she asked.

"Not sure. Not sure what to do." He continued to stare down at his plate, but when he looked up, he said, "I figure I should git on up to Richardson's and have a talk with Burt."

"Sounds like a good idea, Roy. You want me to go with you?"

He shook his head. "Nope," he said, pushing himself away from the table. "I figure this is my business." At the front door, he pulled on his rubber boots, settled his baseball cap on his head, then turned to go, but at the last moment he turned around and said, "Cinnamon."

"Cinnamon."

He nodded. "Cinnamon and lemon peels."

She stood by the front door, her arms crossed, her eyebrows raised.

"For the ants," Roy said. "Them ants don't like cinnamon and lemon. Just sprinkle a bit around your cupboards." Turning, he started down the porch steps to climb in his car and head out to the Richardson farm.

• • •

By mid-morning she could no longer concentrate. It was time for a break. After slipping on her sandals, she strolled down Milburn Corner's Main Street to the village store. As usual, Ethel was intent on narrating the local news. Like others in the community, she was both energized and horrified by the fire. Although she already knew this, Aleda heard again that the Richardson family had lost the entire old timber frame section of the barn, their complete crop of early-cut hay and, most tragically, all forty-one of Dorrie's sheep: eighteen milking ewes, the lambs and a ram.

"Tragic, just tragic," Ethel exclaimed as she packed Aleda's groceries into a brown paper bag. "They're still trying to figure out the cause of the fire. It was either electrical or spontaneous combustion from the new hay," she said with authority.

Before she turned to go home, Aleda paused to say good morning to three old men who sat side by side on the green steel bench in front of the store. She walked past the mailboxes on the corner, past Roy's tidy perennial gardens and Grace's brick bungalow. As she wandered home she realized, with a start, that there was something that Ethel didn't know. She hadn't heard that Dorrie was missing.

After stowing away her groceries — most of them unnecessary except for the cinnamon, which she sprinkled in her cupboards — Aleda wandered to the back veranda, slipped on her rubber boots, strolled over to the door of the old stone church shed, lifted the bolt and slid it back. She scooped ground meal out of the grain bin and dumped it into the trough in front of her old pet horse, Tracker. "Good morning, merry sunshine. Did we sleep well?" she murmured to the old horse as he turned his great shaggy head toward the meal.

She had pulled her van across the grass alleyway that lay between the church and the parsonage — the only escape route from the backyard — and it was her little secret, or so she thought, that she let Tracker out into the back garden of the parsonage to enjoy a little freedom and fresh air.

"He never does any damage," she had quietly explained to Roy. "Just walks to the same spot and hangs his head over the corner of the fence, facing the swamp."

"Can't see no harm in that," Roy had mumbled. She nodded, thankful that Roy had been her advocate when she first asked permission from the church Board to keep an old horse as a pet in the church shed.

Now, brushing the mottled gray hair on Tracker's swayed back, listening to him grind the meal between his worn teeth, she wondered how long she would have him. How long did horses live? Should she call Dr. Patel and ask her to do a health check on Tracker?

Aleda shovelled manure into the wheelbarrow, spread fresh straw in the stall and then, giving Tracker a friendly slap on the rump, she said, "Out you go, old boy. Get on out there and enjoy some sunshine." But, for the first time since she had taken him in, Tracker was reluctant to leave his stall. She wondered if the old horse was not feeling well. She slapped his rump again, but Tracker wouldn't move.

In that moment, she became aware of the stench of smoke clinging to the village. She remembered hearing that horses often return to a burning barn rather than flee from a fire. Is that what had happened with Dorrie's sheep? Had they huddled together under the burning hay loft, unaware of the danger, afraid to leave? She now wondered if Dorrie and Burt had tried to chase them out of the barn but the animals kept returning, running back to what they thought was safety.

Aleda stood looking at Tracker, then shrugged her shoulders and considered that today, with the stench of the fire in the air, perhaps Tracker felt safer indoors. She left him munching on his ground oats and turned back toward the veranda.

When she had settled into her office chair, she reached for her favourite brown leather-covered Bible, but it wasn't there. She had used it Sunday. Where was it now? Perhaps she left it in the church. Sighing, she pushed her feet into sandals and reached for the heavy antique key that unlocked the wooden church door.

As she mounted the front steps, she stopped, her hand clutching the railing. When she peered closer, she could see that the door was ajar. This was most unusual. The church was always locked on weekdays. She stepped inside and tiptoed up the steps leading into the sanctuary. When she peeked around the corner, she was startled to see Dorrie, alone, perched in a centre pew.

For a moment she stood still, then moved forward, shuffling her feet to alert Dorrie to her presence. Dorrie looked up at her. "I had to come here," she said. "I couldn't stand the smell."

Aleda sank down into the pew. "I know. I understand," she murmured. She reached out a hand and lay it over Dorrie's.

"I had a key from the days when I was president of the Ladies Guild," Dorrie explained. "I shouldn't have come, but I couldn't stand the smell, you see."

"Really, Dorrie. It's fine for you to be here. In fact, it's the best place to be right now. I just wish," Aleda added, her voice taking on a wistful tone, "that more people would think to come to the church in times of trouble. This is a safe place to be. Stay as long as you like."

The two women sat together in silence until Aleda turned to Dorrie and said in a soft voice, "You must be hungry. Why don't I go back to my house and bring you a snack? You must be hungry," she repeated.

Dorrie continued to stare straight ahead and when she didn't answer, Aleda rose and walked slowly to the back of the church, then rushed down the steps and hurried into her house. She would fix a bran muffin for Dorrie, but first she had two important phone calls to make. She must contact both Burt and Roy and let them know that Dorrie had been found, safe and well, sitting peacefully in Milburn Corners Community Church.

It was only after she had made her phone calls and carried a bran muffin and a mug of hot tea across to Dorrie that she realized something important.

Both times when Aleda had entered the church, Dorrie had been staring straight ahead, looking up at the only piece of art in the sanctuary. It was a large painting in a heavy wooden frame hanging behind the choir loft. The canvas depicted a kindly loving representation of Jesus wearing a flowing white robe, his long brown curls falling onto his shoulders, his dark eyes and olive skin a contrast to the blue sky beyond. Jesus was not looking out though; he was looking down. His face shone with concern, love and tenderness as he cradled a small lamb in his arms.

5

Friends

EARLIER IN THE SPRING, ALEDA HAD STUMBLED INTO A SATISFYING FRIENDSHIP WITH two newcomers to the village, Laura and Martin. When they first met, they realized that they had some things in common. All three were relatively new to the area and, for various reasons, they were all living alone. Aleda and Laura were both single and although Martin was married, his wife lived in their home in Guelph while he spent his summers at his farm near Milburn Corners. Together, Martin, Laura and Aleda had developed a pact to eat dinner together on Friday evenings. The companionship, Aleda thought, seemed as rewarding to both of them as it was to her.

It had been difficult for Laura to return to the village where she had grown up and where her father, the local doctor, was still revered and honoured. At first, isolated and unhappy, Laura was impatient and housebound as her broken ankle healed. It hadn't been easy for Martin either, although the four summer months were a break from his work as an agricultural innovator with the University of Guelph. His farm provided him time and space for his current passion: ecological experiments with composting dead stock. It was a sad but inevitable reality of farm life, he said, that farmers sometimes lose their stock through disease or accident. Unfortunately for Martin, with the exception of the veterinarian, Dr. Patel, local people seemed to think his composting experiments were just a little crazy.

When Laura called Aleda to confirm their Friday night plans, she proposed that they invite themselves to Martin's farm for the evening. "It's upwind," she explained. Though several days had passed, the reek of the Richardsons' fire continued to cling to draperies and backyard clothes lines; the odour seemed suspended in the mist that hovered over the swamp at the north end of the village.

"Good idea," Aleda agreed. "I don't often use this word, but the best description of this air is nauseating." She sighed and heard a corresponding sigh from Laura in her home at the top of the hill.

"I'll call Martin and see if this works for him. I've picked up hamburgers and buns," Laura added.

"Why not? I suppose he has a barbeque."

After they had settled into lawn chairs in what passed for Martin's back lawn but was really a swath of open field, Aleda turned to Laura, laughing. "No need for entertainment tonight." Their eyes darted back and forth following the antics of three robust puppies, the offspring of Buddy, a dog Martin had nursed back to health after she had been injured in a hit-and-run car accident. The puppies rolled and tumbled, falling as they chased after the toys Martin flung into the long grass. Buddy, as if worn out from the demands of mothering, exhaled noisily and lay down on her side, close to Martin's chair.

"What will happen to the puppies?" Laura asked. "Have you found homes for them?"

"Working on it," Martin responded and, after watching the puppies play, he added, "I can't imagine life without this little canine family."

"But surely you can't keep them," Aleda said.

"Oh, no. I have to find homes for them, and Buddy needs to get spayed and move back across the road where she belongs with Callum. She *is* his dog, after all, and that kid is very fond of Buddy," Martin said. "The problem is, I've grown rather attached to the dog and the pups, too."

"We totally get it," Laura sympathized. All three had been involved with Callum, Roy and the village teenagers when the dog had been injured. So many people were caught up in helping the dog, it seemed as if these puppies truly belonged to the community.

After the sun had dipped behind the western cloud bank, the mosquitos arrived. The whining, blood-sucking insects made any summer social gathering around Milburn Corners a torture. After Aleda had first arrived in the community, helpful people had suggested ways to repel them. Grace told her to plant geraniums in her flower beds, as mosquitoes hate the scent of their leaves. Roy had advised planting herbs — catnip, rosemary and anise — and, before settling down in the evening, to squeeze the leaves in her hand and rub them on her neck. Others said that the only deterrent for mosquitoes was a good smoky bonfire. The problem was that this only proved effective when sitting directly in front of the fire. The question then arose: which is more annoying, smoke in the eyes or mosquitoes? Ethel Aylmer swore by her homemade remedy — a combination of lemon and eucalyptus. "Mosquitoes hate it!" she had declared, but Aleda muttered that it was not so for the giant immune mosquitoes who lived at her end of the village. It was all useless advice.

On the beautiful evening of July 5, 2002, the three friends solved the mosquito problem in the only sensible way: they moved indoors.

Aleda and Laura had been into Martin's farmhouse kitchen on only one other occasion, when he had invited them to meet Buddy's newborn pups. The women now sat at a square pine table in the centre of the kitchen, waiting as Martin grilled three burgers on an old barbeque near the back steps.

Laura leaned across the table to Aleda and whispered, "Not much wonder his wife doesn't like to come here for the summer."

The women looked around at the old cupboards, the sink with streaks of rust in the basin, an ancient refrigerator and a pot-bellied stove set up on a red-brick platform. Along one wall was a buffet cluttered with files and a rocking chair lined with a floppy cushion. The women smiled, examining a chair that Martin had repaired with bailer twine and duct tape. When he entered the kitchen holding the tray of browned burgers, he stopped and demanded, "What is so amusing to you two?"

Aleda answered in a joking voice, "Just admiring your masculine decor."

Laura laughed. "This is perfect. Perfect for you."

"Hey," he said, grinning, having taken no offense, "I call my design style 'postmodern-rural-man-doesn't-really-give-a-shit'." He set out the buns and retrieved ketchup, mustard and relish from the refrigerator. "Help yourself," he said, then added, "Oh, yes. Plates."

When they had finished their burgers, Laura announced that she had a surprise, producing a square white box. Aleda exclaimed in mock surprise, "Oh, what on earth can it be?" Laura smiled and lifted the flap to reveal three gooey, rich, maple butter tarts.

"Do you have more plates?" Laura asked, looking from Martin to the cupboard.

"What's wrong with these?" he exclaimed, glancing around the table at the three plates smeared with ketchup and mustard. He gathered the dishes and rinsed them off in the rusty sink, muttering, "Women." They laughed as he wiped the plates dry and set them back on the table.

"The only thing that would improve Grace's fresh butter tarts would be a butter tart dipped in chocolate!" Aleda quipped.

"Well, why don't we?" Martin responded, jumping up and pushing back his chair. He reached into a cupboard and pulled out a block of chocolate. Plunking the chocolate into a small pan, which seemed to reside permanently on the top of the stove, he turned on the burner. The women made a wry face to each other.

"I was just kidding, actually," Aleda said mildly.

"I wasn't!" Martin replied, turning back to the cupboard to retrieve coffee beans and an old wooden grinder.

As the coffee was dripping, he carefully lowered the top of each butter tart into the molten chocolate and set it back on a tray. "The only thing that would improve Grace's fresh butter tarts dipped in chocolate would be a large dollop of ice cream."

Both women laughed and groaned, holding their stomachs in mock horror, but neither objected when Martin produced a tub of ice cream from the freezer.

When the butter tarts and coffee were ready, Martin sat down, suddenly serious. "Laura," he said, leaning toward her. "I have a little surprise of my own. A confession, really." She tilted her head quizzically.

"You remember last month when you redecorated the Doctor's house, to make it your own?"

"Of course!" she responded. "I love it. My new fresh white living room."

"You remember that you didn't know what to do with the old furniture?"

"Of course!"

"You remember," he continued, "that Callum and his father had no furniture in their living room and dining room across the road, so we loaded up all those lovely old solid oak pieces and moved them there." He gestured with his arm toward the derelict old farmhouse that was home to the boy and his father.

"Of course, of course," she answered. "I was glad that someone wanted to take them." She hesitated for a moment, glanced over at Aleda and turned back to Martin. "What's your point?"

"My point is," he said slowly, "turns out the furniture was just a big nuisance in that house across the way. The chairs got in the way of Callum's rock collection and they like to store their potatoes and carrots in bins in the dining room, so the oak chest was just taking up way too much space." He stared down at the chocolate-coated butter tarts where the ice cream had begun to melt and pool around the edge of the pastry. "One day," he added quickly, in a hurry now to make his confession, "I was over at their farm and they had moved all those lovely old pieces of furniture out into a shed. I … well, I guess you could say that I rescued them."

Martin abruptly stood and Laura stared up at him. "Won't you two wonderful women grab a cup of my finest java and a freshly decorated butter tart and join me in my living room?"

When Laura followed him down the hall into the front room, it was as if she had stepped back into her old life. The room was full of heavy, dark, substantial old furniture; it was flooded in maroon and green, velour and plush, and on the sideboard sat the ticking china clock that Laura had known from her childhood. For a moment she was speechless, and when she turned toward Martin, she could see that a line of perspiration had formed above his upper lip.

It had been only a couple of months since Martin confessed to Laura that, as a child, he had been playing in a closet and discovered a hat box full of old love letters to his mother, Rose. He was shocked to see that they were from Dr. Browning — Laura's father — but Martin had kept this secret throughout his childhood and youth. Rose confessed to Aleda that she and Dr. Browning had been lovers when they worked together as a doctor-nurse team and that he was the father to both Martin and her other son, James. This news had been as startling to Aleda as it was to Martin. But it was a well-kept secret; Rose was determined that both her family and Dr. Browning's family would remain intact and unharmed by this liaison.

When Martin told Laura about this relationship, she, too, had been deeply shaken by the revelation and still struggled to make sense of it. How could the two families have lived within walking distance of each other in the village and this situation had not been noticed? How could she have grown up thinking that she and her brother, David, were the precious children of her father while, at the same time, he also supported Rose and her sons? And how could she bring herself to accept this entanglement when Rose had become such a good friend, offering her captivating books, intellectual stimulation, fresh cinnamon buns and, above all, the closeness and camaraderie that she had never enjoyed with her own mother?

The three friends now stood in the middle of Martin's farm living room, deep in thought. Aleda wondered if the other two were thinking about the very thing that was on her mind. Should she say, perhaps, that this was his biological father's legacy to him, a gift that might compensate, in a marginal way, for what he had missed as a youth? In the end, she didn't need to say a word.

"Martin!" Laura declared. "This is wonderful. Quite wonderful. It's like coming home, in a way. I'm so glad this furniture ended up here." Aleda glanced at Laura and noticed that her friend had never seemed more serious.

"You missed out on so much, not having much of Father's attention when you were growing up," she said. "He chose each of these pieces of furniture. They meant a great deal to him, mainly for the reason that you value them, I imagine." She trailed her hand along the side of a buffet. "They are solid, good, enduring pieces, items that will outlast all of us. They are made from the wood of this land — oak and maple and pine, but mainly good solid oak. They really seem to belong here and I'm glad that you will have them as a remembrance of ..." she hesitated, "our father. Besides," she added, smiling a little, "now I don't need to feel guilty about giving this furniture away."

Aleda noticed Martin's shoulders relax, and his grim expression dissolved into a smile.

"Sit down. Do sit down," he urged. "Let's eat. These butter tarts are melting."

Drowsy and tucked under her cool cotton sheets, the windows of the parsonage still closed to shut out the barn fire odour, Aleda sighed in contentment, but she also realized that two things about the evening troubled her.

Laura had asked, "Have you met the new woman who moved into the house across from the store?" Aleda and Martin shook their heads. "She seems nice. Friendly and upbeat. She dropped in to my house a couple of days ago and we had a great blab. Someone told her that I had recently done a little redecorating. She wants to redo her living room and seemed very impressed with my new decor." Laura's voice had risen in enthusiasm. "I was wondering if we might invite her for Friday nights, since she's new. Maybe a little younger than we are, but I think she would love an invitation."

Aleda wondered if her silence had seemed churlish; she was ashamed to admit that Laura's eagerness to include a new friend had sent a stab of jealousy through her. Perhaps it was the same for Martin, she thought. After a few seconds of silence, he answered, "Well, let's wait and see."

Another thing troubled her. Martin told them that Burt had dropped in, asking whether the sheep might be composted. "He really seemed to want my help."

"And?"

Martin shook his head. "I told him that I couldn't use my composting method with cattle or sheep because of the risk of spreading BSE — bovine spongiform encephalopathy. What the media calls 'mad cow disease.' Still," Martin continued, "it was a breakthrough that a local farmer even asked. I told Burt that I would help him assess whether the dead animals were in a state acceptable for collectors. Sadly, no. There was no option but burial, so I waited while Burt arranged for a bulldozer to come. When it is safe to remove the charred barn timbers, the bulldozer will push the dead stock into a pit for burial."

This story had deeply troubled Aleda. "Oh my," she said, horrified as she imagined the scene unfolding. Where would Dorrie be when all this was taking place?

6
Religious Differences

WHEN ALEDA WOKE ON THE 12TH OF JULY, HER FIRST THOUGHT WAS ABOUT THE summer Bible study that she needed to prepare for that evening. When her second thought was about Neil Brennan, she felt a barb of irritation creep into her foggy morning thoughts.

She was interested in him, yet their time together often left her mystified and edgy. She found herself asking, "What was that about?" It was as if there were things that should be said but were left unspoken, and the meaning of the words they *did* say to each other seemed buried or fuzzy. But she wondered again, how could she have endured the trauma of Dwayne's suicide last month without Neil's support and steadiness, a steadiness he had attributed to his strong upbringing in the Roman Catholic church?

She sat up, swung her legs over the side of the bed, plonked her feet flat on the cool floorboards and hunched over, staring at her toes. Her day had begun, whether she was ready or not.

In mid-morning, on her way home from the store, she spotted Roy at the side of his carport. "Morning, Roy," she called out. "What are you up to?"

"Not much. Just mulching around the day lilies."

Aleda knew that he not only loved his day lilies but that he roamed the countryside looking for new varieties. The choices were endless, he had explained, because day lilies were so easy to cross pollinate. He told Aleda that he chose varieties whose names tickled his fancy — Stella d'oro, Black-eyed Stella, Rosy returns. This year he had added four new varieties — Cherry cheeks, Happy returns, Lipstick and lies, and Bela Lugosi. Aleda stood beside him, examining the bottle-green blades of his new plants.

"And these ones are …?" she asked, pointing to a clump of orange blooms which he hadn't identified.

"Oh, just the ordinary common orange day lily," he responded, smoothing mulch around the base of the plants. "I keep them for the sake of our history."

"History?"

If Roy heard the question in her voice, he didn't let on. "Nope," he continued, "this here orange day lily is so common that people sometimes call them roadside or ditch lilies."

"Oh yes!" Aleda exclaimed. "I've seen lots of them growing by roadsides."

"In past times, people used to call them the outhouse lily 'cause they made a decorative trim around the old two-seater. Before the days of indoor plumbing," he chuckled.

"Is that what you meant by history?"

"Oh no, not at all. That's a completely different matter," he answered. "Day lilies bloom at different times, but this one," he said, giving the plant a stir with the blade of his shovel, "blooms on the 12th of July. You can count on that. It's always in full bloom for the glorious 12th."

"The glorious 12th?"

"Yes, you know, when the Orangemen have their parade."

She shook her head. "I'm afraid I don't have a clue what you're talking about."

"In the old days," he continued, "we had a strong Lodge here. Just about every man in the church was an Orangeman. Then they started an Orange Lodge for the ladies, too." Roy explained that, on July 12, 1690, there had been an epic battle at the Boyne River in Ireland and William, Prince of Orange, a strong supporter of Protestantism, had defeated the troops of James II who was fighting to establish Catholicism as supreme in church and state.

"Whoa!" she exclaimed. "I'm lost. Why is there a Lodge that keeps alive a war that happened centuries ago?"

Roy looked at his day lilies, his face solemn. "Oh, it's much more than that, Aleda. Folks around here thought it was a good way to keep our Protestant churches alive and strong."

"But surely, Roy," she protested, feeling a blush rise up her neck to her cheeks as she thought about her attraction to Neil, "it must have created animosity between Protestants and Catholics here in the area." She realized that this was the closest she had come to, as they said in the village, "having words" with Roy, the man who was such a wise friend, helpful neighbour and faithful church elder. She truly did not want to argue with him, but something felt quite wrong about the suggestion that tensions still existed between Protestants and Catholics and that the action of some of the villagers might even keep the old animosity alive.

"Well," he said, "can't say that it did much harm. The Catholics just moved away. Settled around Owen Sound." Roy kept his eyes on the cluster of orange petals at his feet, remembering how his grandfather, also an Orangeman, spoke with derision about the grand new St. Mary's of the Assumption church built in Owen Sound in 1870 to accommodate the growing Catholic population. Roy, himself, remembered reading in the Owen Sound *Sun Times* about a new parish centre built onto the church just six years before. These beautiful and substantial buildings symbolized a religious vitality that Roy was unwilling to acknowledge. As he stirred the mulch with his shovel, he contemplated how difficult it was — maybe even impossible — to give up his allegiance to the Orange cause, since it had shaped his own deep allegiance to the Protestant faith.

"But surely ..." Aleda exclaimed again, then stopped herself. They stared down at the green blades and fan of orange petals on the day lilies, both unwilling to continue the conversation.

There was much that Roy might have told Aleda. He might have told her about the ritual of repeating secret passwords at the entrance to the lodge meetings, the process of choosing the Grand Master, the marching in a square around the community centre and the growing excitement as they planned to travel to the location of the 12th of July parade. He chose, instead, to remind her that he was happy to make a pot of tea for Bible study that evening. After a year as minister of Milburn Corners Community Church, she knew that Roy had an undisputed reputation of being the best tea maker in the community.

She turned back toward the parsonage, her mind buzzing with Roy's information about orange day lilies and the Orange Lodge. She had not considered that a Protestant-Catholic divide had been a strong theme in the church and community that she now called home. Surely this type of religious acrimony shouldn't exist in 2002! It was only as she settled at her computer, thinking of Sunday worship, that she realized what a coincidence it had been — or was it? — that her early morning thoughts had been about Neil Brennan. She checked the calendar. Yes, it was July12th — the day of "the glorious 12th".

Pressing her hands against her closed eyes, she remembered the emerald shamrock in Neil's cruiser. The shamrock with its three leaves, she knew from legend, had been used by St. Patrick to teach the Irish people the meaning of the Trinity. Neil said that his friend in Ireland — was she a girlfriend? — had recently made it for him.

Aleda opened her eyes and stared out the window. She tried to envision a lush green shamrock with its wispy fragile white blossoms growing beside lilies with dancing fans of orange petals. These two plants seemed to represent two men who had become important in her life — Neil with his Irish heritage and solid Catholic faith, his strength and stability, his sense of adventure and willingness to take risks, and Roy who was so supportive and encouraging to her, who lived with integrity and whose many acts of kindness and comfort were a direct result of his devotion to his Protestant church. How would she ever manage without the solid, comforting and wise presence of Roy? And, of equal importance, could she ignore the growing hope that, perhaps, her future was tied to Neil's? How could these things be reconciled?

There are certain things, she mused, that are difficult about being a minister in a small village, and this is just one of them. She thought back to some of the things she had been through. By the grace of God and with Roy's help she had somehow survived the fiasco of adopting an aged horse and negotiating with the church Board for him to live in the old stone church shed. She had also survived the transition from using only the organ in worship to including a variety of instruments in the youth praise band. Luckily, she had emerged unscathed when Grace spotted her walking alone through the village at ten o'clock at night, a glass of wine in her hand. She had overcome the gossip when villagers noticed that she had befriended Laura and Martin, strangers in the community. As she gazed out the window, all these things, all these little indiscretions and adventures, seemed to have been incorporated into the rhythm of life in Milburn Corners.

But now she had to face something new. Her life seemed always to be on display. She was not only a minister in a small village, she was also a *single* female minister who was becoming interested in a police officer who was a strong and practising Roman Catholic. Would this, perhaps, be going just a little too far? Or was she silly to worry?

When she had been interviewed before becoming the minister of Milburn Community Church, Aleda was surprised to hear that the church members liked to have a July Bible study — "the summer study" they called it. It was poorly attended, they told her. People were busy with their gardens and farm work. Still, they would like her to continue the tradition for the few who could come.

As she swept down the stairs toward the church hall, her Bible and notebook under her arm, she heard subdued laughter, and when she opened the door, she was surprised to see a stranger sitting with Grace, Roy and Rose. Roy stood up and held out a chair for Aleda, then said, "Have you met Connie? She's new to the village. Grace brought her along."

Aleda smiled and reached out a hand to the woman. She was blond, pretty and something in the way she held her body suggested that she might have been a dancer or a model. "So glad to meet you, Connie," she murmured.

"Isn't it wonderful that someone new to the village showed an interest in coming to Bible study? Connie would like to join our church, too," Grace said. Aleda nodded, recognizing a barb in Grace's comments. Grace had asked her on several occasions to invite Martin and Laura to church, but Aleda had preferred to let them make their own decision on that matter.

The study started with a reading of the 23rd Psalm, a scripture that was familiar to all of them, ancient verses that still comforted and challenged. When Aleda inquired about their understanding of what it would be like to be guided by a shepherd, she became aware that Connie's soft, evenly-modulated voice was dominating. Everyone leaned forward, waiting for her next words.

"Of course, I can't talk about my work as part of the abuse unit of Bruce Grey Child and Family Services ... confidentiality, you understand ... but I would say that damaged children, most of all, need both the experience and example of someone who is a good shepherd in their lives."

"A valid point," Aleda responded, "but is it not true that all of us need the experience of having a good shepherd in our life?"

"Of course," Connie murmured. "My father was a pastor and when we were growing up — me and my three brothers — he was like a shepherd in our lives. We knew and understood our place in the family. We understood that our father was the head of the family and if we followed his leading and instruction, we would be safe. Like the sheep. I think that's part of the problem with the kids we see in our work," she continued. "They don't understand their place in the family. They have too much power and this causes the parents to respond with excessive anger. When that cycle starts, we get calls from teachers who have noticed bruising or other injuries."

"Oh my," Grace said. "How dreadful." Aleda nodded in empathy, for, much as she chaffed at Grace's challenges, she knew that Grace had a tender heart for Callum, a seemingly neglected child, who passed her house on the way to school. Had she not seen Grace pass a packet of cookies or butter tarts to the child almost every day?

"What is dreadful," Connie continued, "is that some parents do not understand how to discipline a child without using excessive force. Every child needs discipline. Believe me, when our father took us out to the woodshed, we understood clearly what we had done wrong. And after our punishment, we didn't make *that* mistake again." Connie's laughter was soft and melodious.

It took Aleda a moment to understand what Connie had just said. "You mean," she said, leaning toward Connie, "your father used to beat you?"

"Oh yes. A royal beating, but as I said, we learned from our mistakes. I seemed to have turned out okay." Connie laughed again.

Aleda inhaled and stared at the cover of her brown leather Bible. Her own parents had never once hit her or punished her physically, and the thought of adults doing that to their children horrified her. Before she could respond, Connie said softly, "You know what scripture says: 'Spare the rod and spoil the child.'"

Silence filled the spaces of the alcove in the church hall where they were gathered.

"Well …" Roy said. The women looked at him. "I don't personally know any shepherds, but I have been on the Richardson's farm often enough to see how they deal with sheep. Dorrie *does* have a staff — a rod they called it in Bible times — but she would never use it to beat her sheep. No, she wouldn't do that at all." The women waited while Roy seemed to be thinking things through. "She would use the rod to guide the sheep away from danger, away from harm."

"Ah," Aleda said. "Spare the guidance and it spoils the child." She glanced around the table and saw that everyone was nodding, everyone except Connie.

7
Jacobi Family

On the morning after the Bible study, she felt uneasy, so when the phone rang, she welcomed the distraction. "I'm wondering," he asked, his voice formal and polite, "if you might find time to help me with a tricky matter."

She met him in *Sulky Joe's* restaurant in Tara. Why is it, she wondered, that everyone stares at a police officer? Are they frightened? Curious? Even the owner, behind the counter, watched as Neil sank into the chair across from Aleda.

"Thank you so much for meeting me," Neil said. "I'm really sorry to bother you, but I have a matter that needs attention and I believe that you're the perfect person to help."

She nodded, perched stiffly on the edge of her chair. "What's going on?" she asked.

"Do you remember the family I told you about a while ago, the one that moved into the dilapidated church on the Bruce Peninsula?" Aleda nodded. "I need to follow up. I had a call from the realtor. He has some cause for concern and wondered if the children or wife need protection."

"But, why me?" Aleda responded. "Surely if children are at risk, the Child and Family Services should be involved."

"I know. But we have nothing much to go on, just a reaction from the guy who sold them the property." Neil stirred the coffee which the owner had brought to their table. "If you are willing to go with me, I believe that you might have more luck in talking with the father, the husband. You remember me telling you that the man had a dramatic religious conversion and he and his wife changed their names, modelling themselves after Jacob and Leah in the Bible? I don't know what to make of that," Neil confessed. "I don't know if it is a problem. Maybe. Maybe not." For a moment, they stared at each other. "You might have more understanding about whether this religious thing is harmful in any way."

Aleda nodded, thinking, perhaps, that Roy might have some insight into this unusual situation. Normally she would have turned to him for advice and counsel. But how could she suggest to Neil that they involve Roy?

She gazed into her mug, then looked up at him. "When do we go?"

As they made their way down the rutted country lane, the rough, dry grass grazing the sides of the cruiser, Aleda recognized the road leading to the derelict old church. "Once when we were prowling around looking at old churches, Martin brought Laura and me to see this building. It had just been sold and we couldn't believe that a family planned to live here."

Neil eased the police car up to a makeshift gate. They waited a moment, hoping that someone might appear. When no one came, she turned toward him, shrugged, opened the cruiser door and slid out. After squeezing around the gate, she stood inside the property looking from left to right. Further along the stone fence, she spotted two children, their heads bent, searching in the long grass. Glancing up, one of them — a young girl — noticed her and tapped the other child on the arm. Aleda smiled, raising her hand in a small friendly wave. When the children did not bolt away, she pointed to show Neil where she was going and began walking toward them. The boy held a tin cup of wild strawberries and the girl was carrying a basket of field oxeye daisies. Their fingers and mouths were stained red.

"I see that you have found some wild berries," she said, smiling. The children stared at her. "May I have one?" she asked. "I used to love wild strawberries when I was a kid. I didn't have a grandmother so I pretended that the woman across our street was my grandmother. I called her nagymama. My parents were Hungarian, you see."

The children continued to stare at this strange woman who had entered their space and seemed to be endlessly chattering.

"One day," she continued, "nagymama asked me if I wanted to go on an adventure with her. She took me up the mountain in Hamilton to this lovely wooded area and she gave me a little tin cup, just like the one you have." She gestured to the cup that was half full of strawberries. "Oh … those were the sweetest tiny things I have ever eaten." She closed her eyes, and when she opened them, she bent down and said in a whisper, "and I remember when I got home, my mama said that I had berry juice all over my mouth and my fingers … just like you two."

Aleda laughed and, to her surprise, the little girl laughed too. The boy smiled, but Aleda could see that he had begun to back up, edging away from the stone fence toward the church building. When the girl didn't move, Aleda sank down on the ground, in a cross-legged position.

"I've always wondered," she said, pointing to the flowers which the girl had put in her hair, "how you make a daisy chain like that. Will you show me?"

The girl nodded and sat down in front of Aleda. As Aleda watched, the child slit the middle of a daisy stem with her thumbnail, being careful not to break it in half. Slowly, she threaded the stem of another daisy through the slit, pushing the base of the stem through until the flower was snug against the slit. She made a slit in the new daisy and pushed another stem through it and handed the start of the daisy chain to Aleda. "Do you want to try?"

"I would like to," Aleda said as she bent forward.

Neil sat waiting in the cruiser. He knew that she would come back soon, though he had lost sight of her because of the stone fence. When he next glanced at his watch, ten minutes had passed. He opened his door to go in search of Aleda, but then he saw her coming toward the gate, holding the hand of a young girl, both wearing daisy chains in their hair.

"My friend, Dinah," she announced. "She and her brother Levi have been berry-picking; they found a patch of wild strawberries. I'm going inside to meet her family. Would you like to come in with us?"

Neil followed Dinah and Aleda, still holding hands, toward the wooden door. He glanced up at the side of the steeple where bricks had fallen away and lay crumpled in a pile of rubble at the base. The stone steps that led to the door were solid, although overgrown with dandelions and purslane weed that rooted between the crevices.

Dinah broke away and ran up the steps, holding the door open for Aleda. Neil hesitated, waiting outside the door until he spotted a man coming toward them, holding a hand saw. The man scowled, glancing first at his young daughter, then at Aleda, both wearing daisy chains in their hair, but when he caught sight of a police officer outside the door, he dropped the saw, which clattered onto the stone steps. Two small boys playing nearby ran to a room in the corner of the old church.

Aleda extended her hand. "Your children and I met in the berry patch. My name is Aleda Vastag."

"What is it that you people want?" the man demanded, his voice loud and harsh. "All we want is to be left alone. We have a right to live as we've chosen. Do you have a problem with that?"

"Please," Aleda responded, keeping her own voice gentle. "Someone called us, concerned for your family. We're just trying to understand. The way you've chosen to live is so very different. It's difficult for us to understand."

"Did we ask for help?" the man shouted. "I'll thank you to get off my property."

Some instinct made Neil stay back by the door while Aleda edged closer. "May I ask your name?" she said, then waited in front of the angry man who was breathing heavily.

When she had almost given up hope that he would answer, he muttered, "Jacob. Jacob Jacobi. I've just moved in here with my wife, Leah, and our kids."

"Ah. Jacob and Leah. Interesting," she said. "You know, I suppose, that there's a couple in the Bible — in the Old Testament — called Jacob and Leah."

The man jerked away from her in impatience. "Of course. We chose those names for ourselves."

"I'm interested in that," she said. "I'm a minister, you see. At the church in Milburn Corners, south of here, close to Owen Sound. You've been through Milburn Corners?" The man stared at her, suspicious and cautious. "How did it happen that you named yourself after Jacob and Leah in the Bible?"

She waited again for what seemed a long time. Finally, he said, "My life was in shambles." He spoke in such a low voice that Neil could not hear. "A mess. I was drinking and into cocaine. I was a bad husband and a worse father. One night I had a dream. I was crossing a desert and put my head on a stone to sleep. Then, it was like I was dreaming inside my own dream. A strange man came along and started to wrestle with me. When I woke the next morning, my hip was so sore I couldn't get out of bed. I couldn't get to my stash of rye and cocaine, so I just lay in bed for a few days, sweating and cursing. One morning I woke up and my mind was clear as a bell.

"We didn't go to church when I was a kid. My old man had no use for religion. But he did let us go to Bible Camp in the summer, so after my dream, I remembered the story about Jacob in the Bible. Me and Jacob, we had the same kind of experience. That's when I changed my name and my ways. My wife was so relieved that she changed her name too, to Leah, and we renamed all the kids after Jacob's children in the Bible."

It had been a long explanation and when he finished, Aleda exhaled slowly. "Amazing," she said. "Absolutely amazing."

They stood in silence in the centre of the church while Neil leaned against the wooden door. He gazed up at discoloured sheathing and mangled roof shingles that were visible through a formerly striking roundel window, wondering how something that had once been beautiful could now be so repulsive. He thought of his own handsome, well-maintained church in Owen Sound, remembering the satisfying symmetry of rounded windows along the church walls, the pleasing pattern repeated in the curve of the sanctuary cupola. His memory took him to the warm nave where he often sat gazing at the blue stained-glass windows against the pristine white walls, where gold angels heralded a call from the transept, where the expansive altar, adorned in a crisp white cloth, offered the chalice and paten. How different his place of worship was from this desolate and desperate place.

As he stood waiting, he heard Aleda exclaim to Jacob, "Ah! Now I see what you are doing! Now I get it." Her arm gestured wildly around the building. "This building, this old wreck of a building is like your old life," she exclaimed, "and you are making it into something new again."

Jacob stared at her. "I guess so," he said. "But, really, it was all that we could afford."

8

Tracker and Tom

Knowing it was her last week before leaving on vacation, Aleda sat down at her desk to make a list, determined to attend to things that needed attention. She must call her colleague, Robert, and remind him about taking over her pastoral duties while she was away. She also wanted to visit Dorrie. Aleda found herself worrying about her, wondering if she was becoming accustomed to her loss. Was she returning to her former confident state? Poised with her paper and pen, she added "garden" to her list. Perhaps Roy would check on her perennials while she was away.

When she thought about Tracker, she sighed. In an impetuous moment when she had adopted an old worn-out work horse whose owners were about to get rid of him, she had not considered what would happen to Tracker if she were not around. When she had gone away in the previous month, Martin had looked after Tracker for four days, but would he agree to the same thing for five long weeks? It seemed a lot to ask.

And then ... there were the seniors in her congregation. She had been feeling guilty about them for some weeks. She would not see them for another five weeks, so she vowed to visit each person in the week ahead. She pored over a chart listing the names of fourteen members of her congregation who lived in retirement and nursing homes. This time, she decided, she would spend quality time with each one. In the past when she conducted a worship service in the residences, she often rushed in, led the service, shook hands and chatted briefly before leaving. This week would be different. She would take time to really get to know each person. These were not just elderly people with fading memories, content to sit in a wheelchair in front of a blaring television set. No, these were real people with interesting pasts, stories to tell and unique experiences to recall, perhaps even with remarkable dreams for the future.

Thinking of leaving Tracker with Martin led her to call Dr. Patel and inquire about Tracker's health. The veterinarian was quick to ask if Tracker showed any signs of being in distress. Did he seem comfortable? Did he still eat well? "There's really no treatment for old age," Dr. Patel added.

Feeling a little foolish for having bothered the veterinarian, Aleda blurted out, "I apologize for wasting your time. Tracker seems as happy as possible and he still enjoys his ground meal and an apple a day. Except for the time after the Richardson's barn fire when there was smoke in the air, he still goes out into the backyard every day and gets a little fresh air."

"Well, that's the best we can hope for then, isn't it?" There was a pause on the other end of the line and then Dr. Patel asked, "That dog we fixed up — Buddy — the one with the puppies, they're coming along okay?"

Perhaps it was the patient tone in the veterinarian's voice, or perhaps it was the fact that Dr. Patel had taken the time to inquire about the injured dog, or perhaps she was having a slow day … whatever the reason, Aleda found herself rattling on about the puppies. As if one thought led to another, she told Dr. Patel about her plan to visit all the elderly people from her parish in their nursing or retirement homes. "Honestly, when I go there, it makes me sad. Those people — well, they remind me of Tracker. Just hanging out, waiting to die." Now thoroughly embarrassed for rambling on to a woman who looked after a busy veterinary practice, Aleda stopped and took a breath. "What do you think, Dr. Patel? What do you think about people living in retirement and nursing homes?"

"Well, I wouldn't know. In our culture, we don't use retirement and nursing homes. Our parents and grandparents are so precious to us that we can't bear to part with them. They're an important part of our families until they die and they always stay with us in our homes. Even if it's difficult at times, we wouldn't think of putting our elders in a nursing home. It's just not done."

All the way to the nursing home in Owen Sound, Dr. Patel's words echoed through her mind. Have we North Americans got this wrong? she wondered. Do we just shuffle off our seniors into special homes, getting them conveniently out of the way because we don't want to bother with their care? The troubling thought lingered as she made her way down the hallway, looking for the rooms of three parishioners.

When she entered the first room, she realized at once that the woman was sleeping. She glanced at her watch. Of course, people often have a little snooze after lunch. She herself had been known to lie down after a good lunch. When she entered the room of the second parishioner, there was no one there. A woman emerged from the bathroom carrying a cleaning pail and squeeze mop. "Mrs. Johns has gone for her bath," she said. Aleda thanked her and made her way further down the hall to the room of Tom Terrance. She hesitated in the doorway and peeked in.

Tom was sitting in a wheelchair, pressed close to the window, looking at a bird feeder where sparrows fluttered, pecked at seeds, then flew off into a nearby lilac bush.

"Mr. Terrance. Hello." He looked up. "Reverend Aleda Vastag," she said, offering him her hand.

"I know who you are, girl," he said in a grumpy tone. "You do the church service here every month. Call me Tom."

"Sure. Sure, Tom." She paused. "Do you mind if I sit for while?" pointing to a sturdy green chair draped with a colourful afghan.

"Be my guest. Move that damn fool thing out of the way," he said, indicating the afghan. "But you need to know that about this time of day I always take a little snort."

"Snort?"

"Yah, you know, a tip of the old moonshine, a couple of fingers of the old hooch."

"Oh, I see … is that allowed?"

"Allowed?" the old man sneered. "This is my home, ain't it? And can't a man do what he wants in his own home?"

"The staff don't mind?"

"Who knows? Who cares? Once, there was this real snooty girl. She was getting after me for drinking. I was just sitting here minding my own business, watching the birds and having a nip of Crown Royal after lunch when she came in and threatened to take away the bottle."

"Oh my. What happened?"

"Not much really. I gave her a good pinch and that was the last I saw of her."

"You pinched her? Where?"

"Well, really, if she hadn't turned around to pick up the bottle …"

"Mr. Terrance! You didn't!"

"I sure did, and I made damn sure that I found a new hiding place for my rye after that. They never seem to look in rubber boots."

Aleda pressed her thumb against her lower lip, gazing out at the fluttering birds. Dr. Patel's voice echoed through her mind: our parents and grandparents are so precious to us that we can't bear to part with them. They're an important part of our families and they stay in our homes until they die.

"Mr. Terrance — Tom — May I ask you something personal?"

"Hey, now. It's been a coon's age since a pretty girl wanted to get personal with me."

She ignored his comment and continued, "I've been wondering lately if the people here," she flung out her hand to include the entire floor, "would actually prefer to be at home with their families."

"Oh, Lordy love a duck, no!" the old man exploded. "I lived with my son for a bit and that bitch of a daughter-in-law nearly drove me around the bend. And those grandkids of mine. Lazy louts. Need a good kick on the arse. Messy as hell and just sit around playing on them damn fool video game machines. Useless. Absolutely useless. At least the girls in here let me be," he said, shaking his head.

She pressed her folded hands against her mouth, taken aback by his vehemence. A few moments passed in silence and then she lifted her head and looked at the old man, wondering where to go next in their conversation.

"Were you a member of Milburn Corners church all your life?"

"Nope. Not much of a church goer. Never darkened the door. Well, that's not entirely true. Me and the missus were married there and a couple of the kids got done there."

"Done?"

"Yah, you know. Done. Baptized."

"Ah." Aleda paused again, wondering as she gazed out the window how birds can possibly move about so much. It must be exhausting, flitting around like that all the time. "But you said you come to the worship service here in the retirement home."

"Sure do. Never miss."

Aleda nodded, thinking that as people age and mature they may develop more sense of urgency about the end of life, more hunger for spiritual fulfillment, more yearning for eternity. "What is it that draws you to worship here when you never went to church while you lived in Milburn Corners?" she inquired.

"Well, two things," he said, with snorting laughter. "You're a damned pretty girl to look at, and the second thing is ... they always serve chocolate ice cream after the service."

9
Unmentionables

SHE RETURNED FROM THE NURSING HOME FEELING EXHAUSTED AND DISCOURAGED. She had only accomplished one visit and it had been a rather upsetting one, too. She kicked off her sandals, stretched and padded out to the kitchen. Did she have the right ingredients to made a comforting Hungarian dinner? Some bread dumplings or Gundel pancakes with chocolate sauce? Some paprika chicken or bean soup à la Jókai? She was peering into the open door of the refrigerator when she heard a sharp knock on her porch door. When she swung around, she saw Grace standing there.

Aleda frowned a little and closed the refrigerator door. Why do I allow Grace to irritate me? she wondered. She realized that Grace, from time to time, was outspoken, opinionated and even harsh. Yet she knew that she also had a tender side, a kind motherly spirit which surfaced occasionally, especially with children. Why can't I enjoy that compassionate side of Grace and let the sharp barbs go? Why can't I just let Grace be Grace? Aleda demanded of herself as she moved to open the door.

Today, though, Grace seemed subdued and troubled. "Is something wrong?" Aleda asked.

"The strangest thing has happened and I don't know what to make of it."

Aleda nodded and said, "Won't you come in?"

Grace stepped into the porch and repeated, "The strangest thing has happened."

"Yes?"

"You know that I have a clothes line at the back of my house, one of those little ones that go around in a circle."

Aleda shook her head and shrugged a little. She had no idea that Grace had a clothes line at the back of her house.

"Roy put it up for me," she explained. "And he built me a little privacy wall on the west side." She stood gazing at Aleda, then stared down at the floor. "So I could hang out my unmentionables where no one can see them."

Aleda's mouth opened. "Un-mention ..."

"Yes," Grace retorted. "My underwear."

"Ah. Yes, I see."

"I dry my aprons there too," she continued, "and, of course, my dresses and my stockings."

Aleda nodded her head, trying to figure out where this conversation was headed.

"I didn't bring in my laundry last night because it rained a little, you remember? When I went out this morning to take things off the line, some items were missing."

"Missing?"

"That's what I said, didn't I?" she snapped. "But it was the strangest thing," she repeated for the third time. "All my unmentionables were gone. My bras. My underpants. Gone. All six pairs. Only the aprons and dresses were left. And there were boot marks in the mud by the clothesline." Her voice had risen. "Who on earth would do a thing like that? What would they want with my underwear?"

Aleda pressed a clenched fist hard against her mouth. She was worried — in fact, extremely sure — that she was going to howl with laughter. She took a deep breath and shifted from one foot to another until she had composed herself.

"What should we do, then?" Aleda asked.

"How should I know! Why on earth do you think I walked all the way up here to tell you this? You're supposed to know what to do."

Ah, Aleda thought, with an inward sigh. This is why it is difficult for me to let Grace be Grace. She can be a truly annoying person.

After Aleda finished her dinner, she had a second visitor, but this time she smiled. "Rose! What a nice surprise. Do come in. You have something on your mind?"

It did not take long, Aleda had already discovered, for news to travel through the community of Milburn Corners. Once, when she, Martin and Laura had been prowling through the countryside exploring old churches,

Martin had explained that the church bell, in pioneer times, had an important function. When it was rung during the day or at an unusual time in the night, it was a signal that people should hurry to the church for news. Something was wrong: a child was lost or a house was on fire. Maybe a wild animal was prowling close to the sheep pastures or someone's milking cows had broken through a fence and wandered away. Now, it seemed to Aleda, there was no need for the alarm of a church bell. People had become adept at passing along community concerns in a rather efficient fashion. She noticed that many decisions of her church Board were discussed and decided before or after a meeting while people stood outside talking. "Parking lot meetings" were one of the realities of ministry in a small, rural community. Aleda understood that.

Rose, it seemed, knew all about Grace's dilemma. It became obvious from her conversation that Roy knew, too, although the topic of Grace's underwear had been handled with some delicacy. Ethel, of course, mentioned the problem to everyone who dropped into the store to pick up milk or butter, so even Martin had heard of the situation, Rose told her.

"I'm confused," Aleda said. "Is there something I'm meant to do about this situation?"

"Something has me worried," Rose confided. Aleda tipped her head, her shoulders lifting. "It's what the people are saying. The others in the village."

"What on earth are you talking about, Rose?"

"I'm afraid, my dear, that people are pointing their fingers at the teenagers in the village. They think that the young people just don't have enough to do this summer. They're saying that the teens probably thought it would be very funny to steal an old lady's underwear."

"But that's nonsense!" Aleda cried out, her mind flashing to Michael who worked long hours at the campground, then spent his evenings cutting lawns for people in the village. She thought about Savannah working as a lifeguard with children. The other three teens in the village, she knew, were all babysitting long hours and helping on farms during haying season. "That is utter nonsense!" Aleda repeated, angry that the teens she had come to know and love were being viewed with suspicion. "How did people jump to such a conclusion?"

"It seemed to make sense when Grace suggested it to me," Rose murmured. "You remember what it was like to be young, don't you, Aleda? Those long, hot summer nights with nothing much to do. It's an invitation to make mischief."

"Still! What right does Grace have to start such a rumour?" Aleda exploded, thrusting out her arm in an angry gesture.

"I know, I know," Rose continued in a soothing way. "You have to understand that this situation has upset Grace and she's just trying to figure out who is responsible. It's embarrassing to her that someone has her underwear and that the whole community seems to know about it. We're all trying to figure this out." Rose stood up to leave but at the door she turned toward Aleda and said, "It's upsetting to all of us, but we need to ask, 'Would we want someone sneaking into our backyard in the night to steal something, especially something as intimate as our underwear?'"

After Rose left, Aleda found it hard to settle down. She looked over her to-do list, then flipped it onto the kitchen counter. She wandered into the backyard, a hoe in her hand, and stared at the tangle of weeds that had crept around her phlox and echinacea, then turned away, setting the hoe against the railing on the back porch. Perhaps I should call the teens together for a bit of a chat about this, she considered. But even as that thought crept into her mind, she became angry at herself. "I'm as bad as the rest of the village," she moaned. "I'm absolutely positive that the wonderful kids in this village would not do anything so silly and mean-spirited."

But if it wasn't the teens, then who could it have been?"

10
Lion's Head

Two more days until her vacation. Her shoulders were tense, her mind unfocused. She stood, stretched and wandered out to the back porch. Her Sunday worship service was prepared, but now Saturday afternoon stretched out before her, undefined and unstructured. She dropped into a chair on the porch and folded her arms, lost in morose thoughts.

At the beginning of her ministry she had suffered from low-grade anxiety on Saturdays, a miasma of apprehension settling around her. Seventeen years of experience had not extinguished this unease. Often the best antidote was distraction — a movie, a shopping excursion or a quick trip to a new community. But, now, she could not stop thinking about the peculiar thing that had happened in Milburn Corners. Who had stolen Grace's underwear, and why? This confusion only added to her Saturday malaise. Why do I feel so tired? she wondered now. I really must need a vacation. Her energy seemed depleted. How could she summon enough strength to help others in the village figure out what had happened?

She rubbed the skin between her eyebrows where a tightness seemed to be pushing toward a headache. She felt overwhelmed with worry. Somehow, she had to get Tracker to Martin's farm. She had to meet with Robert about her pastoral duties while she was away. Dorrie's situation still worried her. Her confused feelings about Neil troubled her. The visit to the Jacobi family had left her unsettled, and something about the new villager, Connie, made her uneasy. She had eleven more elderly parishioners to visit and only two days left.

It was all too much. Aleda reached behind her neck, massaging her tense shoulder muscles, wondering if she should crawl back into the bed, which she had not had the energy to make that morning.

Her unhappy thoughts were interrupted by the ringing phone. "Can I not have a moment's peace?" she grumbled, turning toward the kitchen.

She immediately recognized Neil's voice. "I have the day off. If you're free this afternoon, I'd like to take you for a drive up the Bruce Peninsula. There's something I'd like to show you." How could her gloomy thoughts shift so rapidly after hearing one short question over the telephone? An unexpected trip in a red convertible was surely a positive antidote to worry.

Within a half hour the red Mustang was in the driveway behind her old van. Roy, mowing his front lawn, glanced up Main Street toward the parsonage. "That's the second time," he muttered. "That's the second time I've seen her go out with that policeman."

Aleda hadn't noticed Roy pausing in his work to stare after the red convertible that zipped west out of the village. Instead, she was thinking that it had been a long time since she had felt so free and happy, her hair dancing in the wind. Neil smiled at her and shifted into third gear. He drove with confidence, slowing down as they entered the village of Hepworth. They zipped on through the community of Clavering, through the town of Wiarton and on toward a hamlet called Ferndale, then turned right heading east toward Georgian Bay.

He drove slowly now, calling out "Lion's Head" and gesturing toward a tall granite rock formation towering over the water's edge. He pulled into the parking lot at a small sandy beach. "People think that spot looks like a lion's head," he explained, pointing up at the jutting rock of Niagara Escarpment.

"Ah," Aleda said, tilting her head to one side, then to the other. "I'm afraid I don't see that."

He switched off the car engine. "Look out there," he instructed. Reaching behind her head, he placed his hands flat against her temples, turning her toward the tall rock, his fingers extended out beyond her face forming blinders that directed her vision. "This is what they do for horses," he said, laughing. "Can you see it now? The lion's head?"

"Yes, yes, I can," she answered, although she still wasn't sure that she would describe what she saw as the head of a lion. At the moment, the only thing she was aware of was the sensation of his strong arms resting on top of her shoulders and his warm hands pressing her face toward something that she could neither name nor define.

After a walk along the sandy beach, they settled at a wooden picnic table, watching children splash within a roped-off swimming area. "Water is very deep and cold here," he said, then added, "Have you ever seen anything like this place?" He stared up at the rocky cliff, then tilted his head to look at the lower rock formation where gnarled evergreen trees clung tenaciously to the rocks. Below, the water against the shore was rippled aqua-green, gradually melding across the bay into swaths of indigo blue.

"This place has blown my mind since I first came here," he said, still staring toward the rocks and the water. His Irish accent, it seemed to her, was more pronounced at times like this, times when he seemed emotional about something. His face shone, and he looked as if he had been transported to a new space, a place that only he could see. Or maybe I just imagined that, she thought. Perhaps it was only the reflection of sun and water and rocks.

The afternoon was waning as they wandered through the town and along the rocky water break to see the prim white and red lighthouse. Neil told her about the ninety-kilometre Bruce Trail that ran through Lion's Head. He told her about the time when he had been hiking near Hope Bay and discovered potholes, places where glacial meltwater had carved out holes in the soft dolostone rock. He told her about his canoeing and kayaking adventures on Georgian Bay. He explained that he had been to Lion's Head in all four seasons. "Some people object to winter up here," he said. "It can be cold, real snowy and blustery. The west wind whips across the peninsula from Lake Huron and the north-east wind comes in off Georgian Bay. A sure formula for a snow machine," he laughed, but then added, "There's a strange quiet beauty here in the winter, though. It's simple and sharp."

"Did you know," he told her as they walked along the shore, "that Ontario has sixty-one species of wild orchids and forty-four of them are here on the Bruce Peninsula?"

"Good heavens! Forty-four! I did not know that."

He nodded solemnly. "Lots of wildflowers here — Indian paintbrush, trilliums, marsh iris, marsh marigolds."

"Mmm ... marsh marigolds. We have those in the swamp in Milburn Corners, too."

Neil turned suddenly, gazing at her intently. "What do you think, Aleda? Do you like this place?"

She hesitated, wondering if he meant, do you love this place as much as I do? "From what I've seen, it seems amazing," she answered.

"Come." He put his hand under her elbow and guided her back to the car. "I've left the best to the last."

The red Mustang began a long, slow climb up a forested trail which, he told her, was cut into a cliff that was two hundred feet tall. When the trail ended, he stopped the car and said, "Come with me. I'm about to show you the best view in the world."

It was, as he promised, a spectacular view. Although it was late afternoon, the vista was still clear. Standing as close as they dared to the edge of a granite outcropping, he pointed out Cape Dundas and Barrier Island to the south. "Look this way," he said, pointing north. "There. See those cliffs? That's White Bluff. And over there is Cape Chin and Cabot Head. Nice lighthouse there, too." After he had pointed out Whippoorwill Bay, they stood for a time, gazing from south to north and out across the aqua-navy expanse of Georgian Bay.

"Look there," Neil said now, his Irish accent returning once more. "Look over there, Aleda, along the shore line. Do you see that cottage, the white cottage with the blue shutters?"

She turned her head, squinting in the direction he pointed. There was, as he said, a white cottage with blue shutters and, although it was built securely on rock, it offered the illusion, from the angle where they stood, of floating out over the bay. She stared, nodded again and exhaled.

"That's it, then. What do you think?"

She swung around to face the man who was still such a mystery to her. Looking up into his face, she raised her eyebrows.

"It's mine," he said quietly. "I put in an offer last week. The owners accepted it yesterday. My new home," he said with a sweep of his hand toward the white cottage.

11
Bench

Something woke Aleda early on Sunday morning. Was it the garrulous robins who persisted in building their family home over her front porch light? For weeks she had woken up to a chorus of "Zeeeeup! Peek … Tut, tut, tut." Most morning she put her pillow over her ear and drifted back into a snooze, but on this day sleep eluded her.

She lay in bed thinking back over her day with Neil. Why had he taken her to Lion's Head? Had he wanted to show off his new acquisition — the white cottage on the cliff? But even as the thought came to her, she knew that, unforthcoming as he was at times, he was not the type of man to show off. She rolled her head from side to side on the pillow. She tossed and turned, then muttered, "I have to get up. I have a sermon to look over."

Although she had come to expect early morning interruptions on weekdays, she had never before been disturbed on a Sunday morning, so she was startled when the telephone rang at seven forty-five.

"Aleda? Reverend Vastag?" Aleda recognized the voice of Ethel Aylmer.

"I'm surprised to hear from you!" Aleda exclaimed. Although Ethel was a long-time member of the community, she had made it quite clear that she did not attend church. Her store, she told Aleda, was open six days a week. Sunday was the only day she had to herself and she liked to stay quietly at home.

"Is something wrong?" Aleda inquired.

"Well, no. Yes. Maybe. I guess you could say so."

In the privacy of her kitchen, Aleda threw up her hand as if to say, Well, what is it? A problem or not?

"It's my bench, you see."

"Your bench."

"The one in front of the store where the old men sit."

"Yes, of course, I've seen them sitting there many a time. What's the problem?"

"It seems to have happened in the night," Ethel continued. "It's not terribly serious, but still ..."

"Ethel! What on earth is wrong with your bench?"

"Well, that's the thing. Someone has come by in the night and painted my green bench orange."

"Orange!"

"Yes, orange."

Aleda frowned and massaged the space between her eyebrows. She could not risk a headache just before worship. "But why?" she blurted, then stopped short, a terrible thought entering her mind. Orange ... Surely Roy wouldn't ...

"Beats me," Ethel said in a puzzled tone. "I can't make head nor tails of it. But really, Aleda, we can't have people doing this sort of thing, can we? It's vandalism. Would you want someone sneaking into your front porch and painting a piece of *your* furniture?"

In her seventeen years of ministry, Aleda had had to conduct some difficult worship services. There was a time when she had a bad head cold. Another time she had slipped on ice and hurt her back, having to take pain killers that made her head fuzzy. She recalled, too, many difficult and challenging funerals, especially one only two months before for the troubled teen, Dwayne, who had hung himself in the church bell tower. If I survived that one, she thought now, I can surely get through this service.

Her mind was buzzing with worry and confusion as she headed across the parsonage lawn toward the church. She unlocked the front door, walked to the front of the sanctuary and placed her brown leather Bible and sermon notes on the pulpit. The teens had taken the summer off from playing in the praise band, so she spent a few minutes chatting to the organist. She hadn't heard Rose come in, but when Aleda smelled the sweet, spicy, honey-musk of roses, she swung around.

"Beautiful," Aleda said. "Yours?"

"My roses have never been more prolific or fragrant. It's perfect weather for roses — hot and sunny with a good drink of rain once a week."

"It's good of you to bring them so we can all enjoy them," she said, taking Rose's arm and leading her away from the front of the sanctuary into the small side vestry. "Rose," she whispered, "there's something on my mind. Something I'm trying to figure out."

"What's that, Aleda?"

"It's Roy, you see."

"Oh, yes. He called me this morning before I left the house."

"He did?"

"Yes. He said to pass on his regrets. He won't be in church this morning. He said that he had a bad night and was just not feeling up to coming today."

Aleda nodded slowly. "I see."

Rose reached out and placed a warm hand on her arm. "You okay, Aleda?"

"Yes, just a little tired, I'm afraid."

"Roy said that you're heading out for a much-deserved holiday. You look quite worn out. I'm sure a vacation is just what you need."

On Sunday afternoon, Aleda packed her suitcase and piled a laundry basket full of clean sheets for the house guests she expected.

When, some months before, she had been wondering what she might do on her vacation, she had discussed her plans with Robert and his elegant wife, Patrice. They always offered her practical and constant guidance, for which she was thankful. She knew that they owned a cabin on Cape Breton Island. When she asked them how they settled on that location, Robert and Patrice glanced at each other and laughed.

"Compromise. There's a lot of that in marriage," Robert had responded.

"Well … hardly, Robert," Patrice said in a tone that suggested some complexity in the decision.

Robert confessed that, when he was younger, his idea of a good vacation was wilderness camping and visiting big league ball parks. It had been, Patrice added, a good time for Robert and their boys, but in time she put her foot down.

"Look at me!" She used her hands to sweep down her silk pantsuit and glittering high-heeled sandals. "Do I look like a person who enjoys camping and baseball?"

Aleda laughed and agreed that sports and the outdoor life might not be high on her list of favourite activities. They had worked out a compromise, buying a property on a high cliff on rugged Cape Breton Island where the setting was wild enough to appeal to Robert while the cabin provided a modicum of domestic comfort for Patrice.

"Why is it, Robert," Aleda demanded, "that ministers for generations — centuries even — have had the luxury of an entire month of holidays? Most people today get only two weeks, three at the most. And farmers, when do they get a vacation?"

He rubbed his cheek thoughtfully. "But I recall you telling me about a farm family in your congregation who took a two-week cruise to the Caribbean last year in February, and about that other farmer who took his family to Switzerland for a couple of weeks."

"Yes. You're right, of course. But those farmers grow cash crops — corn and beans. What about the dairy farmers? They have to milk twice a day. What about farmers like that?"

"You have a point there," he murmured. "I suppose they have to hire someone to take over, and that can't be easy."

Returning to her original question, he explained that the tradition of a month's vacation for clergy had come from a desire and commitment to have erudite and scholarly ministers. The local minister was expected to be one of, if not *the* best educated person in the community. Ministers, he expounded, need ongoing study. "Even though we have a fine seminary education, there is always more to know and discover about scripture and theology and life. There are always new things to learn. When I was at seminary," he mused, "there were no computers, no world-wide web, no global village. Those things have changed our outlook in so many ways. Younger ministers like you bring that mindset to the interpretation of scripture. A month of vacation is a good time to reflect on how the culture of today and the ancient scriptures intersect."

Aleda sat in silence for a moment, her lips pursed, but then she inquired, "So ... what about you, Robert? Before you retired, did you spend your month of vacation in your cabin on Cape Breton Island studying the Bible and planning out your sermons for the year ahead?"

He threw back his head and laughed. "Good heavens, no. I do what makes me happy. I go fishing. To tell you the truth," he confided, leaning forward, "my father was a Presbyterian minister and he studied on his vacation. We had a cottage. Every day, rain or shine — and it *was* mainly sunny — my father went to his office in the cottage and worked from nine until five. My mother and my brothers and me — we all had fun on the beach. That memory stuck with me. I vowed that if I ever had children, I would do interesting things with them on vacation. Poor Patrice. All those golf courses and ball stadiums." He shook his head in mock remorse. "That's why," he whispered to Aleda, "I only do what Patrice wants now."

"Ha!" Patrice exploded. "I heard that!"

12
Bluebird Cottage

TWO WEEKS BEFORE GOING ON THE FIRST PART OF HER VACATION, ALEDA HAD DECIDED to drive to Kincardine and research the cottage on Boiler Beach that she had rented, sight unseen. There was something about the exceptionally reasonable rental fee that made her feel uneasy.

As she pulled into Port Elgin, part way to Kincardine, she spotted a sign pointing to the local beach. She parked, hauled out her folding lawn chair and cooler, and ate her lunch as she watched the waves roll onto the shores of Lake Huron. Ah, she sighed, how peaceful and soothing. Is this what it will be like at Bluebird Cottage on Boiler Beach?

When she got to the town of Kincardine, she pulled off the highway and followed a curving road toward the lake. She drove up and down the side streets of Kincardine looking for a sign pointing to Boiler Beach. She passed a grand old mansion, now converted into a retirement home. She drove past a fish and chip shop called the *Erie Belle*, an ice cream kiosk, a pristine red and white lighthouse, a harbour filled with boats. In the centre of town, she drifted past a grassy square where an old cannon and a bandshell stood under shade trees. She saw signs telling her where to access a hiking trail, where to find the Rotary Park, but nowhere did she see a sign pointing to Boiler Beach.

Frustrated, she pulled her van into a parking spot on the main street and, spotting a man sitting on a street bench, she made her way toward him.

"Hi. I'm wondering if you're from around here?" When he nodded, Aleda inquired about directions to Boiler Beach.

"You won't see signs for Boiler Beach here in Kincardine," he replied. "That's because it's south of town. You'd be wanting to go to there, then?"

"Yes, I would."

"Well, it's easy enough. You just turn around here and get back down the main street, down past the gas station that sells the Indian food. Get past the school and you come to a stop sign. The cemetery is straight ahead. That's where my wife is buried. Well, half the town is buried there, as a matter of fact. The rest of them is down at the pub." The man chuckled, delighted with his own joke. "Turn right there by the cemetery and go past the church. You'll come to a stop sign. It's a real good idea to stop." He paused, chuckling again. "You just keep going straight ahead, straight down the hill and the road curves to the south. Be careful on that there hill. There's more than one person lost his life on that hill. In the winter it's slick as glass, what with the waves crashing up over them big rocks. Before long you'll see Boiler Beach on the right-hand side. I don't think there's a sign, but there is a cairn. Nope, I don't remember a sign, but if you look, you'll see the boiler off through the trees."

"The boiler. Oh, my. That sounds dreadfully complicated."

"Oh, not at all," the old man continued. "Everybody knows where Boiler Beach is. By the way, what do you want with Boiler Beach?"

"Well … um … I'm wanting to look at a cottage for rent called 'The Bluebird.'"

"Yup. Know the place. Know the place well."

Breaking away from the information overload, she thanked the man and returned to her van. "I seem destined to find this stupid beach on my own," she grumbled.

Following the vaguely specific instructions rolling around in her head the best she could — cemetery, turn right, down a hill to the lake, watch for a cairn — she assumed she must be close to Boiler Beach. Just as she was about to give up the search in frustration, she saw a small blue cottage tucked into a grove of trees. The "For Rent" sign was a dead giveaway.

On her way home, serious doubts crept into her mind. "These are not sober second thoughts," she grumbled. "I'm having grave reservations. What on earth is the matter with me? Why did I consent to rent for two weeks without even seeing the place?"

The owner had shown her the interior of the cottage — more a cabin, she realized — but they had not lingered long inside. The owner stepped quickly back out into the sunshine and enthused about the stretch of sand in front of the cottage, the long sweep of beach leading to Kincardine, the waves lapping against the shore. "The sunsets," he exclaimed, "are world-renowned. When you are here, you spend most of your time outdoors. This beach is perfect."

She thought back to the glimpse she had into the dark and dreary interior of Bluebird Cottage. The owner, seeing her hesitation and worried that he might lose the deal, had offered a further reduction in rent. Aleda stood in front of the cottage looking out toward the sunshine sparkling on the waves of Lake Huron. "I suppose that when you're here, you *do* spend most of your time outdoors," she said.

"So true! You'll spend hours on the beach. And the sunsets … well, let me just remind you, don't forget your camera!"

She had pulled onto Highway 21 leading north out of Kincardine when a disturbing realization exploded in her mind. "There was no bathroom in that cottage! I've just rented a dingy, dark, airless cottage for two long weeks, and it has no bathroom!"

She still had misgivings, but what choice did she have? She was ready. Her suitcase was stuffed with shorts, t-shirts, sandals, running shoes, swim suits and, in case it turned cool or rainy, jeans, thick sweaters and the splendid yellow rain poncho that Roy had once given her. Packing the poncho reminded her that she had promised to stop at Roy's house and drop off the key to the parsonage before she left.

When she saw him shuffle to the front door, she felt her stomach contract. "Are you all right, Roy?" she asked, reaching out a hand to steady him.

"I'll be right as rain in a day or two, Aleda. Don't you be worrying about me. Just a flare-up of the old arthritis. You get on your way now and have fun," he said.

"It will be great fun," she told him, hoping that if she repeated it often enough, she would begin to believe it.

As she travelled down Highway 21 in the mid-afternoon of that day, she was grateful for the heater in her old van and glad that she had remembered to pack hot chocolate and to throw in her cozy pink afghan from the front porch. The cool rainy day depressed her spirit, but she thought it would be comforting to curl her hands around a mug of hot cocoa and snuggle up on the couch in her little Bluebird Cottage.

There was no mystery this time about finding Boiler Beach. After arriving and pulling close to the cottage, she hurried through the downpour and struggled to open the door, the rain dripping off the roof eave onto her back. She rushed back and forth between the van and the open door of the cottage, thumping items onto the cracked linoleum floor — suitcase, laundry basket full of sheets and towels, box of books and bag of groceries. When her van was emptied and locked, she hurried back inside and leaned against the back of the door, panting and staring into the bleak interior.

Aleda rarely swore. Her parents had reminded her repeatedly that swearing, however mild, demonstrated a lack of good grace and a definite shortage of good judgement and civil manners. But on this occasion, she was totally overcome.

"Oh, damn it all to hell!" she shouted. "What on earth have I done?"

Pressed against the back of the door of Bluebird Cottage, she surveyed the front room. To her right were an ancient refrigerator and a metal side table that supported a two-burner hot plate set on a scarred asbestos pad. A green sideboard with open shelves held a collection of assorted dishes and a tub of cutlery. In the corner was a round beige chrome table, the legs spotted with rust. Beside the table hung the previous year's calendar, its pages curling from humidity. On the other side of the room was a sitting area with a plaid sofa, an orange plastic tub chair and a lamp with yellowed pom-pom balls dangling from the shade. In front of the sofa sat a square coffee table ringed with water marks, and in the centre of the table lay a copy of *The History of Kincardine*. Someone — the owner? previous renters with children? — had pasted Christmas cards onto white paper plates and thumbtacked them to the wood panelling.

She slouched against the door, her spirit so despondent that she thought she might cry.

There was no door between the front and back rooms, just an archway. The back room was just as dark and gloomy. There were two sets of bunk beds, the mattresses dark and bare. A chest of drawers sat in front of a small window between the beds.

After a long, dark, dreary moment, she straightened and walked slowly to the archway looking into the bedroom, then turned back into the kitchen and living room area. Her muscles were tense, her fists clenched by her side. "Not much wonder it was cheap," she muttered in an aggrieved voice. "How could I have made such a stupid mistake?"

Only after putting her things away in the chest of drawers and storing her food in the refrigerator and pouring herself a mug of wine — there were no wine glasses — did Aleda ask herself the dreaded question: "Where is the outhouse?"

• • •

It was not an auspicious beginning to a vacation, she knew that, but her mood began to shift as she sipped her wine. Tomorrow, she thought, I'll go into Kincardine and buy a few things to make some modifications to this cottage, but first I have to locate that outhouse. Grateful that there was still light in the western sky and that the rain had eased, she made her way out the front door, turned to the north and followed a wood chip path into a copse of trees. And there it was.

There were some things that she had never before experienced, and using an outhouse was one of them. A little half sliver of moon cut from the front door, she soon discovered, offered only a half sliver of light when inside. She was unprepared for the smell and the reality of being able to see deposits left by previous users. There were two holes. Why? she pondered — would two people actually share this noxious space? Her face was a study in disgust and amazement. A metal bucket full of ashes and a small shovel stood by the door, and on the wall hung a hand-written sign:

> *If just now you poop or pee,*
> *We have rules that number three,*
> *Do your business quick enough,*
> *Use these ashes to cover your stuff.*
> *Thank you. The Management*

How gross, she thought, but then she said aloud, with indignation, "The sign says that there are *three* rules, but there are only two! Do your business and cover it." But then she exclaimed, "Oh, I know the third rule: get the heck out of here as fast as you can!"

Once, when she was in elementary school, she remembered a time when she had been sitting with her parents at the kitchen table in their small house on St. Mary Street in Hamilton. She did not remember, now, what had caused her parents to look so full of despair. Perhaps they had been reminiscing, as they sometimes did, about their struggle to become settled in Canada after the Hungarian Revolution in 1956. They often talked of how difficult it was to learn a new language and new customs, to find work and to know — the greatest indignity of all — that both of them worked at jobs far below the level of which they were capable.

Aleda knew that her father was studying to become a doctor and her mother a lawyer when they had to flee from Hungary. Now, it seemed, life was a daily challenge, finances were a constant worry and both parents missed their families and old friends from their student days before all the troubles. They had been lucky, they knew, to escape across the border. Shivering and hungry, they hid in a wooded area until, after bribing the border guards with two bottles of palinka, they had escaped, free but desperate, carrying only a few possessions in their backpacks. Many of their university friends had not been so lucky.

Aleda did not understand what her parents had gone through. She only knew that, in that moment in their kitchen, they were sad, and their sorrow weighed on her. They had been speaking in Hungarian, the language of her heritage but a language she did not fully understand. Even at home, her parents spoke to her in English, perhaps hoping to improve their own English skills, aided by their bright young daughter.

"Mama, Papa," she had said, speaking in her halting Hungarian, "there is always tomorrow." It was an expression she had heard from their own lips, but now, when she said it back to them, they turned to her, startled.

"Yes, darling, you are right." Papa had said and then repeated in Hungarian, "There is always tomorrow." Across the table, her mother was smiling but her eyes shone with tears.

Alone in the musty, dreary little cottage at the beginning of her vacation, with the rain dripping off the eaves, she raised her mug. If there was a point of redemption about the cottage, it was that the entire front west-facing wall was glass, offering a splendid view of the sandy beach and rolling waves.

"To a wonderful vacation," she said aloud. "There is always tomorrow … you scummy little Bluebird Cottage."

13
Transformation

ALEDA VASTAG WAS QUITE SURE OF ONE THING: TRANSFORMATION HAPPENS ALL THE time and in a great variety of shapes and forms. But, still, it often took her by surprise.

As she woke and stretched on the first full day of her vacation, she lay in the bunk bed remembering a teenager in her former congregation. The girl had complained bitterly to Aleda that her father never had time for her. One night, though, on a rare occasion when she was home beside him on the living room sofa watching the late-night news, the girl noticed the creases and fatigue in her father's face and realized how hard her father felt he must work to provide for the family. The girl began to see life from her father's point of view and her attitude changed.

Aleda wondered now what transformation might happen in Dorrie's life. How would the shroud of grief and detachment be lifted? She wondered about Grace. What might soothe the harshness that surfaced in her words? And what of Connie? Aleda did not understand what might need transforming in Connie's life, but something suggested that all was not well.

And what about herself, she wondered. Why was she preoccupied lately with considering how to define happiness? Did her interest in happiness reflect something amiss in her own life?

These things sifted through her mind as she stirred awake on her dank mattress in Bluebird Cottage. She realized that she had been granted yet another transformative opportunity. She could make some alterations to the gloomy Bluebird Cottage, but of more importance, she could transform her attitude. After all, living in a run-down cottage for two weeks was not the end of the world!

She looked around the double-bunked bedroom, surprised to see a broad band of light in the space between the beds. She stared at the sunshine on the bedroom wall, noticing that the sun's rays created an arc of colour. When she turned her head sideways toward the long window in the front room, she could see a white seagull, soaring and swooping above the beach.

"Okay, God," she said aloud. "I'm ready. The first full day of vacation. The day after the rain. I'm going to transform this disaster of a cottage into something more pleasant. I can do it. I may need a little help with my attitude, though."

By mid-morning, after enjoying a cup of coffee and breakfast in her lawn chair on the beach in front of Bluebird Cottage, she grabbed the keys for her van. She had intention in her stride. She had a list in her hand. She was on a mission.

The first stop was at a store on the highway where she discovered an array of colourful home decor items. She gathered into her shopping cart a round Hawaiian table cloth which she would use to cover the beige chrome table, a red throw to cover the sagging plaid sofa, a red and orange beach cushion for the seat of the plastic tub chair and, best of all, three colourful beach pictures, mounted in pine frames — a photo of red cottage chairs, a picture of a sunset, and a photo of a wharf lined with painted boats. Perfect replacements for the Christmas cards thumbtacked to the walls.

Heading toward the cashier, she saw something else that she could not resist. There, in a feature display, were hurricane lanterns with wooden lifters. When a candle was lowered, the flame would be protected by the plexiglass sides and would not blow out in the strong beach winds. Perfect for twilight campfires on the beach, she thought, putting two into her cart.

As she turned onto the curving road toward downtown Kincardine, Aleda suddenly thought about Margie and her teenage daughters who would arrive the next day. She pulled into a plaza parking lot and turned off the van. Alone in her vehicle, surrounded by all the colourful things she had purchased to transform Bluebird Cottage, she was filled with self-doubt.

Had it been a mistake to invite two teenage girls? She pressed her hands together against the space between her eyebrows. She knew, with certainty, that she and Margie had much to talk about, much that they shared in common, but what would two girls do in a dank, dark, bathroomless cottage for three days? There was swimming, of course, and beach walks, but they couldn't do that all day long.

When she looked up, she realized that she had parked in front of a pharmacy. Ah, she thought, perhaps I could find something for the girls in there.

She browsed in a perfume aisle, down the row of hair products, then, feeling discouraged, moved toward the front of the store where magazines sat erectly in little wire cages. She paused to flip through a monthly review of movie stars, then returned it to the rack. As she was doing so, another magazine caught her attention. There, directly in front of her, was a glossy cover with the title "Makeup solutions." She snatched the magazine out of the rack and flipped through it. Perfect, she thought.

With the magazine tucked under her arm, she headed to the makeup aisle, a plastic shopping basket looped over her arm, and began to gather up the needed items: eyeliners in different shades of blue and black, lip gloss, blush, mascara, foundation, moisturizer, and a magnifying mirror on a swivel base.

Now there were only two more things she needed to buy to complete her shopping — a shower curtain and a small plastic tub. She was ready to transform Bluebird Cottage and, she hoped, her attitude toward it.

Aleda seldom ate in a restaurant — her parents had been frugal about that in her childhood — but this being the first full day of her vacation, she decided to treat herself to lunch at the *Erie Belle*, the fish and chip shop she had noticed on her first visit to Kincardine.

As she sat on the front patio waiting for her food order to arrive, enjoying the view of the lake and the warm sunshine on her arms, she was distracted by a man sitting at a nearby table. He was engaged in an animated conversation on his cell phone. She soon determined that he was a real estate agent in the process of closing a deal.

She stared in fascination at the man's phone. Some of her university friends from twenty years ago — the friends with wealthy parents — had owned early cell phones, big awkward devices too large to fit in a jacket pocket. Some were shaped like bananas, which she remembered from watching the movie *The Matrix*. She recalled that, soon after that, cell phones became smaller, had a touch screen and a flip top. Now, staring at the real estate agent speaking into his little silver phone and making notes on a pad of paper on the patio table, she heard him say, "I'm on my cell phone at the moment but I can check that information on the internet. Yes, I understand your concern. I can e-mail you a photo of the kitchen from my phone."

Amazing, she thought, as she dipped her battered fish into a puddle of tartar sauce. She began to think about the ways in which a cell phone would be helpful in her work. A cell phone would be handy for rearranging or making appointments while she was away from home. She could call Laura or Martin if she was running late. But, of most importance, she would have a way to call for help if she had a vehicle breakdown with her old van, especially if she were alone on a country road at night.

After paying for her lunch, she wandered up to the main street where her van was parked. There, directly beside her vehicle, was a store window with a selection of cell phones. The brand names meant nothing to her. Staring through the plate glass window, she only knew that she liked the little silver one, one similar to that of the real estate agent.

She had spent a great deal of money on her shopping spree and was reluctant to spend more. A childhood of caution about money left her with a malaise, a pervading guilt, when she shopped. Still, she thought with a shudder, what *would* happen if her old van broke down in the snow and sleet on a country road at night? What would happen if she had a flat tire?

Twenty minutes later, she returned to her van, surrounded by her purchases of the day. In a compact box beside her on the front seat sat a new silver cell phone. How would she ever learn to use it? Did she really need it or was it only a self-indulgent impulse purchase? Dear God, she thought, partly in prayer, partly in exasperation, sometimes I wish I could turn off my mind!

14
Margie

"I'M SO EXCITED TO SEE YOU! WE HAVE SO MUCH TO CATCH UP ON," ALEDA ENTHUSED when Margie and her girls crawled out of their car. Margie's daughters, who had been listening to music and staring out the car window for the morning, looked sleepy and languid.

"Oh, Jana and Teresa!" Aleda exclaimed. "How you've grown!" Then she added in a hurry, "Oh, I'm sorry. I used to hate when people said that to me when I was young." The girls smiled politely. "Grab your bags and I'll show you into the cottage."

As the girls followed her, they caught sight of the beach and the rolling waves. They stopped abruptly, bumping into each other.

"Wow! Awesome!" they exclaimed together.

"Why don't you change into your swim suits and jump in?" Aleda suggested, smiling at them.

She realized that she had worried in vain about the girls. Everything about Bluebird Cottage seemed a great joke to them, especially her account of the Christmas cards mounted on paper plates and thumbtacked to the walls.

"We get to sleep up there?" they giggled, peering up into the upper bunks in the dank bedroom.

"Um, yes, and there is something else I need to show you, down the wood chip path," Aleda said. To her relief, the girls thought that using an outhouse was the most hilarious thing that had ever happened to them. She showed them a washing area near the bunk beds that she had created using her new shower curtain and plastic basin. "Some days," she said with a wave toward the lake, "that big bathtub out there is just too cold."

Aleda had asked the girls if they would like to go into Kincardine to explore or shop, but they seemed content to hang out on the beach, lying in the sun and playing Frisbee in the breaking waves. When they spotted some children digging in the wet sand, they helped to build a moat around a sandcastle and found twigs and coloured stones for turrets and windows.

The girls were as easy to feed as they were good natured, she discovered, and were content with hotdogs roasted over the beach fire. On their rambles through the clumps of trees that dotted the shoreline, they found sticks which they meticulously whittled, squabbling and teasing each other about whose roasting stick was more perfect. In the evening, they were happy to light the new lanterns and sit beside the snapping fire, roasting marshmallows and watching the stars come out.

"Are they always this easy to live with?" Aleda whispered.

"Oh, they have their moments, that's for sure," Margie declared, "but in general they're pretty good kids." Her face shone with a sort of self-congratulatory pride. Or was it just reflection from the campfire, Aleda wondered, smiling.

"One of the wonderful by-products of having young people in your life," she observed to Margie, "is that they teach you so many things. It would have taken me weeks to learn how to use my new cell phone if the girls hadn't given me a crash course this afternoon."

"I know what you mean," Margie agreed. "It's a generational thing. I would have hauled out the instruction book, read it from the first to last, then painstakingly tried out each step."

By the third day, both women noticed that the girls were taking longer beach walks and, on their return, were animated and giggly.

"It can mean only one thing," Margie said, her lips drawn into a straight line. "Boys."

"Huh?"

"Must be boys down at that end of the beach."

"Does that worry you?" Aleda asked.

"Well, there's safety in numbers," she replied. "And it's certainly not the first time, so I've had some experience."

Aleda looked over at her friend propped up in a lawn chair, a glass of lemonade in her hand. "I sometimes wonder if I could have been a mother," she said. "I think it would have driven me crazy with worry. Do you think there are more dangers now than when we were kids?"

"Good heavens, no," Margie declared in an authoritative voice. "Don't you remember that creep who used to expose himself to us in the park, and we were too scared to tell our parents? And don't you remember that cul-de-sac where the boys used to hang out to fight, with all the other kids standing in a ring around them? Oh, there were dangers then, too."

"I suppose so," Aleda responded in a tone that revealed her doubt.

Margie lifted her head and looked at her long-time friend. "So ... you've never been tempted to marry after that fiasco with Ben?"

"I've been attracted to a few men," she confessed, "but, honestly, my friend, do you have any idea ... any idea at all ..." she repeated throwing her hands up into the air, "how difficult it is to date someone when you're a single female minister in a village where everyone notices everything you do?" For a moment, she considered telling Margie about her relationship with Neil, but something held her back, something private and tentative, something incomplete. The timing did not feel right.

"But has it been enough, Aleda?"

When the girls returned from the north end of the beach, Jana plopped down on a beach towel. "We just saw the weirdest thing."

"Yah," Teresa confirmed. "A big square metal thing sitting in the sand a few feet out in the water."

"Really?" Margie responded.

"That must be the boiler that I've heard so much about," Aleda said. "The boiler that gave this beach its name. I haven't seen it yet, but I've been wanting to. You up for a walk, Margie?"

With the girls tagging along, splashing through the water's edge, they made their way toward the bulky, rusted boiler lodged in the compacted wet sand. It was both ugly and fascinating.

Teresa moved toward a mounted plaque and read aloud:

Wreck of the Erie Belle

The Erie Belle exploded south of Kincardine, November 21, 1883, killing four men in an attempt to free the grounded schooner "Carter." The boiler remains a lasting memorial to Lake Huron sailors.

"I wonder what really happened here," Aleda mused.

"I'm sure," Margie replied, "that we could find out with a quick trip to the Kincardine library."

But that turned out to not be necessary. As they prepared to return to Bluebird Cottage, a man walking his dog emerged from the opposite way. "Came to visit our famous landmark?" he asked with a smile.

"You know about this shipwreck?" Jana asked.

"Sure do. What do you want to know?"

"Everything, really," Jana replied. "What happened here?"

"Well, the *Erie Belle* was a tugboat, built in Ohio and used in the American Civil War. After the war, the boat served as a passenger and freight steamer. She was a spunky, tough little boat, though," the man added. "In her lifetime, she sank and was wrecked two times, but both times she was raised and rebuilt. In 1879 a Canadian bought her and renamed her *Erie Belle*."

"It was a tugboat?" Aleda queried.

"You ever been here in November?" he asked. All four shook their heads. "We can get some wicked November storms on these Great Lakes. Some of the worst shipwrecks happened in that month. Tugboats were essential, really. They were tough, powerful little boats and were used to guide bigger ships in and out of the harbour, but they also needed tugboats for icebreaking and helping ships in trouble. Like here," he said, gesturing toward the boiler. "The *Erie Belle* was trying to tow the *Carter*, a bigger ship loaded with timbers. It was storming so badly that the *Carter* missed the Kincardine harbour and ran aground here."

"Why did the *Erie Belle* explode?"

"They're not entirely sure," the man responded. "It's possible that the release valve on the boiler was wired shut to produce more steam and power. The *Erie Belle* was having trouble pulling the *Carter* off the sand, so maybe the steam built up to the point where it just exploded."

"That sounds horrible," Aleda said. All five people stood in silence, imagining the scene of wind, snow and men floundering in the churning lake while the tug burned and the crew of the *Carter* scrambled through the icy water to pull out injured and dead crew.

"What happened to the *Carter*?" Jana wanted to know.

"Left right there for the rest of the winter. Frozen in. There was nothing else to do. She was freed later, though. In the spring they took apart the *Erie Belle* but left the boiler. Not sure why. Maybe it was too heavy to easily remove, but here's my thinking: those of us who live near this lake have both a fascination and fear of its power. I think that people wanted to keep alive the memory of how sailors and captains risked their lives when they were out on these waters, especially in a storm."

"That's what it says on the plaque!" Teresa declared. "A lasting memorial to Lake Huron sailors."

The girls told Margie and Aleda that they wouldn't be home for dinner. They were meeting new friends for pizza in front of the boiler. Like dozens of other beach walkers before them, the young people had succumbed to the lure of the boiler.

"Really," Margie fussed as she and Aleda watched the girls head off down the beach, "don't you think that they had on a little too much makeup?"

Aleda only smiled and shrugged, trying not to feel responsible for having supplied the makeup. "It's part of growing up," she replied, thinking that her response was a great deal easier when these were not her own daughters. "If only life changes were as simple as applying makeup," she mused, her mind flashing back to the problems she had left behind in Milburn Corners.

"Do you remember that old movie, *Shirley Valentine*?" Margie laughed. Aleda laughed too, for they had seen the movie together three times. "Talk about a *life* makeover!"

"There was something in that movie that we needed, I guess," Aleda said.

"Well, I certainly did," Margie confessed. "I'd been married four years. Both Mike and I were independent before our wedding, then afterward we seemed to settle into the traditional patterns of our parents. I wasn't happy about it, but I didn't know how to change."

"So that movie gave you courage to make some changes?"

"That movie gave me the courage to think that I *could* change, if I really wanted to," she responded. "Shortly after that, I became pregnant with Jana and things got busy. When she was a year old, I was offered the job as head librarian in Hamilton. I was so excited about that. I set about arranging child care, but just as I was about to start to work, I found out that I was pregnant again, with Teresa."

"I hadn't remembered that," Aleda admitted.

"I was devastated because, of course, I wanted everything … family and a career, fame and fortune!" Margie said with a laugh.

"And, so …?"

"One day I thought to myself, well, why not? Women around the world have babies and keep on working. Somehow," she said, shrugging, "we North American women think we're so special. We think no one can raise our children with quite the same finesse as we can. Not even their fathers. We think we're indispensable." She smiled and shook her head. "So, one night I asked Mike if he would consider taking a leave of absence from his job to be a stay-at-home dad for a while. I'm still amazed that he agreed. In fact, he seemed really happy to have that chance."

"When we get back to the cottage, why don't we take a drive into Kincardine, visit the video store and see if they have a copy of *Shirley Valentine* ... for old times' sake?"

They sat on the droopy old sofa, cuddled close together, engrossed in watching *Shirley Valentine* on Aleda's laptop. After the credits began to roll, Aleda exclaimed, "The best part of that movie is the ending!"

Both women laughed as they remembered Shirley Valentine's husband flying from England to find her in the sensuous Mediterranean, to bring her back to her senses, to take her back home. Sitting alone at a beach patio table, wearing sunglasses and sipping wine, Shirley Valentine had changed so much that her husband did not recognize her. He walked past and she had to call him back. The movie ended with Shirley and her husband sitting side by side, staring out to the sea.

"But what happens next?" Margie demanded. "I just can't decide what Shirley Valentine would do."

Aleda pursed her lips and, for the second time in their visit, was tempted to tell her friend about Neil. Instead, she replied quietly, "Yes, how will it all turn out?"

15

Neil

AFTER MARGIE AND THE GIRLS LEFT, ALEDA SAT IN A LAWN CHAIR IN FRONT OF THE cottage, feeling empty and alone. She gazed out at the lake as two teens sailed south on a laser boat with a white sail, tacking into the wind. A young couple, a baby snuggled in a pack on the father's chest, strolled along the beach, a dog trailing along the water's edge, sniffing right, then left. The sun beat down hot, sizzling on the sand, but a cool breeze from Lake Huron stirred the air. "The world's largest air conditioner," Margie had called it.

Sitting in her chair in front of the cottage, she noticed, for the first time, beach flowers growing with strength and resilience in the sand, defying the sterile ground and the scorching sun. She rose and crouched to examine a small plant with a dot of yellow framed by white petals. Its delicate flowers and slender leaves suggested a fragility that she knew was simply not possible in the relentless northwest wind off the lake.

Turning toward the copse of trees on her right, she spotted a cluster of yellow flowers, similar to dandelions, but standing straight and tall on stems that bent toward the lake. She stared at the yellow flowers. Why do they bend like that? Then she realized that they were growing in fine gravel under the trees and were bending toward the light. How amazing, she thought, staring at the cheerful yellow blooms. What a connection, what symbiosis among the various elements: the sand, the sun, the wind and the weather. It was not a hospitable climate for growth, yet somehow the tiny plants survived and put out exquisite flowers, and when they had finished their life cycle, they would die and add nutrients to the sand.

As she gazed, she began to think that this small plant with its golden bloom symbolized the movement from life toward death and then back to life again, but in its glory moment of living, the response of this tiny plant was to lean toward the light. That's what I must do, she thought now. Regardless of what happens in the future, I must lean toward the light, toward what is good and noble and true. Perhaps, she concluded, that's a good way to describe a truly happy life — leaning toward the light.

She remembered the time when she had discovered philosophy at university. How enchanted she was to read that Aristotle described the desire for happiness as mankind's greatest pursuit, that happiness should be a social and civic desire. Her course in philosophy had almost persuaded her to switch her major from science to philosophy.

But as her study progressed, she began to see some flaws in Aristotle's thinking. The pursuit of happiness — as he described it — was the rightful realm of men and their world; women, slaves and children couldn't attain happiness since men's well-being was derived from commanding, while women's happiness came from obeying. The more she read, the more Aristotle's philosophy seemed to lack heart and compassion. She remembered staring in disbelief at the page where Aristotle declared that mentally challenged people could never attain happiness.

Around the same time, she had been attending worship services at the university chapel. When the chaplain spoke about Jesus' teaching in the beatitudes, all starting with "happy are those," she realized that, only four hundred years after Aristotle, the message of Jesus — complete inclusion of the poor and vulnerable, women and children, the sick and hurting — was both evolutionary and revolutionary. It had been a turning point in her life. The power of the beatitudes had drawn her toward ministry. Happy are those … she now thought, trying to remember the sequence of Jesus' teachings.

Back in Bluebird Cottage, as she was preparing a sandwich for lunch, she remembered how the girls had shown her a feature of her new cell phone — the ability to call home to retrieve messages from her landline. She imagined the telephone in the silent, stuffy parsonage kitchen and, eager to try out her new phone, she smiled and dialed her own familiar number. There were two messages. The first was a reminder about a library book she had ordered some weeks before, but the second …

"Aleda, it's Neil Brennan calling. Not sure if you're already off on your vacation, but I've had another call about that family we visited in the dilapidated church. It seems that a store keeper in Wiarton saw the father shopping with the little girl and one of the boys. The boy had a bad nose bleed and bruises on his legs and seemed to have trouble walking, so he was leaning on the shopping cart." She heard the concern and hesitation in Neil's voice. "I have to go back out there again." He hadn't asked her if she might go with him, but she thought he had implied it. He left two numbers where he could be reached.

She stood for a minute, the silver phone balanced in her hand, thinking about Neil's concern for this unusual family. The father had claimed to be a changed man, but if that was true, why had someone placed a call to the police station? It was difficult to understand why a man wanted to keep his wife and children isolated in such a remote and uncomfortable place.

She reached him at his home and explained where she was. He said, "I have a day off. Do you mind if I take a drive to Kincardine and we could talk a bit about this situation?"

"Oh, that would be fine," she stammered. She set down the cell phone and gazed out to the lake. She wondered if she had been prudent to get drawn into the worries that she tried to leave behind on her vacation. Did he really need her help? She suddenly felt like a teenager again, scolding herself for feeling nervous and flustered.

She watched him pull off the road into the little parking space behind Bluebird Cottage and step out of the red Mustang. He stood taking in his surroundings, gazing first toward the lake with its rolling waves, then back to the little cottage with the lawn chairs sitting beside a boxed grill resting over an outdoor fire pit. He spotted her in front of the cottage, smiled and headed down the path.

The afternoon passed quickly. They strolled north on the beach, discussing the curious and disturbing details of the family in the dilapidated church near Wiarton but arriving at no conclusion. When they reached the boiler, they settled on a bench and she told Neil the history of the *Erie Belle* disaster.

"It must have been exciting but also dangerous to sail the Great Lakes," he said. Aleda heard the combination of fascination and envy in his voice.

"But surely … your work," she began. "Every day you must have excitement and danger. Does that never get you down? Does it not stress you out?"

He smiled and looked out across the lake. "Sometimes. It's true, we police officers often see humanity at its worst. I try to stay healthy — exercise, get my sleep, and eat properly. Don't always manage that," he laughed. He seemed lost in thought. "I make sure I take my vacation time. Ireland or kayaking or canoeing in Algonquin Park or Georgian Bay. I go with the priest at St. Mary's," he added, looking down at her. "He's been a good friend to me. And I guess I don't have to tell you how important it's been to have a faith to hold me up when things get tough." She nodded, thinking that there were so many things she wanted to discover about this man.

The sun had begun to slip into the top of a deep cloud bank at the edge of the western sky. "It will be a beautiful sunset, again," she said, waving to the west. "When the cloud formation is like that ..."

"You chose a beautiful spot for a vacation, Aleda."

"As beautiful as Lion's Head?" she teased, but he just smiled and didn't answer. "I picked up some steaks and mushrooms for dinner. Are you able to stay?"

"Love to," he answered, smiling down at her.

To her surprise, he was a skilful cook, intrigued by the possibility of preparing the steak on the boxy grill over an open flame. While he coated the cast iron fry pan with oil, he called out, "You have any barbeque sauce, Aleda? Any pepper? Any chance you have some blue cheese? Some haloumi?"

"Nope," she called out from the open door of the cottage, busy tossing a salad in a granite cooking pot — the closest thing she could find to resemble a salad bowl. "But I did take a trip to Pine River Cheese Factory up the road and I have some smoky bacon cheese."

"Perfect. Bring it on."

While the steak sizzled and hissed on the grill, the mushrooms toasted to a golden brown. Aleda set up lawn chairs, draped the Hawaiian cloth over the rusty table near the water's edge, and lit the hurricane lanterns.

"What do you drink? I have red wine and cold beer."

"Wine for me," he said, turning over a juicy steak.

People strolling along the beach, catching the last glimpses of the pink and orange clouds, smiled and called out, "Great place for dinner!"

When the sky had darkened, when the wine bottle was empty, when the air had begun to chill, Neil suggested a walk along the beach in the moonlight. As they walked, Aleda found herself telling him about her reflections on the meaning of happiness and her critique of Artistotle's definition. She told him about the stubborn and strong little beach flowers.

"Ah," he said when she described the plants. "Sounds like you stumbled upon lyre-leaved rock cress and lakeside daisy."

"Huh?"

She saw him shrug in the dusk. "A hobby of mine. The wildflowers of the beaches of the Great Lakes."

"A rather esoteric interest, I must say," she teased.

They strolled down the beach in silence until Neil said, "Aside from what we learn at school and in church, we discover a lot about life from nature. Don't you think so, Aleda? I'd like to have more time to study plants and water and the stars. You just can't ignore a starry night. It fills you with wonder. Don't you think we become wiser from studying nature?" She responded that she was not at all sure that she would ever be completely wise — she hoped so — but she valued the natural world because it took her outside time, outside the small and focused sphere of herself.

When they came to a sheltered area where large logs lined the sides of a deserted fire pit, Neil asked, "Want to sit for a while?" They settled on the still-warm sand, leaning against the logs and gazing up. "Almost a full moon," he said, smiling at her. "This is about as much of a definition of happiness as I could ever hope for."

She smiled too, looking into his face, and when he put his arm around her brown shoulders and tilted her suntanned face toward his, she closed her eyes and experienced a kiss that was full of both tenderness and passion. He gathered her toward him, wrapping both arms around her in the warm sand. Aleda looked up at him. "Remind me again why you came?"

He kissed the top of her head. "I don't know." But then he added, "To see you, of course."

16

Doubts

After they walked back along the beach toward Bluebird Cottage, he asked if he might stay over. He didn't want to drive after he had been drinking, he said. "But," he added quickly, "I'll get away early in the morning. I have a shift in the afternoon."

Bedtime might have been awkward but, she later thought, what did I expect? Honestly, she berated herself angrily, what *did* I think would happen?

He had a gym bag in his car. "I work out six days a week," he confessed, "so I never go anywhere without it." While she prepared for bed — why, she demanded of herself, had she only her oversized T-shirt for nightwear — he used the outhouse, and when he returned wearing his gym shorts and a white T-shirt, she smelled a minty waft of toothpaste.

"Good night, Aleda," he said gravely, and crawled into the lower bunk bed across from her.

It was dark in the cottage, but the light from the moon shone in the space between the bunks. She stared at the shape of the large police officer on the opposite bunk, wondering what would happen next, but in a few minutes, she heard his breathing slow and saw him turn over, facing the wall. She wondered again how this man who was so intriguing to her and with whom she had shared an intimate evening could be so hard to understand.

She woke to the smell of wood smoke and coffee and the snap of bacon sizzling in the cast iron fry pan over the square grill. She eased out of her lower bunk, noting that the sheets and blankets she had given Neil were neatly folded at the end of his bunk bed. She poked her head out the cottage door. Not seeing him, she staggered to the outhouse, then back to her small shower-curtained area where she washed her face, ran a comb through her hair and pulled on fresh clothes.

By the time she walked out the front door again, she spotted him coming up from the beach, his gym shorts wet and clinging to his thighs. She stared at his sculpted chest, mottled with freckles. Oh my, she thought, watching him approach, that man does indeed work out six days a week. A police officer's body and strength, he had explained to her the night before, are his second-best weapon. "What's your first?" she had asked jokingly, expecting him to name his gun, but he had replied, tapping his temple, "My brain. I try to think ahead, outsmart the bad guys."

"Morning," she called out, making a determined effort to look at his face. "You're up early."

He walked toward her, his face grim, his expression sombre and troubled. There was no hint of the intimacy and warmth of the previous evening. She felt a flutter of panic in her stomach. What had happened?

"I'll get dressed and serve up breakfast," he said, disappearing into Bluebird Cottage.

Despite the wonderful aromas, breakfast was quiet and subdued. There was no conversation, the silence broken only by the gentle lapping of waves and the clanking of their cutlery. At first, Aleda felt confused, baffled and hurt. Then she began to feel angry. She set down her plate and fork with a clatter.

"What has changed?" she asked. "Last night ... well, it seemed perfect, but this morning you look distant and serious. I don't understand what's going on."

Neil glanced at her, then carefully set his breakfast plate on the sand in front of his lawn chair.

"I believe you owe me an explanation," Aleda demanded. She could hear that her words were hard, her voice made high by her shallow breathing.

"I'm sorry," he said. "You deserve better."

She frowned, her burst of anger replaced with bewilderment. "Perhaps you should start by telling me what on earth is going on in your head."

He sat hunched over on the edge of the chair, staring down at his clasped hands. "It *was* a wonderful evening," he said, at last. "And you are a wonderful woman. Smart, pretty, caring." He glanced at her, then turned his head toward the lake. "But I don't see how we can have any kind of a future together." He turned away from the lake and stared into the dying coals under the grate. "You are a career woman and I want something different, a family life. You went to university for six years," he added, remembering her exposition on Aristotle from the previous evening. "Me, I just finished high school and became a cop." She stared at him, but he continued to look into the fire pit. "Then there's the matter of our religious differences. You Protestant and a minister too, me Catholic. Those are important things to us. Those are big differences and we're not going to change them," he said, glancing up at her.

She sat in silence, then stammered, "But surely there are different ways." She searched for ways to describe that she may have gone to university for six years but had no knowledge of the wildflowers of the Great Lakes. She looked for ways to say that she preached about good and evil, but he had to deal daily with the realities of malevolence. She wanted to say that his strength gave her courage, made her want to venture and stretch beyond her comfort level. She sorted through her scrambled thoughts. Did the dissimilarities between them really matter so much?

"It seems that there are too many barriers to overcome, too many differences in our lives," he said, shaking his head.

She found herself unable to answer, but then a worrisome image came to her. Her mind flashed back to a short time before, when she had been sitting in his police cruiser on a hot sunny day. She had picked up the hand-knit shamrock for a moment and cradled it in her hand.

Now, sitting by the dying embers, she turned to him. "You're thinking of going back to Ireland, aren't you?" When he didn't look up at her, she stood, her hands on her hips. "You're thinking about marrying that woman, Mary Bridgette, aren't you?"

He grasped his gym bag in front of him and stood up, ready to leave. Then he reached out as if to touch her arm. "Aleda, listen to me carefully. You must not … and I mean under no circumstances … you must not go swimming today."

She looked up at him, shocked and puzzled by the sudden twist in their conversation.

"There's a dangerous undertow today, quite close to the shore. If you see a child swimming today, or if you see people floating on an air mattress, you must stop them."

She stared up into his face, confused.

"I've seen too many people drown in conditions like this. Will you promise me," he pleaded, "that you will not go into the lake today?"

• • •

The red Mustang had scarcely disappeared when she turned back toward Bluebird Cottage and began to cry. Standing by the dying embers of the breakfast fire, the bacon now congealing on her plate, the coffee cold and bitter, she stared up the road where the car had disappeared. Raising her fist in an angry gesture, she shouted at the top of her lungs, "Neil Brennan, you're one maddening son-of-a-bitch!"

Almost immediately, she stretched her arms up toward the sky. "Sorry. Sorry, God. I know you don't like that sort of language. Sorry, Mama and Papa. Sorry that I swore." Turning toward the beach, she said, "Sorry, strollers. Sorry for my bad language."

But there was no one there to hear. There was just an empty strip of sand and the relentless pulling of the waves.

17
Regina Davis

SHE BROODED OVER HER TIME WITH NEIL. AT SOME POINT, THINGS HAD CHANGED and she had a hard time figuring out what had gone wrong. Storming around Bluebird Cottage, sweeping and mopping, she alternated between anger at herself and resentment toward Neil. Within a time-frame of twenty-four hours, she had moved from certainty about the meaning of happiness to a state of disintegration — all over a man.

This is nonsense, she scolded herself. I'm forty-two years old and reacting like a teenager. Perhaps, she considered, emotions don't mature as fast as bodies, but then she reminded herself that it is human nature to feel disappointment when relationships fail or falter. Still, she was frustrated with herself for having fallen apart, remembering that back in Milburn Corners her parishioner Dorrie was struggling with *real* problems.

She longed to go for a swim, but she had been warned to stay out of the lake. What right does he have to tell me not to swim? she fumed. When her cleaning projects did not diffuse her confusion and energy, she decided to take a long walk into Kincardine.

After reaching the town, she wandered up the main street, pausing occasionally to browse the summer reading offered in the window of Fincher's Book Store, to look at shoes on display in another store, to enjoy a whiff of hamburgers and French fries in front of a restaurant. After she had walked through the centre of town, she decided to turn back to Boiler Beach, but just then she spotted a sign pointing to Knox Presbyterian Church.

Curious and feeling drawn to a church which represented comfort and hope in her life, she turned east and there, set high on a knoll, was an imposing stone and brick structure. She stood at the end of the sidewalk gazing at the lofty building. It seemed that the pioneers had done their best to create a commanding cathedral-like church in their small town. The heavy wooden doors reminded her of the doors on her own church in Milburn Corners. Suddenly overcome with sadness and weariness, she walked up the broad stairs leading to the main door and slumped down.

She had to start her long trek back to Boiler Beach, but the calves of her legs ached. Perhaps there was a taxi company in town. As she was about to rise from the steps and head back to the main street, she heard the throaty rumble of an approaching motor bike. She caught a glimpse of the riders — a man and a woman — as the bike slowed and stopped on the side street next to the church. The driver set his legs firmly on either side of the bike to hold it steady as his passenger dismounted. The woman unsnapped her helmet and shook out blond hair streaked with a wide swatch of purple. Aleda stood up as the smiling woman approached.

"Hi!" the woman called out, her voice cheerful and friendly. "You look a bit lost sitting there on the steps. Is there any way I can help you?"

"Oh, no, no," Aleda stuttered as she stared at the woman who stood dangling her motorcycle helmet. She was wearing pants rolled up to her calves and a long-sleeved shirt — protection from the sun and wind, she supposed — but it was plain to see that she had a tattoo above her left ankle. "It's just that …" Aleda faltered but sensed somehow that an explanation of why she was sitting alone on a church step was expected. "I'm vacationing close by," she continued. Did she really owe this complete stranger an explanation? "I went for a walk, and I guess I've walked a little too far. I'm wondering if there is a taxi company in town? I'm thinking of getting a lift back to the cottage I've rented on Boiler Beach."

The woman threw back her head and laughed. "Surely not that dreadful tourist trap called Bluebird Cottage," she said. When she saw the stricken look on Aleda's face, she was suddenly grave. "Hey, I'm sorry," she said, reaching toward her, lightly touching her forearm. She leaned in and added, conspiratorially, "It's just that it has a bit of a reputation. But don't worry. I live just around the corner. I'll grab my car keys and give you a lift home."

"Oh, please, no. I don't want to be a bother!" Aleda protested.

"No problem at all," the woman said, dismissing the objection with a wave of her hand. "It's my husband's turn to cook dinner. It'll give him a bit of time to get the barbeque fired up. I'll just slip home and tell him what I'm up to."

As she snapped together the catch on her helmet and slung it over her forearm preparing to leave, Aleda blurted out, "Are you always this kind to total strangers who happen to be sitting on church steps?"

The woman spun around, her helmet clanging against the iron railing. "Oh! I am so sorry! I didn't even introduce myself." She reached out a hand to shake with Aleda. "My name is Regina Davis. I'm the minister here," she said, sweeping her free hand upward toward the grand, imposing steeple.

When she had recovered from the shock of discovering that Regina was not only a minister but also a female colleague in her own denomination, Aleda was amazed at how quickly they connected. It was a short drive from the church to Bluebird Cottage, but it was enough time for them to discover that they liked each other and that this might well be the beginning of a friendship which would blossom and continue.

Arriving at the cottage, they sat in the car continuing to chat about the many things they had in common — the unexpected funerals, the weekly challenge of preparing an inspiring and faithful sermon, the joys and burdens of church administration and meetings, helping youth stay involved in the church, keeping abreast of modern theological shifts, the trials of maintaining confidence in difficult pastoral situations.

"This has been a serendipitous meeting," Regina said. "Why don't we meet up again after worship tomorrow? Grab some lunch on the patio at the Bruce Inn. My treat. I insist. My husband is off with some friends for the afternoon. Besides," she added, leaning over toward Aleda, "I don't know if it's the same for you, but after worship I'm both pumped up and exhausted at the same time. It would be great to go out to lunch with someone who might understand that feeling."

"Oh, I totally get that," Aleda responded in a somber voice. "Completely know that feeling."

As the evening approached, she sat on the beach reviewing the unusual turn in her day. It hardly seemed possible that only that morning Neil had stammered out an explanation of how futile it seemed to continue the tenuous relationship they had established. Not much wonder I was furious at that, she fumed again, thinking of how intimate and wonderful their previous evening had been. She remembered their conversation and the tender and passionate kiss they shared, his fingers intertwined with hers as they leaned against the log by the fire pit. And then she remembered his parting words.

Could she let go of her anger toward Neil? Before her resentment could mount again, she forced herself to recall the unexpected encounter with Regina

Davis. What would tomorrow bring? She didn't know, but she looked forward to attending worship, sitting in a pew, being spiritually fed and not having to do the feeding. How different tomorrow afternoon would be from a Sunday afternoon in Milburn Corners. Tomorrow, she thought with a stir of anticipation, she would sit on a warm sunny patio and enjoy lunch with a female colleague, a new friend.

They settled at the edge of Bruce Inn patio overlooking the aqua lake, a table umbrella sheltering them from the hot sun. "This is perfect," Aleda said.

Regina turned toward their waiter, a young woman who greeted her with familiarity. "The usual to start?" the girl asked with a smile.

"Aren't you so clever!" Regina replied, laughing, then added, "the same for my friend as well." The waiter returned with two opaque glasses. Regina bent toward Aleda and whispered, "I don't feel free to order a nice cold beer or an iced chardonnay right after church," she confessed. "I worry a bit about what people might say. You know what I mean?"

"Oh, I do," Aleda answered, thinking of the time when Grace had spotted her wandering through the village on a Friday night with a glass of red wine in her hand.

"I've worked out a little system with the waiter," Regina continued. "She mixes up a nice stiff mimosa and if any of the local people or my parishioners come in for lunch after church, they think I'm having a lovely glass of orange juice. That cute young student is in on my secret and I always reward her with a generous tip. It's a win-win situation," she said with a laugh. "I hope I haven't presumed too much in ordering for both of us," she added, nodding to Aleda's drink. In answer, Aleda lifted her glass with a grin and took a sip of her mimosa.

Over lunch they again talked about the many things they had in common: experiences and joys in their ministry, frustrations and roadblocks.

"I can't believe that we went to the same seminary but have never bumped into each other before," Regina exclaimed.

"We were there at different times, I suppose," Aleda murmured before the conversation swept on to other things. When she glanced at her watch, she was surprised to see that it was two thirty in the afternoon. Other diners had come and gone and, with the exception of the waiter who stood behind the bar polishing beverage glasses, they were alone in the warmth of the patio.

"You've never married, then?" Regina asked.

It was all Aleda needed. She heard her story tumble out, how she had fallen deeply in love with Ben at seminary and how he had broken her heart when he dated another student who became pregnant. She told Regina about meeting him again after eighteen years, and inviting him to visit in Milburn Corners where he bitterly disappointed her again, this time by making advances toward her good friend Laura.

"What a rat," Regina declared in sympathy. Aleda nodded, staring down morosely into her empty coffee mug. Perhaps it was the effect of the mimosas, the lazy warmth of the afternoon sun and the accepting openness of her new friend, but she found herself telling Regina of her interest in Neil, the man who just seemed to keep popping up in her life over the past few months.

"You really think this man is the one for you?" Regina asked.

"I don't know, really," she responded, her voice hesitant. "I'm definitely interested in him. He's so steady, but he also has an exciting edge of danger in his work and hobbies." She told Regina about his kayaking adventures and his story about swimming through the deep grotto at Cypress Lake. "It's a heady combination — steadiness and danger," she confessed as she traced some circles on the glass-top patio table with the tip of her finger. "He's thoughtful and interesting, too." She told Regina about the time he had applied to the Police Benevolent Fund to help a destitute grandmother pay for a funeral. She told about the red Mustang, the cottage in Lion's Head, his interest in the wildflowers of the Great Lakes. She found herself telling Regina about his love and devotion to his Roman Catholic faith, and she talked about his strong and steady guidance through the agonizing time of a teen suicide in her village. "What kind of a police officer," she exclaimed, "would call up and leave a phone message suggesting that I use Chopin's Prelude in E minor or Dietrich Buxtehude's 'We pray now to the Holy Spirit' for a funeral service?"

The two women sat in silence for a minute, both lost in their own thoughts.

"Wow!" Regina exploded. "What's the problem? He sounds terrific!"

"He is terrific," Aleda said, frowning, gazing out over the lake. "It's just that he seems to think that he and I don't have a future together. We have too many obstacles to overcome, too many differences. That's what he said."

Regina leaned toward her. "Well, maybe there's a problem here or maybe not. I'm not sure how it will all unfold, but do yourself a favour, Aleda. Ask yourself this: Is he worth fighting for?"

18
Neil and Phillip

NEIL LOCKED HIS CRUISER AND WALKED TOWARD THE BACK DOOR OF THE POLICE station. It had been an uneventful shift: he had issued two speeding tickets and later acted as a crowd control presence at a sports event. He was ready to spend an hour at the gym, go home, take a shower and cook something for dinner.

He heard someone bark his name as he entered the station. "Neil! Constable Brennan, sir!" Scanning the room, he saw his colleagues preparing to take over the next shift. One was checking out a piece of equipment, another going over an inspection report and another officer was busy with some administration. "Neil!" he heard again. He swung his head toward the desk in the next office where the police dispatcher sat.

There were several dispatchers who alternated shifts in the office, but Neil was particularly fond of Vivian. She had the firm demeanour of a drill major when dealing with unruly members of the public, and even sometimes managing bad tempered officers, but she was also capable of empathy and compassion when people called in, crying, distraught and often incoherent. He knew that she had honed the skill of discerning the kind of emergency response that was needed or when, in fact, no response was needed at all — just a listening ear.

"You need me, Viv?"

"Come and sit down for a minute," she said. "I need to go over something with you."

Neil pulled a wooden chair close to her desk and stared in surprise. Usually calm and in control, today she seemed upset, her cheeks mottled and flushed, her brow frowning. "Something got you upset, Viv?"

"Damn right," she said, sweeping a pile of notes toward him. "You can look these over because it's going to be up to you to follow up on this nasty business."

Neil looked at her and said, "Tell me."

"First," she began, "I got a call from a social worker, a man called Phillip. His name and phone contact are there in the notes. Someone placed a call to Bruce Grey Child and Family Services — an anonymous call. Someone from Wiarton." She explained to Neil the details of the report, things he had heard before — the shopping expedition, the bleeding nose, the frail boy whose legs were covered with bruises. "Good God," Vivian muttered, her face flushed, "I can deal with just about any ugly thing that comes my way, but the idea of child abuse just boils my blood." She scrambled around in the notes. "Seems they moved up here from Dundalk recently and there are quite a few kids. Eight or so. They live somewhere between Allenford and Wiarton on a side road, and this is the crazy thing: they live in some kind of old abandoned church."

Neil tapped his index finger against his lips. "Yes," he admitted. "I've had a bit of contact with this family." His mind flashed back to the scene of a little girl and a beautiful smiling woman, approaching him, both wearing daisy chains in their hair. "What's the scoop on the Children's Aid worker? This Phillip?"

"He's very concerned about the boy. He believes the kid is in grave danger and needs protection, but he's new to the job. A kid himself, just out of college. Can you get on this right away? Go see the family? Better take that Phillip guy with you. You're going to need a second pair of hands, I suspect."

He sighed. "Thanks, Viv. I'll be in touch with Phillip tonight and get on this first thing tomorrow."

It was noon by the time Neil and Phillip turned into the overgrown laneway leading to the derelict church. The police cruiser bumped along the narrow gravel road lined with untrimmed trees, the leaves brushing against the windows of the vehicle. Phillip peered out at the roadside where dry grass from the previous year stood in a tangle of Scottish thistles and wild carrot.

"Perhaps we're catching them at a bad time," Phillip said, glancing over at the tall, somber police officer. "Lunch time, you know." There was a nervous quiver in his voice. "I've been wondering if I should have let my colleague, Connie, come instead of me. She's so much more experienced and would know what to do."

Neil shook his head slightly, wondering if he had ever seemed as young and naive when he was a police rookie. "There'll never be a good time." He steered slowly toward the makeshift gateway that prevented them from getting close to the building. Although he had seen it before, the desolation of the place struck him again. He shut off the motor and whistled through his teeth. "Oh, bollocks," he said, exhaling softly.

The two men stared at the old church. Four arched Gothic windows on the side of the building had long ago lost their glass and were boarded over, but even the wood that covered the windows had been smashed or rotted away. The buttresses were covered with gnarled vines that crept up the ends of the building to the high-pitched roof where tiles had blown off, exposing blackened wooden sheathing.

"What an isolated place," Neil said, "and what a mess. It's hard to believe that a family is living here." A "Sold" sign sat in a tangle of tall grass, wild brambles and overgrown lilac trees. As they waited, they noticed movement at the rear of the building. The girl, Dinah, wearing a long dress that resembled a nightgown, came cautiously toward them. Bare-footed, she picked her way around some broken bricks, then stood just behind the gate.

"Perhaps you might go to meet her?" Neil suggested. "Maybe a police officer would frighten her."

Phillip swallowed hard, then eased out of the police cruiser. Neil watched as he slowly approached the child. The girl seemed to indicate that the rest of her family were inside the church building.

Phillip returned to the cruiser. "We can go in," he said, and behind him the girl tugged open the gate. The men followed the child around the edge of the building, walking slowly and staying back from her so she wouldn't be frightened. When she disappeared behind the wooden door, the men stood looking up at the wide, square steeple with its pointed-arched windows and crumbling turreted top.

"Is it safe?" Phillip asked.

"Oh, not likely." Just then, the door opened and the girl stepped out, holding the hand of a man.

"My papa," she said, speaking to Phillip. Jacob wore a loose tunic and cut-off blue jeans and, unlike the little girl, he wore a pair of steel-toed work boots. They had obviously interrupted him at a woodworking project; his arms were covered with wood shavings and sawdust.

"May we come in?" Phillip asked. "My name's Phillip and I'm from the Bruce Grey Child and Family Services. This is my colleague, Constable Brennan." The man remained silent, but he moved so that his legs were set far apart and his arms folded in a defiant and defensive position. "Someone called us, worried about your son. They wondered if he needs help."

"Which one?" the man barked. "Which son?"

"We're not sure," Phillip continued. "A boy who has nose bleeds." The man continued to bar their way into the church, so Phillip repeated, "May we please come in?"

Slowly the man stood aside. When Neil and Phillip stepped inside the church, they stood in silence, staring. "Oh, my," Phillip whispered.

The chancel furniture had been removed but, part way back in the sanctuary, old pews with curved ends, the straight backs now darkened from rain and snow, had been arranged in a large square creating what seemed to be a cleanly swept play area for the children. Near the back door, Neil and Phillip could see that the man had been putting drywall on the outside of a large room. There was no doorway on the room yet, but they could see that it served as a communal bedroom and living space. Cots, a crib and mattresses were arranged on the floor at one side of the room, and a cupboard and table stood against another wall. A child was lying on one of the cots and, nearby, a cluster of children crowded close to a woman.

Phillip and Neil began to cross the sanctuary, but Neil kept his head turned slightly, aware of the heavy thud of the man's boots on the wooden floor as he followed. Phillip and Neil waited until the man entered the bedroom, then they, too, stepped inside.

For a moment, everyone stared at each other. Neil's eyes swept over the young boys who had been playing with some sticks, until his gaze fell on the boy lying on a cot, his thin legs protruding from a brown blanket, his dark-circled eyes staring up at him. An older girl standing near the table had been interrupted in the task of washing dishes in a plastic tub.

Phillip nodded to the woman and forced himself to smile at the children, whose faces were full of worry and fear. He inched over and crouched down by the cot where the boy lay. "What's your name, son?"

The boy looked up at Phillip, then at Neil who was standing by the doorway. His eyes searched out his father, then swept back to the police officer. He blinked, his gaze dropping to the gun in the policeman's holster.

"Can you tell us your name, son?" Phillip repeated, but still the child didn't answer.

"Look!" the man behind them exploded. "This is my family and I look after them well. All we want, all we've ever wanted, is to be free to live the life we've chosen. You have no right — no right at all — to come barging into our home." When they heard their father's raised voice, the small boys moved behind their mother, their hands bunching her skirt.

"But, sir," Phillip began, standing up.

"Shut up!" the man roared, before Phillip had time to continue. "Just shut up and get out." Startled, Phillip stepped backward. The man stomped over and stood in front of the boy's cot, his arms out. "We have our own ways. The boy has had some nose bleeds and is a bit under the weather, but we're treating him with herbs and he'll get stronger. Now, I'll thank you to get off my property."

Neil motioned Phillip toward the doorway and they stepped out of the room and moved across the broken-down sanctuary. When they reached the door where they had entered, Neil suddenly stopped, staring at something hanging on a nail near the doorframe. "You see that?" he muttered and both men stood gawking at a leather strap, the type that Neil remembered from his school days in Ireland. Phillip was too young to remember such an object but, for Neil, a muscular, tall, self-confident police officer who had had to deal with just about every type of violence imaginable, that leather strap still had the power to strike terror into his heart.

Turning toward the defiant man who had followed them to the front door, Neil said, "We will be back."

19
Laura

As she had promised, Laura arrived to spend a few days at Bluebird Cottage with Aleda. In the evening, juggling the Hawaiian table cloth, glasses and cutlery, Laura set the table near the lakefront while Aleda seared perch with almonds and lemon in the cast-iron fry pan. Laura sensed Aleda's need to talk, to tell a good friend about the events that had unfolded in the days of her vacation on Boiler Beach.

"Okay," Laura said as they sat down to dinner. "I want to hear it all. Start at the beginning."

She began by telling Laura about the wonderful days she had spent with Margie and her girls. Because she had not told Laura and Martin about Neil, she began to hesitantly explain her new and confusing relationship with him, including her trip to Lion's Head and her disturbing visit to the family living in the old church.

"I wonder," Laura commented, "if Connie might be helpful in this situation, dealing with the family in the old church, I mean."

Aleda inhaled and fell silent, staring out across the expanse of Lake Huron. Why did the mention of that name send an uneasy feeling through her? Aleda felt the old familiar stab of jealousy as she sensed Laura's interest in Connie and remembered when Laura suggested inviting her into their social circle. After a few minutes, she began to tell Laura about meeting Regina Davis and the friendship that had started to grow between them. Laura, in turn, fell silent. When Aleda realized what was happening, she turned to her and blurted out, "I really don't know what I would do without you, Laura. You've been a great friend." Then she added, "When I was a kid, we had little autograph books and once a year our friends would sign their names in them or write a little poem. There was one that I liked in particular:

Make new friends, but keep the old,
One is silver and the other gold."

Laura smiled and nodded, thinking but not daring to say that it felt quite silly for a grown woman like herself to feel possessive when she heard of Aleda's new relationships with Neil and Regina. Somehow the long-time bond with Margie seemed more natural, less of a threat to the stability of her own friendship with Aleda.

"Well, my friend," she said, "I do believe that it is the duty of a silver or gold friend to help you see things clearly, so may I remind you, Aleda, that it was only a couple of months ago that you reconnected with Ben? You do remember, don't you," Laura said, shaking her head, "how you fell head over heels for him again?"

"You must really wonder about me. I stupidly fell for him again after all these years. What a charmer," she said bitterly. "But I just as quickly woke up to the fact that he had essentially not changed. He was still a real jerk. Imagine him making a pass at you when he and I had just reconnected! What kind of a man does that?"

Laura wondered what she could say to her friend. She was having a hard time understanding how Aleda could have moved in such a short space of time from rejecting a former unfaithful lover to being so interested in a police officer she had known for only a few months.

"Aleda," she said finally, "I trust your judgement. I really do. But, as you once advised me when I was making up my mind about whether to take early retirement and stay in Milburn Corners, it's always good to take a temporary step before the permanent one."

"Yes," Aleda acknowledged, looking down, "I did suggest that. And what have you decided about teaching and retirement?"

Laura saw that Aleda had deftly deflected attention away from herself and put the focus back on Laura.

"I've requested a year's leave of absence," she told her.

"Wow. That's awesome, at least for me. You're okay with that decision? You won't miss your students or your life in Toronto?"

"I'm happy with the decision. It seems to be what I need just now, a quiet life in the village where I grew up." Both friends, sitting in lawn chairs, stared at the lapping waves. "Did I tell you that Rose has called the first meeting of the Milburn Corners Book Club? Starts in the second week of September. I'll have some reading to do every month."

"Really. I hadn't heard." Aleda began to visualize her September calendar filling up with commitments — meetings, book club, special worship services, the Friday evening youth meeting, pastoral calls. "Who will be part of the book club?" she inquired.

"I haven't heard yet, but you can count on an invitation."

"And what about you and Rose? Have you been able to talk about things with her?"

"You know how upset I was when I learned about her relationship with my father," Laura said. "The most peculiar thing happened, though. One day, shortly after you left to come here, Rose popped over to my house with a library book and a pan of sourdough cinnamon rolls. She brought me a book that came out last year — *Atonement*, by Ian McEwan. You've heard of it?"

"Heard of it but haven't read it."

"It will be first on the book club list, Rose said. I asked her what she liked about the book. She said, 'You know, Laura, we all have parts of our lives that need redeeming. We make mistakes and need to feel that we've been forgiven or delivered or rescued in some way.' This is where things got strange. She said to me, 'I have something in my background that should cause me to atone. I had a long chat with Aleda about it and that certainly helped. But the truth is, I don't feel all that sorry about it. Perhaps in the eyes of society and the church what happened was wrong, but it just felt so wonderful and right.' That's what she said to me."

Aleda turned her head sideways and gazed at her friend. "And then?"

"I took a direct approach. I said, 'Rose, what are you talking about?' She told me everything, bit by bit. Slowly. I think she didn't want to shock me. She told me about working as a nurse with my father and how they became close, how my father helped to care for her injured husband and how he took an active interest in Martin and James, paying for their university education and staying in touch with them. She told me how hard she and my father worked to keep both families intact. It was certainly a well-kept village secret. I didn't confess to her that Martin had already told me about it just a couple of months ago. When she was done, I just said to her, 'Rose, thank you for telling me this. You and I — we have a lot in common, and now we have one more thing in common. We both loved my father, and neither of us seems able to let him go.'"

As a rule, Aleda tried to have a quiet Saturday night. She liked to stay focused on Sunday worship, on the day ahead. But this Saturday night was quite different. Tomorrow would bring no preaching responsibilities, no pastoral cares.

"When I met Regina Davis last week," she told Laura, "she told me about an old tradition in Kincardine. Every Saturday night there's a bagpipe parade. We need to go."

Shortly before eight o'clock in the evening, they found themselves in Victoria Park in downtown Kincardine. The park was teeming with people — old and young, babies in strollers, children wearing tiny kilts and beating small drums. Along the main street, a throng of local people and tourists stood on the sidewalk or sat in lawn chairs or in parked cars, their windows rolled down, waiting for the drone of the pipes. Aleda and Laura stood among the mass of gathering people in the park, looking around, waiting for something to happen.

"What goes on here?" Aleda asked a woman who looked as if she had been there many times before.

"Oh, we just march along the main street behind the pipers," the woman answered, smiling. "This your first time?"

"It is," she confessed.

"When the pipers start," the woman said in a breezy manner, "just fall in behind them." Aleda nodded, smiling. "And don't forget the ice cream," the woman added. "The pipers stop for a break about four blocks away and the crowd rushes toward the ice cream stand. Then we all turn around and march back here to Victoria Park. That's it in a nutshell. Kincardine on a Saturday night!"

"That's it? Then people just go home?"

"Oh, the band plays a bit more back here in the park, and if you're lucky, someone might invite you for a pint or, as they say around here, 'a wee dram.' It's the most wholesome entertainment in all of southwestern Ontario," the woman concluded with enthusiasm.

Aleda turned to tell Laura about the ice cream, but Laura had disappeared. She moved through the crowd, searching for her, then turned back toward the band shelter where the kilted men and women were gathering. She spotted Laura admiring a set of pipes held by a man.

When the marching started, they fell farther and farther behind the pipers because of the masses of people who joined in from the sidewalks along the main street. Laura linked her arm through Aleda's and whispered in her ear, "If you can do it, so can I. I've just met the most interesting widower. Maybe I'll take up the bagpipes," she said with a laugh. "He asked me to meet him at the ice cream stand during the break. He wants to introduce me to Kincardine's most famous person."

"The mayor?" Aleda asked, but Laura just shrugged and raised her eyebrows.

When the drone of twenty bagpipes and the rat-a-tat of eight drums had stopped for the mid-way break, Laura pulled Aleda forward through the crush of people toward the ice cream kiosk. Before they got there, they heard a man's voice behind them. "Ah, there you are. I was afraid you would forget." The man smiled at Laura, a plaid bagpipe collapsed under his right arm. "Come and meet Kincardine's celebrity."

He took Laura's arm, steering her through the crush of people. Laura motioned for Aleda to follow and the three inched their way to the edge of crowd. The women found themselves staring down at two huge fuzzy black feet. Their eyes moved up to a white cylinder, topped with a wide black smile, a gargantuan red nose, bushy black eyebrows. On the top, instead of a hat, there was a structure with windows, a light bulb flashing through the cracks. The man who had taken Laura by the arm made a courteous gesture toward the creature. "I'd like you to meet Blinkey the Lighthouse," he laughed, as the mascot waved a large red-gloved hand back at them. "Only in Kincardine."

As the woman in the park had suggested, there was an invitation to the Legion Hall for a wee dram following the parade. They were returning to Bluebird Cottage when Laura exclaimed, "I can't believe it! I've just signed up for chanter lessons this fall."

"Chanter lessons?"

"Apparently you have to learn the chanter before you learn the bagpipes."

"Laura!" Aleda exclaimed. "I had no idea that you are interested in the bagpipes."

"I'm not, but I'm very interested in the handsome widower who teaches the chanter." Then, glancing over to her friend and laughing, she called out, "Aleda Vastag! You have a nerve to look shocked!"

20
Re-entry

After packing to go home, Aleda made a confession to Laura. "Despite my misgivings about this dingy cottage, the two weeks have flown by and were filled with many wonderful moments."

"What will you do for the rest of your vacation?" Laura inquired.

"I've booked myself a week at home, then another two weeks in a lodge in the Muskoka Lake district. I hope it's a bit more upscale than this," she said, gesturing toward Bluebird Cottage. "But on second thought, it was cheap too." She sighed, then added, "I'm not sure it was such a great idea to return home for a week. What if I get drawn back into things again — Dorrie's troubles, church problems, the Jacobi family? Maybe I should have decided to go straight to the lodge but, at the time, I was thinking about laundry and regrouping."

"I'm sure it will work out fine," Laura said in a soothing voice. "If it helps, you can stay at my house. Your house will be hot and stuffy and there's probably no food in your fridge. Besides, I'd love the company."

"What a good friend you are! I think I'll take you up on that offer." As they bumped along the road between Tara and Milburn Corners, Aleda confessed that she had always had trouble with re-entries, with transitions."

Laura nodded. "I understand. One year I had a boy with autism in my classroom. He had such trouble fitting in at times. The worst times for him were the beginning and ending of the class. He would literally throw a temper tantrum every time he came in or left. It was very difficult and upsetting for me and all the other students. A few weeks into school, his father came in for a parent-teacher interview. He was a single dad and I guess he didn't want to leave his son at home, so he brought him along. I was busy with another interview, but I could hear the father outside the classroom. He just repeated every minute or so, 'We're going into the classroom to see your teacher.' Over and over he said it. When it was time for them to enter, the kid just walked in, calm as could be."

"Really? What made the difference?"

"That's exactly what I wondered. Then a few minutes before we were about to finish the interview, the dad repeated over and over, 'In a minute, we'll be going home.' And then, they just walked out of the classroom, unruffled and peaceful."

Aleda lifted her eyebrows in surprise.

"You can bet that the first thing I did next day was call up that dad. All he said was 'Transitions. My son has trouble with transitions, so I repeat things. It helps him get ready for the next change.' After that, it was a piece of cake in the classroom. I had one of the other students stand outside with the boy and repeat over and over, 'Soon we're going into the classroom,' and I had another student do the same toward the end of the class time. Girls are great at that sort of thing," Laura added. "Many of them are natural helpers."

"And, my dear friend," Aleda said, "I believe you are trying to tell me something that is not very subtle."

"Aleda, my friend, you will soon be home in Milburn Corners where things are slightly different ..." Laura said, repeating the sentence two more times before both women broke down laughing.

"After we've settled in, I'd like to walk down the hill to check on my house," Aleda told Laura as they hauled their suitcases in the back door.

How often she had taken this walk, she thought as she started down the hill, but tonight it was with uncertainty and dread. She glanced toward the east and saw Connie standing on the sidewalk talking with Rose, and as she turned the corner, she could see that before she reached the parsonage she would first need to get past Grace.

"Things have not been good here lately," Grace said bluntly as Aleda approached. "That Ethel Aylmer at the store. She's impossible. We've had a falling out and now we're not speaking."

"But Grace ... the butter tarts and pies and muffins ... surely ..."

Grace made a sound through her nose that was like a mixture of a grunt and snort. "As if this trouble with Ethel is not enough," she complained, "nobody has figured out who stole my laundry. Someone should to be held accountable! How can people just sneak around the village stealing and vandalizing things? Why isn't something being done? That's what I'm wondering."

Aleda shook her head slowly, easing away from the angry, complaining woman, relieved to see Roy crossing the road. "Nice to see you home, Aleda. You on your way up to your house?" he asked. When she nodded, he said, "That's good then." Roy's voice took on a sombre tone. "There's been a little trouble at the church with Robert."

"Robert? Robert is having trouble? I find that hard to believe. He's so …"

"Maybe it will blow over. It's Connie, you see. The new woman across from the store," he said, gesturing up the street where Connie stood with Rose.

"Whatever do you mean?" Aleda demanded.

Roy was silent for a minute. "Well," he said, "I think it would be better if you hear it straight from Robert. I'm afraid he's on the verge of quitting and finding someone else to fill in here until you're back."

Aleda stared at him, glanced quickly up the street, then back to Roy. "Quitting!" she exploded.

Roy pressed his finger against his lips, a signal that she should not speak so loudly. "It's what she's been doing for days now," he said in a quiet voice, leaning in closer. "She goes around the village at night talking to people, trying to get them to side with her against Robert." Aleda gaped at Roy. She could hardly believe that this trouble had erupted in such a short period of time. As if to confirm her concern, Roy continued, "We've been a peaceful village. I just don't like the idea that people are taking sides. It's not a good feeling, and it certainly isn't what church should be about."

After checking on the parsonage — it *was* hot and stuffy as Laura had predicted — Aleda turned back toward the centre of the village, ready to head up the hill to the quiet respite of Laura's home, but as she approached the main intersection, she heard someone call her name. It was Rose, hurrying down the sidewalk toward her.

"How nice to see you," Aleda called out.

"Aleda, I'm sorry to trouble you, but there's an urgent matter. I think you should come and see for yourself." Urgent? Rose never uses words like "urgent," Aleda thought.

"It's unnerving," Rose said as the two women stood in front of the roses by her walkway. "It happened two days ago. I noticed it right away. How could you not notice this?" They stood staring at the bed of roses where, at irregular intervals, the flowers had been snapped off, mangled and, in some cases, twisted off and scattered on the soil.

"I've gardened roses all my life," Rose continued. "I love them for their colour, beauty and fragrance and, of course, because my mother named me after these wonderful flowers. But roses are not, by nature, friendly creatures. All those thorns." She smiled ruefully. "When I go out to garden in my rose beds, I go armed. I have my thickest garden gloves. I always wear my rubber garden coat with long sleeves and I always use my sharpest secateurs."

"Secateurs?"

"Gardening shears," she explained. "There's nothing more unpleasant than gardening roses when the thorns are grabbing at your hands and arms. It's really painful." She paused, frowning. "It will be easy to repair this bed. I'll just prune them back and they'll put out new shoots and buds. But what worries me is this — I think that whoever broke off these rose bushes twisted them off with their bare hands. Whoever did this," she said, turning to Aleda with a look of distress on her face, "is covered with bad scratches. This person is hurt."

Rose stared into the tangle of broken branches. "Something very bad is happening in our peaceful little village, Aleda. These things — Grace's stolen underwear, painting the bench at the store, and now my roses — they all happened under the cover of darkness. Nobody in this village is out prowling at two or three in the morning. We'll all in bed, sound asleep," she exclaimed, then added, "Except the teens, of course. It's hard to say what they are up to. They don't seem to need much sleep."

Aleda stared at Rose. Surely, she had not succumbed to the speculation that the teenagers were responsible for disturbing and damaging their own village.

It might have ended there, but there was one more piece of bad news in her day. After she returned to Laura's house, longing for a quiet end to the evening, she discovered Martin's rusty grey truck in the driveway. Tracker had developed an abscess in one hoof, he told her. Nothing to worry about, it had been drained and treated by Dr. Patel, but he was sure that she would want to know.

The sun had set when Aleda crawled into the bed in Laura's guest room. All she wanted, at that moment, was to be back on the shores of Lake Huron, listening to the steady lapping of waves on a sandy shore, inhaling the musty air of Bluebird Cottage. She wondered if she should stay home from her two weeks of vacation at the lodge and help to straighten things out in Milburn Corners, but then she remembered a conversation she had with Robert before leaving for her vacation. She had admitted to feeling guilty and uncomfortable about going away when Dorrie needed support. Besides, she told him, she hadn't finished her visits to the retirement and nursing homes as she had promised, and what on earth would she do with Tracker? Robert had listened carefully to all her complaints, then asked, "You've been on an airplane before, Aleda?"

"Of course! Many times."

"What is it that the flight attendant says after pulling down the oxygen mask? What are the instructions?"

"Oh, I really can't remember," Aleda had answered in an impatient voice. "What? Tell me, Robert."

"The flight attendant says, 'If you're travelling with a small child, secure your own oxygen mask first. Then assist the child.'" He sat back while she stared at him. "There's no way you can help people if you're deprived of oxygen yourself," he added.

She remembered this as she lay in Laura's guest room. I hear you, Robert, she thought. I've been away for two weeks and already I'm drawn back into problems at Milburn Corners. I need to finish my vacation and return with strength to face what comes next. But can I do that? Can I just let it all go?

21
Crisis

THEY HAD JUST FINISHED BREAKFAST WHEN THEY HEARD A SOFT TAP AT THE KITCHEN door. There stood Burt Richardson. Both women agreed later that they had never seen a more despondent man.

He shuffled his feet in apology. "Hello, Aleda. I'm sorry to bother you when you're visiting a friend and I know you're just back from holiday. But it's Dorrie, you see. I'm real worried and I don't know what to do."

"Please," Laura urged. "The patio is warm and shaded. I'll bring out coffee. You can talk there."

When they had settled, Aleda asked softly, "What's happening with Dorrie? Tell me."

It's a terrible thing when a grown man cries, she thought afterward. For a moment she didn't know what to do. Burt sat in a lounge chair, his hair dishevelled, his bib overalls dirty. He sobbed into a red-checkered cloth handkerchief which he had retrieved from the pocket of his pants. It seemed a long time to her, but then he abruptly blew his nose with a great honking noise, did a vigorous swipe of his eyes and nose and, without looking up, began to talk.

"It started just after the fire. She would go missing. I never knew where she was, but that first day … you remember … you found her in the church. Then a couple of days later she disappeared in the night. Toward morning I heard her creep in and she crawled into bed, cold as ice. In the morning when I was going to the barn, I noticed a plastic bag by the back door. It was full of women's underwear." He paused, looking down at his hands, then glanced up at Aleda, who listened patiently. "I says to her, 'Dorrie, I know the fire has been a terrible shock, but is there something that you need to tell me?' but she just looked at me with that blank look that's come on her since the fire."

Aleda nodded, absorbing Burt's revelations. So the mysterious underwear theft hadn't been the teens. How could Grace have planted that suspicion in everyone's mind? she thought with indignation.

"A few days passed," Burt continued, "and I thought things were really getting better. She slept all through the night. I was so pleased that I got up early each day to make her a cup of tea just the way she likes it — piping hot, with lots of milk — heated, she likes the milk heated, and a half teaspoon of sugar. Then one night I wakened just before dawn. She was gone again. I didn't know where she was and I got real worried, but just as the sun was coming up I saw her walking up the road from the village." He paused again, raising his head to look at Aleda. "It's a strange thing, but she was carrying a can of paint and a paint brush and when she got home her running shoes were all splattered with orange paint."

Aleda sat up straight. Orange paint. As she slumped back, waiting for Burt to continue, a niggling shame crept into her mind. She had been as bad as Grace, suspecting Roy of painting the bench orange when she should have been looking for solutions to a problem, when she should have figured out that a hurting, traumatized woman was calling out for help.

"Things seemed to get a little better," Burt said. "Then a couple of nights ago I woke in the middle of the night and she was gone again. I couldn't get back to sleep. Toward morning I felt her crawl into bed and there was a strong metallic smell about her, like blood. In the morning, I saw there were bad scratches and cuts all over her hands and arms. 'What the hell?' I said. 'What happened to you?' But she never told me anything. She didn't try to hide a thing. She just didn't tell anything."

Aleda and Burt sat together in the silence of the morning, enveloped in a shared fear and uncertainty. She was worried for Dorrie, but she couldn't help the wash of relief that flooded over her as she realized that the local teens had not been responsible for the vandalism upsetting the village. Clarity of mind, Aleda, she silently reminded herself. Quietness of spirit and clarity of mind, that's what you need at this moment. She took a deep breath. They needed to turn their best attention toward Dorrie, who desperately needed their help.

Aleda cleared her throat. "Burt, I'm so very sorry. This is a distressing situation. What do you think is best to do for Dorrie?"

He slowly shook his head, but after a time he said, "One thing I've noticed lately, she often gets in her car and drives away. I thought about following her, to see where she goes, I mean."

Aleda sighed. "I suppose it's a good start. We need to keep her safe until she's through this crisis. Are you planning to follow her today?"

"I was thinking of that," he replied, "but I was wondering if you would come with me. Company, like."

"Of course," she agreed readily. "I have a new cell phone. I'll jot down the number for you."

They worked out a plan. If Dorrie left the farm in her car, Burt would call Aleda.

The call came at three o'clock in the afternoon. "She's headed down the lane," Burt said in a breathless voice. "I'll pick you up in a minute."

Dorrie was not a fast driver, so Burt and Aleda had barely left the village heading east when they spotted her car. They saw her turn left at the Rockford intersection. There was a moment of panic when a transport truck pulled out of a side road and they lost sight of her car, but when they could safely pass the truck, they soon spotted her again, turning left onto 10th Street in Owen Sound. Staying behind at a discreet distance they turned left, then right, then left again. Then, in an instant, everything changed.

Dorrie pulled into a street where a yellow checkered sign announced that it was a dead end. Burt hadn't noticed and he pulled around the corner, just metres behind her stopped car. Stomping toward them with a scowl, Dorrie snatched up a fallen leafy branch that lay by the sidewalk. With both hands, she lifted it over her head and slammed it across the hood of Burt's truck. Burt and Aleda jerked backward, but before either had time to do anything, Dorrie was at the open window, shouting, "You stop following me, Burt Richardson. I know what you're up to. You just stop following me." With those words hanging in the air, she tramped back to her car and backed up with such ferocity that Burt barely had time to reverse to get out of her way.

Her car roared off down the street, travelling far faster than the posted speed limit. Aleda grasped her shaking hands together, then glanced over to Burt, who was staring down the street at the racing car. "Burt, it's time to get help," she said.

It had been hard to get Dorrie to go to their family doctor, and when they finally arrived at the office, she had refused to let Burt go into the examining room with her. Nervous and impatient, he paced back and forth until the doctor came out and said quietly, "Burt, I wonder if you might come in for a moment."

Dorrie was lying on the examining bed looking calm and peaceful, with a flannel sheet wrapped around her. Burt stood looking back and forth between the doctor and Dorrie.

"We need some special help here, Burt. Dorrie has had a terrible shock, as you know. I've contacted the Psychiatric Urgent Care Clinic. There are good people there who are well versed in trauma-based therapies; they'll help her through this. In the meantime, I've given her something to help her mind and body relax." The Doctor put his arm around Burt's slumping shoulders. "She'll be fine, Burt. In time and with some care, she'll be fine."

On the following day, Burt called on Aleda's cell phone early in the morning. "Would you slip in? Would you just go in to the hospital and see that she is okay? It would relieve my mind."

She had never been to the part of the hospital that helped patients with mental health and dementia problems, so when she inquired for Dorrie's room, she was told that the staff would speak to her through an intercom to give her a code to enter the ward. After punching in the required numbers, she stepped inside and heard a firm click as the door closed behind her. She stood motionless, trying to decide where to go.

"May I help you?" a nurse inquired.

"I've come to see Dorrie Richardson. She was admitted yesterday and I'm her minister." Aleda showed her clergy identification badge. "I'm wondering if I might have a short visit."

"Of course. Follow me. She's in Room 303," the nurse said, leading her down the corridor.

Dorrie was lying in a bed, covered with a patchwork quilt. Aleda stood in the doorway, glancing around the room; it seemed comfortable, almost home-like. There was an easy chair in the corner with magazines on a side table and a chest of drawers holding a bedside lamp. The windows let in a soft filtered light. She took a step into the room and walked softly around the bed. Dorrie's eyes were closed, but when she sensed movement next to her she stirred and raised herself up on an elbow.

"Hello," Aleda said, softly as she reached for Dorrie's hand and grasped it.

"I'm so happy to see you," Dorrie said, but before she could say anything more, her eyelids began to droop, as if she might drift back into sleep. No doubt they have given her medication and it is making her drowsy, Aleda concluded.

There was a metal chair by the bedside, so she pulled it closer and sat. Still holding Dorrie's hand, she bowed her head, praying, asking God to give strength and restored health to Dorrie. The sun warmed the quiet room and as the moments passed Aleda realized that Dorrie wasn't the only one who was drowsy; she, too, felt as if she might nod off. But just at the moment when her head began to sink forward, she felt a twitch from Dorrie's hand. Aleda's eyes snapped open.

"I was wondering if you would sing for me?" Dorrie whispered.

"Sing?"

"Yes."

She leaned closer. "What, Dorrie? What would you like me to sing?"

"That one about the shepherd leading," she said.

"The shepherd leading," Aleda repeated slowly. "The Lord is my shepherd … he leads me beside the still waters …?"

"No," Dorrie murmured. "I have another one in my head. I just can't think of how it starts."

Aleda sat thinking, Shepherd … lead us … The hymn tune surfaced in her mind.

Down the hall in the nurse's station, a nurse wearing a pink tunic sat entering medication records in a computer while a doctor in a white coat, a stethoscope around his neck, looked over a patient's chart. Together, they heard the first wavering, plaintive, quivering notes drifting through the doorway of Room 303.

"Saviour, like a shepherd lead us, much we need thy tender care;

"In thy pleasant pasture feed us, for our use thy folds prepare."

Then, as they paused in their work, tilting their heads toward Room 303, they heard two voices join together, singing softly,

"Blessed Jesus, blessed Jesus! Thou hast bought us, thine we are.

"Blessed Jesus, blessed Jesus! Thou hast bought us, thine we are."

Aleda tucked the blanket around Dorrie's neck and shoulders with great tenderness, shaping the cover around the arm and side of the drowsy woman. "Sleep well my friend," she said softly, then bent to smooth back the tangled hair and kiss the woman's brow. "God bless you, Dorrie. The Good Shepherd is with you."

22
Simeon

On her fourth morning in Laura's guest bedroom, Aleda nestled under the comforter, amazed that this room was so different from the musty bedroom in Bluebird Cottage. Silk georgette sheers stirred and billowed at the window, brought to life by a cool northern breeze. The sheets, patterned with tiny dots, were crisp and fresh. She mounded the pillow to hug her head and gazed at an antique oak dresser with a bevelled mirror and brass pulls, the polished top gleaming in the morning sunshine. A small white lamp sat on the bureau along with a curved vase of fresh lavender. The floors were pine, wide and softened to a rich golden patina. Not much wonder Laura loves this old house, she thought. It overflows with peace, tranquility and beauty. A place of refuge.

Languidly, she rose from the bed, grabbed the fluffy pink towel that Laura had given her, and headed to the shower. The aroma of coffee drifted from the kitchen. She and Laura would start the day in a civilized way, with conversation and breakfast. But as she finished dressing, she heard an unusual noise, like soft chiming. She swung around and tilted her head. Someone was calling on her cell phone. Was it Burt? Was there more trouble with Dorrie?

She recognized Neil's voice at once. He spoke in an uncertain, tentative tone. "Aleda, I am so sorry to bother you. Are you still at Boiler Beach?"

"No. I got back to Milburn Corners a few days ago," she said, her own voice stiff and formal, still hurting from the memory of the way things had ended between them at Bluebird Cottage.

"I'm sorry to intrude, but I have something tough to do," he said, his voice hesitant, his words stumbling out. "I wouldn't have asked you … I don't want to bother you on your vacation … but I really need your help. I need to go to the old church and remove the boy who is having the nose bleeds. I believe — we all do — that the child is in grave danger. I could take Phillip, but he's been overwhelmed with the situation. He asked me to take his colleague, Connie …" Aleda felt the muscles of her shoulders tighten. "But the truth is, I'd rather have you come with me. You were great with the little girl and you are the only one so far who has been able to have any kind of reasonable conversation with the father. The rest of us just make him go ballistic. I've seen you in action in a very difficult situation — Dwayne's funeral," he said, referring to a suicide death in Milburn Corners. "I have confidence that you can help in a way that neither the social workers nor I can. It's just that I'd like to do this peacefully. I don't want a physical confrontation with Jacob and I don't want to create more trauma for the other children and their mother. The last thing that family needs is to see him wrestled off in handcuffs."

"Well ..." she could hear the hesitation in her own voice.

"If you don't feel comfortable doing this, I could ask Connie to go with me."

"No. Of course I'll do it," Aleda said quickly. "When do we go?"

Events at the derelict church-home did not go smoothly. On their second encounter, Jacob scowled at Aleda, shouting, "Just because you're a minister doesn't mean you get to side with the law when they're doing something wrong." She was not used to being yelled at and felt her knees shaking. She took a deep breath. She realized that perhaps to Neil, Jacob seemed to be a dangerous angry man, but, somehow, to her he seemed more like a wild animal, a protector willing to fight for his offspring.

"Please," she said. "We only want to help your family, especially your son." Breathing deeply and pushing down her panic, she smiled at Leah, who was holding a toddler. "This is ...?" she asked, taking the child's hand.

"Joseph," the woman answered. Then, touching another small boy on the shoulder, she said, "Zebulun. We call him Zeb for short, sometimes Zebby."

"And you are ..." Aleda said, reaching out her hand toward two red-haired boys. "You must be twins. You look exactly alike."

Leah answered, "Issachar and Judah. I guess you've already met Dinah and Levi." She pointed to the two children whose lips and fingers had been stained with berry juice when Aleda first met them. Aleda did not look toward Jacob. She stayed focused on the children.

The only children left in the room whom she had not met were a tall girl who seemed to be the oldest in the family and the boy lying on the cot. The girl had been sweeping the floor, but she stopped, cautious and anxious, when Neil and Aleda had come in with her father. Aleda approached the boy on the cot and knelt down. "And you are ...?"

When the boy did not answer, Jacob stepped forward and said in a strident voice, "This is my son, Simeon, and we will not allow him to be separated from our family."

Aleda nodded, but did not stir from the boy's side. "Jacob," she said, addressing the father but gazing at the child, "you know that God is good. You know that, don't you Jacob? You know that God gave you a second chance. That's what we want for Simeon. Right now, he is unwell. We want to give him a second chance. Can you be gracious like God, Jacob?"

The man was silent, scowling, until he repeated in an angry voice, "I won't have my son separated from our family."

Aleda stood up, glancing first at Jacob, then over to where Neil stood leaning against the doorframe. She moved away from the child's cot, confused, wondering what else she might possibly do. To her surprise, Neil strode into the room. Startled, Jacob took a step forward, but in three long strides Neil was in front of Simeon's cot. They watched in astonishment as Neil dropped to his knees in front of the child, his large boots bumping against the floor, something on his uniform belt rattling as he knelt. Everyone stared at the police officer, who folded his hands on the side of the cot as if in prayer.

"Jacob and Leah," Neil said, speaking to the parents but looking at the boy, "I am a man of honour, a man of my word. I've always believed that children are a gift from God. Really one of the most wonderful gifts God gives. I've never had a child of my own, but you have been blessed with eight. I want very much for this boy, Simeon, to be well and happy. If you give me permission to take the child to a hospital to get help, I give you my solemn word that I will do everything in my power to help him become strong again. I will personally visit him every day in the hospital and I will treat him as if he were my own family. You can count on me." Neil paused, still on his knees. Then he made the sign of the cross and stood up.

Aleda, her eyes blurred with tears, looked at Neil. Jacob stared at him, too. Leah clutched the smaller boys to her and everyone waited.

At last, nodding to the oldest girl, Jacob said, "Reubena, fetch some warm water and soap. Simeon will need to be bathed."

Because Jacob had been reluctant to leave the family unprotected in the dilapidated church, it was decided that Reubena would accompany Simeon to the Owen Sound Hospital so the boy would not be lonely and frightened. But, when Neil had gathered the boy in his arms and it was time to leave, Aleda could see that there was a problem. Reubena had no shoes. The children, Leah explained, wore boots in the winter but preferred to go barefoot in the summer. The truth was, although Leah was too proud and embarrassed to admit it, their meager income from Jacob's occasional work as a carpenter did not provide enough money for shoes. They used what little money they had to buy flour, oil and milk powder.

"We can stop at my house in Milburn Corners on the way to the hospital," Aleda told the family. She set her own foot alongside the foot of the girl. "They'll be big, but better than nothing."

They waited in the emergency room at the hospital until Phillip arrived. When the social worker walked in, he saw a police officer cradling an unhappy and bewildered boy. Beside him sat a waif wearing a long, flowing caftan and orange flip flops, and a tanned woman clutching a tattered hospital magazine.

After completing a mountain of paper work, Phillip, Aleda and Neil settled the children in a room at the hospital. The boy looked small, frail and frightened, tucked into the crisp white sheets, until Reubena folded a warm flannel blanket around his body. Aleda arranged to have extra blankets so the girl could sleep in the recliner chair beside the boy's bed, and she brought in a bundle of magazines from the waiting room.

After Phillip said good-bye, Neil and Aleda prepared to leave, too. They stood in the doorway, having assured the children that they would be back by eight o'clock in the morning. "In time for breakfast," Aleda said, smiling at them, reassuring them once again that they would be safe.

The children had been given mugs of warm cocoa and Reubena, settling beside Simeon on the bed, began to read him a story. She was a good reader — they were home-schooled, she told Aleda — and the inflections in the girl's voice made Aleda smile. "You may become a famous actor someday," she said, returning to the bedside to hug the girl.

"Or maybe a world-famous preacher like Aleda," Neil added.

They confessed to each other that they both needed to debrief, to talk over the events of the day. Sitting together in the dusk on a bench near the harbour, Neil said to her, "That was a tough day. I'm very grateful to you. It would have been much more difficult if you hadn't been with me."

"It was your action that saved the day." She shook her head, feeling her eyes mist with tears as she remembered him kneeling before the cot.

They looked at each other and when he saw the tears in her eyes, he said, "We did it together. At least the boy is where he'll get help." He glanced down to where her hand lay on her lap. "I'm very sorry to have drawn you into this, Aleda."

"Don't worry about that. I was glad to help. I had already decided to stay in Milburn Corners for the week before heading off for the next two weeks of my vacation."

"Tell me," he said, "you were so good with Jacob. All of us — me, Phillip, the realtor, the store keeper in Wiarton, even Vivian my dispatcher — we had all concluded that he was beating the child." Neil paused, thinking about the strap hanging by the back door. "What made you take a different approach?"

"It was the little girl — Dinah. While we were making our daisy chains, we had time to talk. She told me that her dad keeps a leather strap hanging at the back door. She said that he keeps it there for two reasons. If the coyotes came too close, he has a weapon to shoo them away. And," she added, "the second reason was that Jacob's father used to punish *his* children with a strap. When he had children of his own, Dinah told me, Jacob made a promise to God and to Leah that he would never punish his children, only love them and guide them."

Neil looked at her in surprise. "She told you that?"

"I even asked, quite casually I think, 'You mean, when you children are naughty, he never hits you?' The girl was quite shocked that I would even think of such a thing. I don't think that children can fake that kind of reaction." She was silent for a moment. "That's why I thought that probably something was physically wrong with Simeon; it was a medical emergency, not abuse. I don't know what's wrong, but it's something that herbs won't heal." Aleda shrugged out the tension between her shoulder blades. "It slowly dawned on me that Jacob had been telling the truth all along. He simply couldn't bear to have Simeon separated from the family."

Neil nodded and peeked over at her face. She was not smiling. In fact, she looked almost grave. She was remembering the tenderness and compassion on his face as he knelt, as if in prayer, at the bed of the frightened boy. She remembered the tears that welled in her eyes as he made a solemn promise to God and the family. Then she remembered the words of her new friend, Regina Davis, as they sat on the patio at the Bruce Inn — "Aleda, ask yourself this: Is he worth fighting for?"

23
Roy

True to her word, Aleda arrived at the hospital at eight in the morning, carrying orange juice and breakfast sandwiches for herself and Reubena. Simeon had not slept well, Reubena told her, nor did he want to eat his breakfast. A bowl of cornflakes sat on a hospital tray and a silver lid partially covered cold scrambled eggs and toast. "I'm not hungry," he complained.

"Would this help?" Aleda asked, pulling from her pocket a bag of coloured marshmallows. The boy shook his head. "I'll leave them for Reubena. She'll be hungry later."

As she was getting a fresh glass of water for the boy, Neil poked his head in the door, then headed to the empty metal chair beside Simeon's bed.

"You're not working today?" Aleda inquired, noting that he was wearing jeans and a sports shirt.

"I've taken a week off," he said. "I still had a week of vacation for this year, and yesterday I made a promise to Simeon's family. I need to honour it."

When the lab technician came in to take blood samples, Neil held the boy's hand and talked to him, distracting him from the prick of the needle. At ten o'clock, Phillip popped in, bringing with him one of the hospital social workers who, he said, would check in daily. Before noon, the doctor appeared too.

"I'm Doctor Coulter," he said to Neil and Aleda. "Are you Simeon's parents?"

"No," Neil answered. "But this is his sister, Reubena. We are … well, we're friends of Simeon's family. His parents couldn't be here, so we offered to stay with the children for a while." Aleda nodded in agreement.

The doctor frowned. "I'll need to speak to the parents. I'm going to need a thorough family medical history. I wonder if you would come with me for a moment," he asked, nodding at Neil and Aleda. "Reubena, will you kindly take good care of your brother for five or ten minutes?"

They settled in a reception room at the end of the hall. "Okay," the doctor said, "I'd like some information about what's going on here. Where are the parents and why aren't they here?"

Aleda and Neil explained who they were, then filled the doctor in on the details of the situation, including the story of their struggle to get the child to a hospital for assessment.

"I'll need to do some further tests and I'll need the parents' permission for that," the doctor said. He sat tugging at his lower lip.

"Leave it to us," Aleda said. "We'll work something out."

"That's good. That's good," the doctor murmured, nodding his head slowly. "I won't know until we do some more tests, but based on the preliminary blood work, it seems to point to leukemia — acute lymphocytic leukemia."

Beside her, Aleda heard a soft exhalation from Neil. "Holy Mary, Mother of God," he breathed.

The boy needed his parents beside him, but how would that be possible since the family had no car and there were so many children? It would be unwise and problematic for Leah to stay in the dilapidated church with all the other children if Jacob were to join Simeon. Neil and Aleda walked together to the hospital cafeteria. It was a difficult situation, but they understood that they needed to provide some guidance and solutions.

"After this week, I'll be away for two weeks at a lodge," Aleda said. "Would it be possible for the Jacobi family to stay in the parsonage? I have a place to stay with Laura if they need to move in earlier."

"I suppose. But Milburn Corners is ten kilometres from Owen Sound and they have no car."

"True," she admitted, staring into her coffee mug. After a moment of quiet reflection, she looked up at Neil and said, "Maybe it's time to visit Roy."

Neil nodded, although he was not entirely sure what she had in mind. "Maybe I'll have a talk with Phillip and see if there is some temporary housing in Owen Sound. I'm afraid there might be a longer period for diagnosis and treatment than we expected."

Aleda threw open the screened windows on the porch of her house, turning on a fan to circulate the stale air. Flipping open the back door, she glanced at the closed shed door where Tracker normally resided, wondering how the old horse was doing at Martin's farm. She stood staring at her tidy perennial beds — thank you, Roy! she breathed — then began to prepare for a visit to her neighbour.

She had not been in Roy's backyard in the summer, only caught glimpses of it from her kitchen window. She glanced around, searching for him, and when she saw a hoe leaning against the side of his garage, she started down the brick path between the garage and the house. "Roy! You there?"

"Well, land's sake, Aleda. What a nice surprise. Come on in." He turned around and gestured toward a bench in the backyard. She stepped into the garden, stopped and gasped. Roy swung around. "What? What's wrong?"

"What's wrong? This!" she exclaimed. "This blows my mind!" She waved her arms wildly around, sweeping over the expanse of the yard.

He smiled. "This is her living room," Roy told her. "Pink. She loved pink, my wife did." Aleda took in the curved bed displaying every shade of pink in the colour palette. "The coneflowers have just started to bloom and the summer phlox will be out next. These here are rose mallow and I have a nice swath of cosmos there. Here at the front there are pink dahlias and some pink alyssum. Some would say that petunias are too common, but I like them. They're like a little work horse in the garden. Never give up."

"And this?" she asked, squatting down.

"Dianthus. This variety smells like cloves."

For each of his garden "rooms," Roy had painted a bench to match. Aleda trailed her hand along the top of a bench that reminded her of the colour that might result from stirring raspberry juice into a cup of milk.

"And this?" she asked, pointing to a dazzling array of yellow.

"Sunshine," Roy responded. "My wife loved sunshine. Oh, she hated rainy days. This here is her sunshine room." Aleda stood staring as Roy pointed out the varieties of yellow — towering sunflowers with their heads beginning to form in a mass of seeds and fringes of gold, leopard's bane, yellow loosestrife, yarrow, coreopsis and corydalis, and in the front were yellow plants with magical names like basket of gold, goldenstar and Pacific Beauty calendula.

"Amazing," she said, inhaling deeply.

"My personal favourite," Roy said, leading her to the back corner. "The shores of Lake Huron room. My wife did love the shores of Lake Huron."

Aleda gasped. "Roy, I've never seen anything more beautiful." She gazed over a band of every shade of blue and azure, every hue of cobalt, navy, sapphire and indigo. Nestled in the middle of the garden was a pond, the water splashing gently over field stone. Around the edge of the pond was a small, shimmering sandy beach.

"Some say that blue is a cold colour, but I don't agree. Blue keeps me calm," he said.

"Roy," Aleda gushed, "you are truly the most amazing person I know." He looked a little embarrassed to receive such exuberant praise from her, but at the same time, pleased. Standing now in the heart of his picturesque garden, so lovingly fashioned in memory of his wife, Aleda felt remorse and shame remembering that she had even for a moment suspected him of doing something as despicable as sneaking around to paint a bench in the night so he could change something green into something orange.

"Sit down," he invited, gesturing to a cerulean blue bench. "What's on your mind?"

She explained the situation of Simeon's illness and her intent to let the family stay in the parsonage for two weeks while she was on the rest of her vacation. "You don't think the church folks will mind, do you?" She realized suddenly that perhaps she should have gained permission.

"Oh, it's a good turn, Aleda. We'll just make sure that the Chairman of the Board knows, in case there's an emergency or something."

She nodded, relieved. "Roy, I simply don't know what I would do without your wise counsel. It's really important that one of the parents is at the hospital with Simeon as much as possible. The problem is …" she paused, glancing over at him, "the family has no car. The father has a driver's license, it seems, but they simply can't afford a vehicle."

She remembered the moment when she and Neil had been preparing to take Simeon to the hospital. Neil had asked Jacob for the child's surname and the family's health card. Jacob hesitated, then said, "Jacobi." Neil had asked if this was the legal name for the family or one that they had adopted. Slowly, Jacob pulled a wallet from his back pocket and passed a driver's license and the family's health insurance card to Neil. Both cards belonged to someone called John Smith. "We'll put that on the admission form at the hospital. May I?" Neil asked the child's father, holding up the health insurance card. "Simeon Smith." It seemed a good compromise — half the assumed name and half the real one.

• • •

Aleda and Roy sat in silence, listening to water splash over the field stone, watching the koi and goldfish gliding near the surface of the water. "I've been wondering if there might be people from the church willing to take turns driving one of the parents to the hospital each day," Aleda suggested. "What do you think?" She sat waiting, having learned long ago that it was neither wise nor helpful to rush Roy.

"Busy time of year, Aleda," he said at last. "Lots of field work and gardening. Summer crop of alfalfa is ready and I saw them cutting the winter wheat up on the town line road." She nodded and waited.

When he spoke again, his voice was soft, perhaps even resigned, she thought later. "Maybe I can do one better," he said. She swung her head sideways, looking at the man who had been such a constant good friend to her. "Seems like I have a condition in one eye called macular degeneration. I started to have trouble last year — some dark blurry things in the centre — and the doctor says that it might happen in the other eye, too. Touch wood," he said, knocking his knuckles on the seat of the bench, "nothing yet."

She opened her mouth to say how sorry she was to hear that, but before she had an opportunity to speak, he said, "I've been thinking lately that there might come a time when I'll have to give up driving. I hope not. Not for a year or two, maybe more. But if I was to lend my car to this family for a couple of weeks … well, it would give me a chance to see what it would be like to have no wheels." She smiled at his use of the term "wheels," something that the teens in the village might say. "Besides," he continued, "I got a lot of work to do in the garden just now, and I can get everything I need to eat right here at Ethel's store."

All that remained was for Aleda to visit the Jacobi/Smith family. It took Jacob only a moment to accept her offer. He had been worrying about how they would be with Simeon. How could he leave Leah with all the other children in the unfinished church? She wanted to see Simeon too, and how would that be possible? Living in Aleda's house seemed a good option.

24

Troubles Brewing

Aleda busied herself making space for the Jacobi family, cleaning out closets and packing her winter clothes into boxes for the attic. Even though she had met all the children, it was hard for her to imagine them sleeping in her bed, running through the halls and slamming the back door. She had just finished making a shopping list of cleaning supplies when the telephone rang.

"Robert! Wonderful to hear from you. I've been home for a few days but have been really busy with … well, I guess you could say it was a crisis."

"Aleda," he said, coming straight to the point, "I really need to talk to you today. Something has come up."

"Oh dear," she sighed. "Roy warned me that something was going on."

"It's better if we discuss this in person. Your place or ours? Can we do it this morning?"

Puzzled by the urgency in Robert's voice, she grabbed her keys, climbed into her van and headed to Owen Sound.

Patrice, her thick white hair twisted into a French pleat and wearing a violet sundress, met her at the door and suggested she join Robert on the back deck. Aleda rushed over to where Robert was sitting. "You have me scared, Robert. On the telephone you sounded so serious." She laughed but Robert nodded solemnly.

"I thought you should know. This has all blown up since you left for Boiler Beach. It happened so quickly, but I suppose that sometimes these things do."

"What on earth are you talking about?"

"It's that new woman, Connie," he said.

"What about her?"

"It started shortly after you left. The first worship service I did in Milburn Corners went well, or so I thought. Patrice thought so too. Roy was happy and

I even got a positive comment from Grace. But after the worship service was over, Connie came up to me and asked if she might have a word. Seems she took great exception to something or other I said in the sermon. I asked Patrice to sit with us in that little area in the narthex. We were both stunned — Patrice and me — when Connie took me on. She did not think that my interpretation of scripture was either adequate or accurate."

"She's a social worker!" Aleda exclaimed. "Hardly an expert in theology."

"She would beg to differ," Robert mumbled. "Her father was a pastor and drilled all his children on proper theology." Robert used his fingers to put quotation marks around his last two words.

"But what was she objecting to?" Aleda asked.

"I did an ecology sermon," he explained. "It being summer, it seemed a good time to do a little series on our God-given responsibility to care for the earth, what with climate change being in the news so much. I started with the Genesis creation story. Connie had come to church carrying her own Bible — the King James Version. According to her, it's the only accurate translation. She said to me, 'The Bible does not *contain* the word of God. It *is* the word of God.'"

"How did you answer that?"

"I said, 'You're right, Connie. The Bible does not *contain* the word of God. The word of God is alive and active in the world.' No, she insisted, we must believe the words of the Bible the way they are written. God inspired everything in the Bible. The words may have been written by men, but God's words flowed through them onto the holy pages. She insisted that my implication that God worked through evolution and time was just plain wrong. Why can't we believe that the world was created in six days and that God rested on the seventh? 'With God, everything is possible!' she said."

Robert rubbed his hand over his brow. "I tried to explain my method for interpreting scripture — how I try to understand what the book or passage actually says, then try to figure out what it meant when it was originally written, and then try to discern what the passage means to people today. 'That just proves my point!' she said. 'The Bible *says* that the world was actually created in six days. When the biblical writers wrote down that creation story, that's exactly what they *meant* — the world was created in six days. And what does that mean to us today? It means that we have no right to go changing things in the Bible. This book,' she said to me and Patrice, laying her hand on her Bible, 'does not contain some truth. It *is* the truth.'"

"Oh, my," Aleda sighed, rubbing the skin between her eyebrows, feeling a creeping headache.

"That's when Patrice spoke up." Robert laughed a little. "'Surely Connie, we have to use our common sense, too. After all, science and common sense tell us that there are some writings in the Bible that shouldn't be taken literally. You know how in Matthew's gospel it suggests that epilepsy is caused by demons. We're not intended to believe that today.'"

"What did Connie say to that?"

"She declared that it is a slippery slope. If you start doubting one thing, you'll start to doubt everything. 'Maybe illness really is caused by demons,' she said."

Aleda felt her stomach churn and a flush creep up her neck into her cheeks. But Robert had one more thing to add. "The most serious part," he said, leaning toward Aleda, "is that Connie has been talking to some of the villagers, even going out to some of the farms, asking the church elders to replace me and find someone else to fill in until you are back from your vacation."

Aleda gasped. "I cannot believe this! What nerve! What absolute gall!" They sat in silence, puzzling over this strange turn of events, until Aleda blurted out, "But, why Robert? This seems a very strong overreaction to a sermon."

Robert nodded. "I thought so too, so I went to see Roy. He'd been talking with Connie, too, and he let me in on a little secret. I don't think he meant to say it, but maybe he did. You never know with Roy. He let slip that when she was talking with him, she confessed that her father had been physically abusive to her and her brothers. It's true that her father schooled them in 'proper theology,' but do you know why she reacted so strongly against me?" Aleda shook her head. "I look like her father," he said quietly.

Aleda discovered that Neil had been as good as his word. Every morning and often in the afternoon and evenings, he dropped in to the hospital to visit Simeon. The boy was frequently alone with his sister, frightened and ill, although he smiled when he learned that his family would soon be moving closer to Owen Sound and that someone had lent them a car so his parents could visit him. Everybody did their best to cheer the boy, bringing puzzles and treats, but it was evident that there was no substitute for his family.

"Would you like me to drive out and get your father so he can spend the afternoon with you?" Neil asked him. Simeon nodded and Reubena, too, looked relieved. Perhaps she was overwhelmed with the responsibility of caring for her brother. But when the doctor came in on his rounds, he asked Neil if he might meet that day with both parents. He wanted their permission and cooperation to start treatment.

"I'll do my best," Neil promised. "It's just that there are six younger children to care for and their situation is ... well ... isolated."

"Please try. I'd like to get treatment started."

Neil was reluctant to call Aleda to ask for help again. He had bothered her too often on her vacation, he thought. There was no choice but to call Phillip. Perhaps the social work department might have a lead on some temporary caregivers who would look after the younger children while the parents were at the hospital.

Neil agreed to meet Phillip in the hospital cafeteria. However, after Neil had settled at a table with a cup of coffee, he was surprised when an attractive blond woman approached him and asked, "Are you Constable Neil Brennan?"

As soon as she introduced herself as Connie, Neil immediately knew who she was, and that Phillip had sent his colleague in his place. When he had explained to her the need for a caregiver, she said, "It will be easy for us to arrange some child support for the family for a day." She told him that she would drive a caregiver to the old church and bring the parents back to the hospital. Would Neil, she wondered, be able to drive Jacob and Leah back home in the evening and return the caregiver to Owen Sound?

"I have the week off," Neil said. "Happy to do that."

Connie smiled brightly and began to gather her purse and notepad. "I suppose you know that I've bought a house in Milburn Corners?" Neil nodded. "Lovely people there," she continued. "They've been very friendly and welcoming to me. I understand that you know some of the people in the village. Roy told me that. Such a wonderful man," she enthused. "And then there's the local minister." Neil stared at her, wondering what she meant. "It must be hard for you. I understand that you're a good Catholic. You must surely realize that women do not belong in ministry. Imagine having a female priest at St. Mary's!" she said, laughing softly. When Neil didn't respond, she continued, "I've met my neighbour, Grace. She agrees with me. Women should not be ministers."

Connie stood up, but before she turned, she added, "We have a meeting tomorrow night at Grace's house. A few of us are concerned about how things are going at the church and are meeting to discuss some issues. You would be most welcome to join us. Seven thirty. The coffee pot will be on."

After Connie left, Neil continued to sit at the cafeteria table staring down into his empty mug. Aleda must be told about this potentially harmful situation that was brewing in her village and church. Connie had initiated a whisper campaign against Aleda that could divide the village and might end badly for Aleda. "Wolf in sheep's clothing," he muttered, thinking of Connie's sleek blond hair, her sweet modulated laughter. Someone needed to warn Aleda, but should it be him?

25
Irish Tea Room

EVEN SIMEON NOTICED THAT NEIL WAS UNCHARACTERISTICALLY QUIET THAT EVENING. "You don't want to play a game of Parcheesi?" he asked Neil.

"Sorry, Simeon." He patted the boy's hand. "I'm a little off tonight. Something on my mind. I'm thinking something through. Maybe tomorrow."

He had to find some way to warn Aleda about the troubles festering behind her back. But, how could he? They had parted in an uncomfortable way after his visit to Boiler Beach and, although they had worked together to help the Jacobi family, she was still cautious, strained and distant with him. Would she be open to hearing from him that she needed to tread with care, perhaps even take some protective measures for the sake of her own emotional well-being and career? Would it not be better to talk this over with Roy? Perhaps Roy could warn her. She certainly trusted and respected Roy. But how could he discuss this with Roy? Did he only imagine that Roy was more than a bit suspicious of him? It seemed to Neil that the tentative rapport he had with the older man was as precarious as his relationship with Aleda.

Driving home from the hospital, he had a sudden flash of an idea.

She had just finished cleaning her closets when she heard the faint chime of her cell phone.

"I'm calling to tell you again how much I appreciated your help with the Jacobi family. I would not have been able to do that as well without your help."

"You're welcome."

"I'm wondering …" Aleda could hear the hesitation in Neil's voice, "if I might offer you an afternoon tea as a thank-you?" He rushed on to explain that he had discovered an authentic Irish tea room near Owen Sound. Would she be so kind as to join him for tea in the afternoon?

Why did I agree to that? she berated herself as she punched the end key on her cell phone. *Is it not enough that he seems to toy with my affections while* he's thinking of returning to Ireland to get married? She was angry and frustrated with Neil, but she was even more angry and frustrated with herself. She dared not have her hopes for happiness raised again, only to be dashed by a broken relationship. And to think that she had agreed to go with him to an *Irish* tea room, where she would be reminded of this business all over again. How could she have made such a stupid mistake?

When they arrived, she could see that the walls were lined with photos and prints of Ireland — many in black and white.

"Would you like to look at them more closely?" he asked.

"Not really," she responded. Then, realizing that her reply was churlish, she added in a light tone of voice, "Oh, why not?" She rose from their table and began a slow circuit of the tea room while he walked quietly behind her. There was an antique map of the island and beside it, in dazzling emerald green, an up-to-date version. In a corner hung a painting of two women bent over, harvesting potatoes, and another of a dog under a single street lamp, sniffing at a wooden crate, fog creeping forward in the background. Hanging beside it was a picture of a contoured farm edged with a stone fence, a cottage nestled in the corner of the field.

Behind her, she heard Neil grumble, "More romantic than comfortable."

"This one?" Aleda spoke for the first time since beginning the tour. She pointed to a castle which seemed to perch on the edge of an island, its shadow reflected on the sapphire blue water.

"Dunguaire Castle in Galway Bay."

"Beautiful."

"Isn't it grand, that castle? Perhaps you'll go there for a visit someday."

"Oh, I doubt that," she said, turning back to their table. "I see our tea has arrived." The waiter had spread the table with coffee cake, biscuits, plum and raspberry jelly, and a pot of honeycomb. Another plate held shortbread and éclairs. Neil poured two steaming cups of amber tea from a pot covered in a green tea cozy.

"We never had such a grand tea at home," he told her. "Mother usually served bread and butter and, if we were lucky, a little cake."

While they were eating, Neil told her about his grandmother in Dublin. "She had a sister who came over to Canada. She liked to send little surprise packages back home for Grannie. One Christmas she sent a box of maple creams and a package of tea bags. Tea bags were totally new to Gran, unheard of in Ireland, and when she wrote back to thank her sister for the treats, she said, 'We sure enjoyed the maple creams but please don't send me any more of those little bags of tea. It takes too long to cut them open.'" Despite herself, Aleda laughed.

When she inquired about Simeon, Neil told her that the doctors were anxious to get started on Simeon's treatment and, with proper care and time, they were optimistic that the boy would recover. "There's an eighty-five percent cure rate, quite high really," Neil said, nodding. "And," he added, "Phillip has a good lead on temporary housing for the family in Owen Sound. They hope to move in two weeks, so that will be much easier for them and you can have your house back." He stared across the room. He couldn't bring himself to tell her about the meeting at Grace's house.

"The boy, Levi," he sighed, glancing over at her. "He seems to be acting out. Phillip told me that he went on a bit of a rampage and smashed everything that was breakable. His parents were upset. You know as well as I do, they don't have many possessions. It's a great loss to them when they have so little. Phillip is helping them replace their dishes from a second-hand store."

"Oh, that's terrible! What is going on with the boy?"

Neil shook his head. "From what I see, everyone has a place in the family — Reubena, being the first born, is a natural helper. Simeon is the sick one who gets lots of attention, Dinah is off in her own little fantasy world, the twins have each other — they're inseparable — and the little boys have their mother. But Levi … he's lost in the middle."

"The lost boy," she said. They sat without speaking for a moment until she inquired, "Did you ever feel lost as a child?"

Neil nodded slowly, his eyes squinted and guarded. "When I was about Levi's age, I started to steal bread from the corner grocery. We didn't need it … we were poor, but not hungry. My mother always made sure that we had bread and butter. Of course, the grocer caught me and marched me home to mother. She grabbed her coat and took me straight over to our old parish priest. 'Father, you need to talk some sense into this boy. What he did was just plain wrong.'"

Aleda could see that, even after all these years, the memory of that time still troubled him. He shuffled his feet beneath the table.

"When my mother left, the old priest put his hand on my shoulder and told me to sit down on a bench. He just sat there beside me, bent over, with his hands folded, looking down at his black oxford shoes. Then he said, 'Do you know that it's wrong to steal, lad?' and I said, 'Yes, Father.' Then he said, 'Will you do it again, lad?' and I said, 'No, Father. Never.' He sighed and said, 'Well then, you can't be held to blame, is all. You have no father to guide you. I think you would make a fine altar boy.'"

"That's it? That was the end of it?"

Neil shrugged. "That was the end of it. The strange thing is, I never really understood why I stole that bread. I just wanted somebody to notice me, to find me a little special. That's all I wanted. That old priest became a father figure to me. I was an altar boy for years, and I missed him so much after he died."

Aleda sat gazing at Neil who seemed lost in his story. "That's surely the answer," she said in a quiet voice. "Levi — he needs someone to notice him, to find him special. He's simply lost in the middle."

After they pulled into the driveway of the parsonage, she turned from the passenger seat and said, "Thank you for the tea." But her eyes widened when she saw the grave look on his face.

"There's something you need to know," he said. Did she trust him enough to hear some disconcerting news? "I hope, for your sake and for the sake of your church and everybody in the community, that this blows over." Aleda stared at him, "It's about Connie," he continued. "There's something I need to tell you about the new woman down the street."

26
Healing

I'M NOT GOING TO JUST SIT QUIETLY BY AND LET THIS HAPPEN, SHE FUMED. SHE STOOD in the front porch of the parsonage, watching Grace's house as seven thirty approached. She couldn't go to the meeting. She knew that. She wasn't even supposed to know about it. How could she fight back if everything was so nebulous? She felt as if she were a victim, but she had no understanding of how to make things change or even if she could transform this situation.

Angry and impatient, she decided that she would not stand lurking in the front porch to see which of her parishioners would show up for a meeting. No, she would drive away, drive into Owen Sound and find something to distract herself.

As she braked on Creamery Hill leading into Owen Sound, she suddenly thought that perhaps she should visit Dorrie at the hospital. Were there visiting hours? She didn't know. She only knew that in that moment she had a real need to escape Milburn Corners, and perhaps Dorrie might enjoy an evening visit.

After she heard the familiar click of the locked door letting her into the ward, she started down the hall toward Room 303, but as she was about to pass the nursing station, a nurse looked up. Aleda recognized her as the same woman who had been on duty when she and Burt had admitted Dorrie for treatment. The nurse held up her hand and Aleda couldn't tell if it was in greeting or in warning. The nurse motioned her silently to follow and led her a small, empty waiting room.

"I recognize you as Dorrie's minister," the nurse said, inviting Aleda to sit.

Aleda nodded and pulled her forgotten clergy badge from her handbag. "How has she been?"

"She was coming along very well," the nurse told her. "We were quite sure that she could go home last weekend. But then her husband came in. Something he said really set her off and she is right back in the catatonic condition that she was in when she arrived." The nurse sighed. "She seemed to need to retreat again for her healing to continue."

"Oh, dear me," Aleda murmured, feeling overwhelmed. If these skilled people couldn't help Dorrie, then who could?

"There has been one glimmer of hope this week, though. I haven't had a chance to talk to her husband yet." Aleda nodded and waited for the nurse to continue. "We have a therapy dog, a lovely golden retriever called Flora. We weren't sure how Dorrie would react when the therapist brought the dog in, but when she entered Dorrie's room, her face opened up. Within minutes she was patting the dog and even helped brush her." Aleda raised her eyebrows in surprise. "I booked the therapist to bring the dog in every day this week. It's the most response we've seen from Dorrie. I'm not sure what triggered that reaction, but any positive thing feels like a little breakthrough."

Aleda sat, lost in thought. "That's great," she murmured.

The nurse leaned forward. "I want to talk to her husband, but perhaps it would be easier for you to see him. I wondered if he might consider getting Dorrie a dog, a puppy perhaps, to ease her re-entry into home."

Aleda nodded. "I'll pop in to see her now, and I'll go up to the Richardson's farm tomorrow," she added. "I'm quite sure that Burt would be open to the suggestion of getting a puppy, and I happen to know a farm up the road where there is a little pup needing a new home."

She and Roy had filled her refrigerator with bread, butter, eggs, vegetables and frozen goods in preparation for the arrival of the Jacobi family. When she swung open the freezer and saw two packages of bran muffins from the corner store — made by Grace — Aleda slammed the door shut. The day before, she had been upset about a church meeting happening behind her back. Today she was angry. Very angry.

She pushed on her sandals and reached for the heavy key that opened the wooden doors of Milburn Community Church.

It was cool and dark in the church as she moved toward the centre of the sanctuary, then sank down, leaning over to press her forehead against the cool wooden pew in front of her. Okay God, what do I do in this situation? she prayed. But sometimes there are no answers. The Bible, she knew, said that God sometimes comes in the roaring thunder and sometimes in a tiny whisper, but in the stillness of the church, despite her fervent pleas, Aleda heard no answer from God.

What do I do? she asked again. She leaned back, folded her arms and let her head sink despondently. Tears began to roll down her cheeks, at first silently, then in great shuddering sobs. She looked up at the painting of Jesus holding the lamb and realized in that moment that she was as vulnerable and in need of healing as Dorrie.

After a time, she reached into a pocket, removed a tissue and blew her nose. She took a deep breath and, as she exhaled, she remembered something that her friend Regina Davis had told her. She said that once she had preached on the silence of God. In her sermon, she told her congregation about a week when she had struggled to prepare a sermon but nothing would come. "It wasn't just preacher's writing block," Regina said. "God just seemed silent. I went for a walk. I read my Bible. I prayed. But there was only silence. And finally, I came to realize that we should not confuse God's silence with God's absence."

"That didn't upset you?"

"No, because," Regina had said, leaning closer, "even when God is silent, we need to remember that God is still there and God promises never to forsake us."

Aleda sat now, gazing up at the Good Shepherd. God is here, she thought. Whatever happens, God is still here.

When she felt calm and restored, she locked the church again and headed back to the parsonage. She would go up to the farm to see Burt and suggest that he consider adopting a puppy, then drop in on Martin to see if he approved of this plan. But when she had returned to the kitchen and was plugging in her kettle to make a cup of coffee, she noticed the red message light on her phone. Someone had called her at eight o'clock. She punched the code to pick up her message, listened, then shuddered. Grace wanted to see her. Could she drop by the parsonage at nine?

The visit to the Richardson's farm would have to wait. First, she would see Grace. She was filled with dread, overcome with fear and anxiety, so when she heard the sharp knock, she took several deep breaths before moving toward the front door.

"Come in, please," she said, feeling not-at-all hospitable. She turned and marched into the kitchen, leaving Grace to follow. Aleda motioned to a chair at one end of the kitchen table while she slipped into a seat at the opposite end. I will not make this easy for her, she thought, folding her arms, breathing deeply and looking at Grace.

Grace looked down at her hands, clasped in her lap. "There's something important I need to say," she said. Aleda didn't respond. "We had planned a bit of a meeting last night, to talk about things. It's Connie, you see, the new neighbour." Still Aleda did not respond. "She's been upset about things. She wants to belong to our church, but it just seems impossible for her. She doesn't care for Robert and she doesn't approve of women being ministers." Aleda shrugged but still said nothing. She continued to breathe deeply; she needed to stay calm. Grace looked uneasy, but Aleda remained resolved to offer no help through this conversation. "Connie told me that six or eight people were coming to our meeting — maybe more — but, when seven thirty came, there was just the two of us — me and Connie."

For the first time in their conversation, Aleda responded, "Just the two of you?"

Grace nodded. "After we talked for a while, Connie went home, but a few minutes later, Rose showed up at my door. I said, 'Oh, Rose, did you come for the meeting? It was at seven thirty. You're an hour late.'" Aleda stared at Grace, who kept her gaze turned down at her clasped hands. "We had a good conversation, me and Rose. She wanted me to come and tell you this." Aleda had never seen Grace look so uncomfortable and unhappy. "Rose helped me see things a different way. Sometimes a square peg won't fit in a round hole, Rose said. Maybe Connie would be happier going to church someplace else, someplace where the teaching fits with hers instead of her trying to change all of us. At least, that's what Rose said."

Aleda nodded. It was the closest to an apology that she might expect from Grace.

"I know it's important to keep the community together," Grace added. "Besides, I want people to keep buying my muffins and butter tarts."

27
Letter

"You're ready then?" Roy asked, reaching out to receive the key for the parsonage.

"Packed and ready," Aleda answered. "It does seem a bit unsettling, going away when Dorrie is still in hospital and the Jacobi family needs support and there's that trouble with Robert at the church. I suppose you heard," she said, tilting her head sideways and studying his face carefully, "about the meeting Connie arranged at Grace's house last night?"

"Now don't you worry at all about that, Aleda. Everyone in Milburn Corners has been more than happy with your ministry. You've been a breath of fresh air to all of us. We don't want to be the type of people who side with one person against the other, but you need to know that you have our loyalty."

"Oh, I see," Aleda stammered. "Well, then … here's the number for my cell phone. Don't hesitate to call if there's a need."

Roy nodded. "We'll be just fine, Aleda," he said. "The important thing is that you have a good rest and come back to us in two weeks. Now, git along on your way before it's too hot."

After checking her van for fuel and stowing snacks and drinks in her cooler, she said goodbye to Laura, thinking that her friend had accepted her decision about going away on her own for two weeks in a calm, even casual, manner. Laura told her that she had planned a week of flea market excursions and summer theatre with Rose. For an infinitesimal moment, Aleda had an insecure reaction — wondering if her good friend cared at all whether she came or went. But as soon as that thought flitted into her mind, it fled just as quickly. She felt a wave of excitement in her stomach. She was about to set out on an adventure, a path that led … who knew where? Anything was possible.

• • •

"Why don't we start close to home?" Rose suggested. "I've heard that the Keady sale is the place to go."

"That's a flea market?"

"More than that, I've heard. More like a giant farmers market and garage sale and antique show and bake shop all rolled into one. They even have boxes of kittens for sale."

"When do we go?" Laura responded, laughing.

It had been hard to find a spot to park in the big open field. "This is amazing!" Laura exclaimed, gazing around at the sea of cars that surely represented crowds of people wandering through the offerings at the Keady sale.

Rose's description had been accurate. They paused to look at one of the largest selections of socks Laura had ever seen. They picked up goat's milk soap at another booth and admired a vendor's collection of bird houses, all built to resemble miniature motels. "How cute is this," Laura said to Rose, pointing to a bird motel with a little swimming pool. They laughed and wandered on to a table where a man was selling freshly roasted coffee beans, then around the corner to where a farmer sold baskets of Harvest apples, pears and peaches. Next to him, a woman was selling medicated ointment.

"That's a brand I haven't seen since …" Rose almost said, "Since your father and I worked together." But she stopped herself, wondering still how Laura had taken the news that her father and Rose had been lovers as well as the trusted doctor-nurse team in Milburn Corners. Of course, Rose thought, as she continued down another aisle with Laura, all that is now history.

When Laura heard her sigh she said, "You okay, Rose?"

"Of course. I was just thinking that each generation has its own challenges. My generation and yours. And no doubt it's the same for my grandchildren. Each generation has challenges; they're just different."

"What brought that on?"

Rose smiled ruefully. "The medicated ointment, I'm afraid."

As Laura was dropping her off at her house, Rose turned to her and asked, "I've been wondering if you've met the new neighbour, Connie?"

"Briefly. Why do you ask?"

"She's been on my mind lately," Rose confessed. "I've been wondering if you would consider inviting her over for a visit — dinner or lunch on the weekend. Perhaps it sounds a little cunning, but I do believe it's important to the life of our village to find out a little more about Connie. What is it that's motivating her to wage such a battle against Robert and Aleda? I think we need to figure that out. Then maybe we'll see a way forward."

Rose was picking up her mail from the communal mailbox when she saw Roy sitting on a bench in front of his workshop. She could see that he was reading and absent-mindedly rubbing his knee, his shoulders hunched forward. Walking over, she called out, "Something got you worried, Roy?"

"Well," he said, looking up at her, then down at a letter in his hand. "It's that Connie woman." Rose waited for him to continue. "Seems like things didn't go well last night. The meeting, you know, to persuade people to get rid of Robert, maybe even Aleda." Rose nodded but didn't confess her part in the failed meeting; she had spent the previous week quietly advising people against attending such a divisive meeting. "Maybe you should read this for yourself," Roy said, handing her the letter. "My eyesight is not as good as it used to be."

Rose's face was solemn as she sat down on the bench beside Roy and began to read. After a few minutes, she said, "With a few phone calls, it seems that Connie has discovered how to take a complaint to a higher level in our church system."

Roy nodded. "She has written a letter to the elders of our church, asking us to forward her complaint to the Presbytery for some action."

"I'm not up on these processes, but I'm assuming that this can't be good."

"No," he confessed. "It's bound to keep things stirred up." They sat in silence for a minute as he rubbed his knee.

"Your knee bothering you, Roy?"

"Touch of the old arthritis, I'm afraid. Either that or too much hoeing."

"I've got just the very thing you need. Picked it up today at the Keady market. I'll go home and bring it back for you. Remember that old medicated ointment Dr. Browning used to prescribe?"

Roy laughed. "We used to say that he recommended it for everything — sinus trouble, aching muscles and piles."

"Wonderful. Simply wonderful," Rose murmured.

"Yes, wasn't it?" Roy agreed, although he was thinking about a tin of menthol medicated ointment and Rose was thinking of happy times spent with the doctor. "I just can't understand why she is doing this."

Rose had been lost in memories but now her head jerked up. "Me neither," she agreed, shaking her head. "Did you tell Aleda about the letter?"

"Oh, no. I wouldn't do that. She needs to have some peace and quiet. No need to worry her when she is heading off for a couple of weeks of vacation."

Instinctively, they both turned, two old friends, two of the longest residents of the village, and stared at the house across from the store — Connie's house. What was happening to their harmonious little village? What was happening to their peace of mind?

28

Rest-a-while Lodge

She swept through the picturesque bayside town of Meaford, thundered by the old mill in Thornbury, rolled past the ski hills, now lush and green, in the town of Collingwood. All these towns nestled on the edge of Nottawasaga Bay were worthy of a visit, even suitable for a vacation. But no, she mustn't stop so soon. She was not even halfway to the lodge.

By the time she got to Barrie and stopped for lunch overlooking Lake Simcoe, she wondered why she had not considered this a good spot to vacation. She glanced at her watch and shook her head. She had further to go.

When she next stopped for a rest and pulled out her map, she could see that she was heading toward Gravenhurst, Bracebridge and Huntsville, all popular summer vacation destinations. Months ago, when she was planning her vacation, she worried about finding an affordable vacation spot among all the classy resorts in those towns. When she discovered a brochure on Rest-a-while Lodge, she was attracted to its rustic wooden exterior, the large screened veranda running around the entire lodge, the wooded path leading to the lake, and the beautiful garden which, she would later discover, the owners, Jørgen and Erika Jenssen, had lovingly recreated from memories of their childhood in Norway. She had especially liked the price. Compared to other lodges on the lake, it was affordable for her.

When she reached the lovely tourist town of Bracebridge, she stopped to enjoy its charming tumbling waterfalls. She glanced at her watch, sighed and climbed back into her van. She was not there yet.

As she drove slowly out of Bracebridge, she saw a billboard advertising Steamboat Bay and Indian River in Port Carling. The locks in Port Carling, the billboard said, connect Lake Muskoka and Lake Rousseau. She pointed her van in the direction of Port Carling. After winding along the edge of Lake Muskoka, she found herself at a T-intersection. To the right was a road into town; to the left was a gravel trail that vanished into a wooded area. She turned left. The road became increasingly narrow and twisted. Was she on the right road? This one seemed to go nowhere, but just then she turned the corner and there it was — Rest-a-while Lodge.

The first thing Aleda noticed was a stout woman with a walking stick marching toward the front veranda, and the second thing she spotted were children racing around the outside of the lodge, screaming and dashing from one spot to another, playing a raucous running game. Ironic, she thought, given the name of the lodge.

The girl at the front desk helped Aleda with a registration form and took an imprint of her credit card, then tapped a little silver bell that sat on the desk. The door to a back room opened, where five or six teenaged girls were busy folding napkins, stacking dinner plates and polishing silver.

"Emily," the girl at the front desk called out, "I'd like you to meet our new guest. Miss Aleda Vastag."

The girl who emerged from the back room smiled and, in an animated voice, said, "Hi! I'll be your waitress in the dining room, and I'll also be making up your room each morning. Is there anything I can do to make your stay pleasant?"

"Um, well, I'm not sure yet," Aleda said.

"We always ask how to address our guests," Emily continued. "Would you like to be addressed as Ms. Vastag? Miss Vastag? Mrs?"

"Please, just call me Aleda."

"Oh, I see. It's just that … well, I'm sorry about this." The girl hesitated, frowning. "With the configuration of guests right now, there's no other choice but to place you in the dining room at the table of Miss Madeira." Emily hesitated again, then added, "I'm sure she will not want to call you by your first name."

Aleda stared at the girl and shrugged. "Is that so terrible?"

"No," Emily answered, but Aleda could see that there was something that she did not want to say.

"I'm wondering," Aleda said, thinking that this day had brought enough excitement, "if I might go to my room, take a hot bath, and have a sandwich and a cup of tea brought up for my dinner?"

"Of course!" Emily said, smiling, suddenly animated again. "Let me show you the way."

The old lodge had no elevator, but Emily was strong. She lifted Aleda's suitcases and climbed the stairs, then turned into a narrow hallway where their footsteps echoed off the wooden floors. The girl opened a door, handed Aleda a key, and opened an inner door to display the bathroom. She turned down the comforter on the bed and said, "If there's nothing more you need, I'll bring up a sandwich in an hour."

Aleda murmured a thank you and looked intently at the bed, hoping that it would be comfortable.

"Breakfast is at eight in the morning. Just come to the dining room door and I'll show you where to sit." Emily, turning to leave, her hand on the door knob, swung back around to Aleda. "Whatever you do," she said in an urgent tone, "don't come late for breakfast. Miss Madeira hates that." Aleda stood staring at the girl, her mouth open. "And it's not good to be early, either. Miss Madeira insists on being first to the table."

"Who *is* this woman? I must say, she sounds quite disagreeable." Aleda noticed that the girl's sunny expression had once again disappeared and she wondered if she had uttered the words harshly.

The girl glanced out into the hallway as if worried that they might be overheard, then leaned toward Aleda and whispered, "Mrs. Jenssen says she's the guest from hell."

The following morning, Aleda was ready early. "This is ridiculous," she grumbled as she glanced at her watch. She was trying to figure out how long it would take her to leave her room, walk down the long wooden hallway, go down the stairs and make her way to the dining room. One minute? Two minutes? What if her watch was not accurate? "This is ridiculous," she repeated, then threw back her shoulders, grabbed her key, locked the room and headed downstairs.

Peering into the dining room, she could see that the tables were set with white linen and cloth napkins. Nice, she thought, wondering if this was the Norwegian way to do things. Emily was standing by the dining room door, clutching a bundle of black menus. She looked relieved when Aleda appeared, her face brightening with a smile. "Perfect! Miss Madeira has just gone in," she said, waving toward a retreating figure making her way to a table in an alcove of the dining room.

Aleda could see that Miss Madeira was the stout woman with the walking stick she had seen the day before. Emily led Aleda toward the table, where the woman was tucking her black flowing dress around her legs and settling her sturdy walking shoes under the table. Despite the fact that she was plump, Aleda noticed that she had disproportionately thin bony legs, giving her a top-heavy look. She looks like Humpty Dumpty, Aleda thought uncharitably.

Emily held out her hand to signal Aleda that they should wait. When Miss Madeira had settled, Emily smiled, stepped forward and said in a formal and precise voice, "Good morning, Miss Madeira. As I mentioned last evening, you now have a table guest. May I introduce … er … this is Aleda, Miss Madeira."

"Aleda? Nonsense, girl. What is her proper name?"

Aleda stepped around Emily. "I'm pleased to meet you, Miss Madeira. My name is Aleda Vastag. Thank you for sharing your table with me."

"Miss or Mrs?" Miss Madeira asked, turning to look at her in a critical way, making Aleda wonder if she had dressed too casually for breakfast. "I refuse to use that term Ms."

"Well, then," she shrugged. "It has to be Miss."

After Aleda had settled into a chair opposite the stout woman, Emily set a black menu in front of her, but Miss Madeira intervened. "Take that away." She made a shooing motion with her hand. Emily grabbed up the menu and stepped backward, clutching it to her chest. "At this table," Miss Madeira announced, "we eat toasted marmalade and bacon sandwiches for breakfast. I bring my own homemade Seville orange marmalade with me."

Soon, Emily was back from the kitchen carrying a tray with two marmalade and bacon sandwiches. Aleda glanced around the dining room, looking at a family with four rowdy children — the children who had been tearing around the lodge on the previous day. All six members of the family were slathering butter over crisp golden-brown French toast, splashing on maple syrup, piling on strawberries and toasted almonds and whipped cream. Across the room, a middle-aged couple were thanking their waiter for plates of poached eggs piled high on English muffins and smothered in buttery Hollandaise sauce topped with fresh herbs. A young couple, newly married, Aleda guessed, gazed into each other's eyes, ignoring their plates of creamy scrambled eggs topped with chives and smoked salmon and hash browned potatoes and glossy thick sausages. Eat, eat, eat, she thought, staring at them, then sighed and turned back to her bacon and marmalade sandwich.

Emily approached with a silver pot. "Your tea, Miss Madeira?" After she had poured, she turned to Aleda to fill her cup.

"No, thank you, Emily. Coffee please. Coffee with cream." Aleda took a bite and set down her sandwich. Miss Madeira was staring at her.

"After breakfast," Miss Madeira said, "we will take an hour to let our breakfast digest. Then, at ten o'clock sharp, we will meet in front of the lodge for a brisk morning walk. We shall have lunch at twelve thirty sharp, then a nap following lunch. There will be cribbage in the sun room at four, one dry martini in the lounge at five — gin, no vermouth, olives, straight up — then dinner at six. The evening, of course, is on your own."

Aleda glowered at her and set down her coffee mug with a thud, splashing coffee onto the clean white table linen. Emily froze behind the serving station, her hands pressed flat against the table top. She glanced sideways, then dropped her gaze and stared down at the rejected black menus.

"Miss Madeira," Aleda began, "I am here for a much-needed vacation. I don't play cribbage. I don't drink martinis. I drink coffee for breakfast, and tomorrow ... tomorrow, I want one of each of those," she said, gesturing around the room at the breakfasts of the other guests. "The one thing I will agree to," she declared, "is to try the brisk morning walk, because I need a little exercise and I love to walk. If it doesn't work out, well ... I gave it a try." Although she didn't want to admit it to the imperious Miss Madeira, she was thinking that the idea of an afternoon nap sounded like a fine thing to do on a vacation, as well.

Miss Madeira glared at her, drew her back up straight and said, "Well!"

Emily exhaled softly, her lips pursed, then turned back to the kitchen, smiling a little.

29
Miss Madeira

MISS MADEIRA HAD BEEN TRUE TO HER WORD. IT WAS A BRISK WALK. FOR SUCH A STOUT woman, she was capable of walking very rapidly. She also had a proclivity, as Aleda was to find out in the days ahead, to deliver a lecture as they walked. It made things easier for Aleda, since she was too out of breath to talk, not that Miss Madeira seemed to notice.

She wondered if Miss Madeira might be a teacher, but it turned out that she was a writer, a syndicated columnist with several Canadian newspapers. She was an expert on nutrition, and it was about this topic that she wrote and spoke.

On the first morning, as they walked, she lectured Aleda on the importance of obtaining enough potassium in her diet. "When I say 'potassium,' what are you thinking about?" she demanded of the panting Aleda, but, before she could respond, Miss Madeira continued, "Bananas, of course. Everyone thinks you have to eat bananas for potassium. There are many sources of potassium in everyday food." Her voice remained strong as they strode up a hill. "Acorn squash," she declared. "One cup gives you twenty per cent of your daily requirements for potassium, and a great deal of magnesium and folate as well. And beans. Plain white beans. People need to eat more beans. Cooked white beans are a wonderful source of potassium and are particularly good if you put some melted butter, salt and pepper on them. Maybe add some roasted garlic and a little fresh thyme. And then, there's salmon. People always think that salmon is only good for its omega-3 fatty acids but, oho!" she exclaimed as they marched along, "one six ounce serving of fresh salmon gives you almost twice as much potassium as that little banana of yours! Now, why do you need potassium, can you tell me that?" But before Aleda could sputter out an answer, Miss Madeira called out in indignation, "Do you want high blood pressure? Heart attack? Stroke? Osteoporosis? No! You need that potassium to keep your muscles functioning properly. You need it to relax the walls of your blood vessels."

Panting and sweating, Aleda strode quickly alongside the pontificating Miss Madeira, wondering if the lodge gift shop sold ear plugs.

By the end of the hike on her first day at Rest-a-while Lodge, Aleda had made an exciting discovery. Miss Madeira suffered from allergies to the great outdoors. In August, moulds were particularly bad for her, she told the perspiring Aleda, the type of moulds that hang around logs and soil and compost.

"That dreadful Norwegian garden," she declared with a sweep of her hand, "is the worst place in the world for me."

Aleda did not know at the time what she was referring to, but this made her more determined to find out.

As they were returning from their walk, Miss Madeira began to sneeze, and when Aleda glanced over at her, she was wiping her eyes and had pulled a handkerchief from her bosom to hold under her dripping nose. The brisk morning walk, as it turned out, was the only outdoor exposure that Miss Madeira could tolerate in a day. Aleda had a plan that she was quite sure would work.

By two o'clock in the afternoon, she was sitting in the sunshine of the Norwegian garden, as Miss Madeira had dubbed it. Nestled close to her lounge chair sat an oversized tote bag full of books and a hamper containing a picnic lunch. Everything I need for complete happiness, Aleda thought, as she settled into her new hiding place.

She pushed her sunglasses up onto her head and gazed around. When she first entered the tranquil garden, she caught a glimpse of the lake, but when she was seated, the garden seemed private and complete, edged on all sides with mature trees — balsam, fir, tamarack, black spruce and eastern hemlock — creating a protective green shield around the lawn and flowers.

In the centre of the lawn, a clump of four paper birch trees with three large rocks nestled close together offered a miniature wilderness vignette. Aleda admired the sweeping flower beds with their gently curving edges, not tangled with creeping Charlie and bindweed like her own garden back in Milburn Corners had been before Roy had given her a hand.

The flowers were all purple, white and yellow, giving the space a peaceful unity. Lounge chairs, painted purple, dotted the lawn. It's a paradise, she thought, smiling. The boisterous children could be heard from time to time, but they were far away, racing around the lodge or splashing in the wading pool or running in and out of the sun room. Not much wonder Miss Madeira calls them "the ruffians, the little barbarians."

Her mind drifted to her own backyard, wondering if it was now full of balls and toys and running children, but she forced herself back to the Norwegian garden. If she could immerse herself in her new vacation experience, she believed she would emerge from it fully refreshed and better equipped to deal with troubles that were brewing back home.

One small thing marred her otherwise perfect hideaway. Another person had also discovered this beautiful, secluded place. A woman — Aleda recognized her from breakfast as the mother of the rambunctious children — sat across the garden reading her own stash of books. Unlike Aleda's, her books were romance, the type with covers depicting a man kissing the neck of a woman, her head thrown back, her dark tangle of curls falling over her bare shoulders, her bodice opened to reveal the top of plump breasts.

Later, when Aleda had a chance to speak to her, she discovered that the woman had a dreamy, absent-minded indifference to the escapades of her children. "I look after them all year long," she told her. "It's their father's turn now." It became obvious to Aleda — and to the beleaguered staff and other guests at the lodge — that the father wasn't taking much responsibility for his unruly offspring, nor did the mother much seem to care. She was here to restore herself for the year ahead. Perhaps the father was here to become rested and re-energized too, and so the children ran wild.

After the second afternoon in the Norwegian garden, Aleda and the woman greeted each other with a perfunctory wave, then settled down with their respective books and their separate picnic hampers.

Aleda's days fell into a predictable and easy pattern. It was only the evenings that were difficult. Restless, she often wandered down to the lake. Once, she ventured into the lounge but beat a hasty retreat when someone suggested she join them at the bridge table. She was too tired and well-fed to read, and it seemed somehow just plain wrong to watch television in this idyllic setting. In the evenings, her mind invariably drifted toward home.

First on her mind was always Neil Brennan. Was he still considering a return to Ireland? If that was so, why had he been so good to her, so constant in his attention? He had taken her to the Irish tea room and seemed genuinely worried when he warned her about the problems with Connie. Why had he taken the time to warn her about the dangerous undertow on the day he left Boiler Beach? Why had he kissed her with such tenderness and passion?

Close behind this worry was always the problem of Dorrie. What do I know about mental stress and suffering? she demanded of herself. And what if the Jacobi family isn't able to move out of my house on time? Where will I go, and what will I do about their situation? What will happen, she thought with a shudder, if Roy loses his eyesight? How would she manage without his practical help and his quiet moral support if he had to sell his house and move to a retirement community? What will happen to our wonderful friendship when Martin returns to Guelph this fall? Will Laura and I carry on as if nothing is different? And what about those puppies? Who will take them in? And Tracker ... if he got an abscess in one hoof, is that the beginning of many small ailments which will lead to one enormously difficult decision? But always, nagging at the edges of her mind, was the issue of Connie. How on earth would that situation be resolved?

But all these concerns were back home, not here, not in her idyllic garden retreat at Rest-a-while Lodge. Despite the nagging interruptions of her evening worries — and the insistent and seemingly endless walking lectures given by the indomitable and autocratic Miss Madeira — it was to be, as she would remember for years to come, one of the most peaceful times in her life.

30

Norway Garden Theology

SINCE ARRIVING AT REST-A-WHILE LODGE, ALEDA HAD BEEN CAREFUL TO AVOID mentioning that she was a Presbyterian minister. She didn't reveal it to Emily, who looked after her so attentively. Nor did she drop a hint of her profession to Miss Madeira — not that the woman would have noticed; she seldom gave Aleda time or space to talk. Aleda rarely saw Erika and Jørgen Jenssen, so it was not likely to come up in casual conversation. She and the preoccupied mother reading romance novels in the garden chatted only in passing. It wasn't that she was sensitive about admitting her profession. She simply wanted and needed a time of privacy, a time when people did not see her through a different lens when they found out.

It took her off guard, then, on a glorious sunny day in her second week at Rest-a-while, when two incidents happened that caused her to fall into a time of deep reflection in her afternoon retreat in the Norwegian garden.

Dressed in a tank top and yoga pants, she had met Miss Madeira in front of the lodge at ten o'clock in the morning. Having learned to concentrate on her breathing and the mental image of oxygen pumping through her lungs and energizing her muscles, she was, by now, able to keep up to the woman who strode along on her spindly legs wearing, always, a long flowing dress — sometimes black, sometimes navy blue.

Today Miss Madeira held forth on the importance of eating ten fruits and vegetables each day and on the absolute necessity of avoiding overly-processed food. Puffing and perspiring beside the striding woman, Aleda's mind flashed to the thick slices of bacon that appeared each morning in Miss Madeira's iconic bacon and marmalade sandwich. Has she not considered that bacon was treated with nitrates to make it last longer and to improve its appearance? Was bacon, although delicious, not loaded with fat and salt? Even if she could catch her breath long enough to pant out these questions, she knew that Miss Madeira would have a snappy repartee ready. Aleda marched along, trying to keep up.

That morning, Miss Madeira led her up over a hill on a route that was different from the path they usually took. As they passed a small cottage perched on the edge of Lake Rousseau, she pointed out the summer home of an Anglican priest, now retired.

"What a lot of nonsense Christianity is!" the woman exclaimed. "Absolute rubbish. The idea of joining the club ..." which, Aleda realized as Miss Madeira continued to talk, meant joining the church, "is to dunk people under water, practically drowning them, then offer them blood to drink and flesh to eat. Craziness. Christianity claims that God is one but God is also three. Christians can't even do basic math. And to call their god a 'father' in this day and age when fathers are leaving their wives and children without a thought in the world is just plain nonsense. Besides," she ranted on, "what kind of a religion believes that a father would just stand by and watch a son be killed? Baloney. Absolute rubbish."

Miss Madeira's views on religion were as adamant and definitive as her views on everything else. Her rant on Christianity didn't upset Aleda, but it made her wonder if others saw Christianity in that way. As someone who loved and cared about the various aspects of Christianity, she found it disconcerting that someone could be so dismissive and sarcastic about the belief system that was central to her life.

After showering and changing into fresh clothes, Aleda was surprised and pleased to experience a counter-balance to Miss Madeira's rant on Christianity.

She had gone to the kitchen door to pick up her lunch. Every day, she eagerly opened her hamper to discover open-faced Norwegian sandwiches that were as beautiful to look at as they were tasty — flatbread spread with cream cheese, radish, tomato and lemon, or rye bread covered in smoked salmon, hard-boiled eggs and fresh dill.

As she turned toward the Norwegian garden for an exquisite afternoon of eating, reading, thinking and napping, she was surprised to see Erika and Jørgen Jenssen sitting under a shade tree enjoying a cold drink. Lunch in the dining room was a cold salad plate, so she assumed preparation was already complete.

"Hello there," Aleda called out as she came close. "I don't want to disturb your rest, but there is something that's been puzzling me." They listened to her question.

"Oh, it's quite simple," Jørgen answered. "When we first bought the lodge, we were trying to think of a suitable name for it. It was winter and we were talking about how nice it was to have a warm kitchen with a fire, a bowl of fish chowder and fresh bread. After supper, we read a chapter of the Bible together ... we usually do. Mark's gospel, wasn't it, Erika? We got talking about how upset Jesus must have been by the things going on in his life. His cousin had just been beheaded, of all barbaric things! And then to think that Herod's daughter presented John's head to her mother as a gift at a party."

"Yes," Aleda agreed. "Horrifying. And just a short time before, Jesus had been baptized by John."

"As we read on," Jørgen continued, "Jesus seemed overwhelmed by the crowds of people all around him, everybody needing and wanting something."

"That's when we read that verse in Mark," Erika said. "Jesus suggested to his disciples that they go away to a deserted place by themselves and rest a while. We turned to each other and said, "Aha! Rest-a-while Lodge."

"It's strange," Jørgen added, "how many times it seems that people come here troubled or harried ..." He glanced into the garden where the mother of the four rowdy children sat reading a romance novel in tranquility. "That's what we want for our guests, that they have a place to retreat and rest a while, then go home refreshed."

"Wonderful. Fantastic vision," Aleda murmured. She felt deeply touched by the Jenssen's story. Their account felt like a gift from God, a glimpse into the way their Christian faith shaped their hospitality, their work and the way they lived.

"You have motivated me to read the Gospel of Mark this afternoon," she said, slinging her bag of books over her shoulder.

"You need to borrow a Bible?"

"I have my favourite one right here," she said, patting her bag.

When they were in their last year of high school, Aleda and her friends had been sitting in the school cafeteria discussing what they might do after graduation. Margie, with her excellence in English and her love of literature was most clear about the path she would take. She planned to major in English at McMaster University, then take graduate studies in Library Science. Their friend Rob was equally confident. His interest in physics had been sparked by a science project about how the sun keeps shining. He became fascinated with the interaction between matter and energy. "Who knows where this will take me?" he declared. "Maybe into space technology or into the energy field." Their friend Will, always quiet and thoughtful, surprised them by saying that he would apply to an electrical engineering program at the University of Waterloo.

Aleda was the most undecided. Her report cards had proved one thing — she had an aptitude for science. Her parents, her father in particular, had supported her in this. He had studied to be a doctor when he was a university student in the days before the revolution in Hungary. To live out his dream through his daughter was a tacit hope. She didn't want to be a disappointment to her father, so she announced to her friends that, like Margie, she would stay at home in Hamilton and study chemical and physical sciences at McMaster University and maybe become a doctor one day.

As she settled into her purple lounge chair, she remembered that discussion and marvelled at how people who had so much in common could have such diverse interests. I certainly would have no interest in becoming a librarian or physicist or electrical engineer or even, for that matter, a doctor, she thought, as she flipped open a theology book, lowered her sunglasses and prepared for a stimulating time of reading.

She loved reading theology. Glancing across at the woman reading her romance novel, she smiled, thinking of how others might find it a dull and ponderous activity, but to her it brought great pleasure.

She didn't read theology books for education — although she did find instruction in the process. It was something deeper than that, something that she found hard to define or describe. While she wasn't searching for theological correctness, she admitted that when she read books with a different theological slant than her own, it helped her reject some ideas, clarify others, change her own way of looking at something.

Perhaps, she thought, theology helps me understand a particular view of God, helps me understand people and make sense of the world. Perhaps it helps me think and live in a way that is a bit more self-sacrificing than would happen if I lived by my personal preferences and ideals.

Oh heck! she thought, settled in the Norwegian garden surroundings with a volume clutched in her hand, I read theology because it's just plain interesting to me.

She opened her book, a commentary on Genesis, and thought, what can be more deeply satisfying than staring at those thrilling opening words, "In the beginning …"? She nestled down to reflect on the sweep and mystery, the majestic and prosaic flow of the story, the account of how it all began.

It was reflecting on the creation story that made her think of Connie. She remembered Robert telling her how Connie had criticized his interpretation of Genesis.

Thinking back to the only time she had been in the Bible study class with Connie, Aleda remembered their discussion about taking the Bible literally. Even Jesus, himself, Aleda had insisted, did not interpret scripture literally. "Think of the many times when Jesus was teaching and he started with these words: 'You have heard it said …' but then he went on to say, 'But I say to you …' Scripture," Aleda had declared, with as much fervour as Connie, "is a living, dynamic word. It's not words stuck on a page. It is the story of how God and people interacted long ago and how God continues to relate to us." At one point, Aleda remembered that she became blunt. "Connie," she said, "we simply have to admit that we have differing interpretations of scripture."

"Well," Connie demanded, "what makes you think you're right?"

In that moment, Aleda realized she could live happily with a church member who believed in a literal interpretation of the Bible. What she was unwilling and unable to accept was that Connie, and others like her, believed that their interpretations were the only valid ones.

That had been a hard lesson, she thought now as she returned to her book, but that experience helped her see that one of the main responsibilities she had as a pastor was to be a good student of the scriptures as well. Hadn't Jesus taught her that?

The days at Rest-a-while Lodge had settled into a predictable pattern for Aleda: breakfast with Miss Madeira, a second cup of coffee in the sun room, the brisk walk that left her both exhausted and exhilarated, a refreshing shower and change of clothes, picking up her lunch hamper, and then an afternoon of sinking into the realm of ideas, thoughts and prayer in the Norwegian garden.

Dinner, it turned out, had taken an unusual twist. As guests arrived and left, table groups were reshaped, and she found herself enjoying dinner conversations with interesting new guests.

Erika Jenssen, though having mastered North American cuisine, still preferred to offer Norwegian dinner fare, things she knew and loved. The evening meal usually started with fiskesuppe — a fragrant milk-based chowder containing cod, carrots, onion and potatoes. The girls then served small crab cakes, accompanied by jars of sour cream and herbs. Mrs. Jenssen believed in a hearty dinner of braised lamb or roast pork, served with flatbread to dip into the gathered juices. Once, she had surprised them with grilled venison wrapped in bacon, much to Miss Madeira's delight.

Toward the end of her second week at Rest-a-while Lodge, she realized that, at the beginning of her time, she had been able to tuck worries neatly away at night, but now they stayed with her, seeping into her dreams, and when she woke her sheets were twisted and moist with perspiration.

It was time to go home.

31
Wife

It had been Neil's habit — partly through instinct, partly because of his upbringing — to turn to a priest for advice or encouragement. So, after his shift and his workout at the gym, he drove up the hill in Owen Sound, heading to St. Mary's rectory.

He had come to think of Father Greg as a friend over the years. Together, they had kayaked on Georgian Bay and enjoyed rigorous canoe expeditions into Algonquin Park. When he considered buying a house on the cliffs of Lion's Head, he had taken Father Greg along to ask his opinion. The priest had requested that Neil call him by his first name; sometimes Neil remembered, but most often he slipped back into the habit of calling him "Father Greg" or just plain "Father." This was one of those nights.

"Father," he began, "you're probably the worst person in the world to ask for advice about getting married." They both laughed. "I could use some guidance about a wife. I'm thinking of getting married, but I just need to sort things out." Neil explained about his unexpected trip home to Ireland to see his ailing mother. He explained about Mary Bridgette who was a former girlfriend and who continued to come into his mother's home to clean a little, to cook soup or simply to have a cup of tea with the ill woman. "Mary Bridgette has been very good to our family. I've known her for years. She always went to mass with me, Carrie and Mother."

"She sounds like a good and kind person. So, what's the problem?"

Neil tried to remember just how the conversation had gone on that last evening before his return to Canada.

It was either the tonic of his presence by her bedside or simply another survived health crisis, but his mother had greatly improved since his arrival. Having enjoyed a portion of the shepherd's pie that Mary Bridgette brought over, she was content to let the younger woman help her into a clean flannel nightgown and prepare her for bed. Neil was boiling water for tea when Mary Bridgette came down the stairs and into the kitchen.

"That's it, then," she said. "Tucked in for the night."

"You're good to Mother," Neil said. "Kind and good."

"Oh, really, it's nothing," she protested. "What else would a good neighbour do? Besides, I'm very fond of your mother."

Perhaps it was the coziness of the kitchen, the shepherd's pie sitting ready for supper, the tea kettle steaming, or the ease with which Mary Bridgette seemed to manage all these things that made Neil think about marriage. He would like this in his life. He would like to come home to warmth, to something more than a television set and a frozen meal from the grocery store.

"Have you never thought of marriage then, Mary Bridgette?" he inquired, glancing up at her. He noticed a flush rise in her cheeks.

"I've been waiting for exactly the right man," she replied.

"I know what you mean, all right. It's very important to marry the right person."

They lapsed into silence as they ate, and it was only when she had poured out two mugs of tea that she asked, "Will you never come back home to us, Neil?"

Her question caught him off guard, for his mother had asked him the same question just hours before. "No," he said, staring down into the steaming tea. "No, I really consider Canada home now. I'll always come back to visit, though," he said, looking up. "I'm sorry that I can't be here to help more with Mother. Carrie and I have arranged more nursing care so it's not so much burden on you."

"Oh really, Neil, it means a great deal to me to look after your mother. Don't worry on my account."

"Is there anything I can do, Mary Bridgette? Anything that would help you along? Something that would make your life better?"

She sat quietly, her hands wrapped around her tea mug. "You could make me a promise," she said at last, gazing at him. "You could promise never to abandon us. You could promise to come back to us."

It was Neil's turn to sit in silence.

Mary Bridgette stood up. "I'll do a little washing up before I go," she said, but before she turned to the sink, she reached into her pocket and pulled out a hand-knit green shamrock dangling from a braid of yarn. "I made this for you.

It's my pledge to you. I will never forsake you. You have my word," she said. "And when you look at this shamrock, I ask that you think of me. Will you hang it in your police cruiser then, Neil?"

That's how the conversation had gone. He was quite sure of it. "Men can be dense about these types of things," he told Father Greg. "But, thinking back, I'm wondering if she felt that I would ask her to marry me. I distinctly got the impression that she wanted me to ask."

"But you didn't. So, something was holding you back."

"Yes," Neil admitted. "It's not that I'm selfish about this. Heaven knows I'm old enough to have gained a bit of smarts along the way. I've wanted to get married for some time. It's just that I want to be very sure that I've found the right woman."

"Would it help if you described the qualities that constitute the right woman?" Father Greg teased. He was visualizing a wholesome, caring, kind Irish woman across the ocean, wearing an apron and making shepherd's pie. But, when Neil next spoke, his mind was on Aleda Vastag.

"I do admire a capable woman," Neil confessed. "One who really knows her mind, a woman who is smart but not so smart that she makes me feel stupid," he said with a laugh. "I hadn't thought of it before, but I admire a woman who is independent, who has a life of her own, but not so independent that she's above spending some time with me."

Father Greg's mind focused on a woman knitting a green shamrock. Neil's thoughts turned to a different scene: lolling against a log on Boiler Beach, warm sand beneath him, the rays of a sunset in the sky above, his arm around tender, tanned shoulders.

"I've always dreamed of having children," Neil said. He sat in silence for a moment, then added, "but lately I've come to think that family can come in many different forms."

Father Greg's imagination took him to a Dublin house with Neil, his aging mother, Mary Bridgette rolling pastry, a cat curled up on the rocking chair, and rosy-cheeked nieces and nephews bursting through the back door, bringing in the cool night air. Neil was thinking of Aleda and Dinah, skipping through the overgrown meadow toward his police cruiser, holding hands, wearing daisy chains in their hair, and instead of a calico cat curled in a chair, he was thinking of a grumpy old horse.

"Now that I've reconsidered it, I can't quite remember why having biological children seemed so important. There are so many ways to be family."

Father Greg nodded, thinking that perhaps Neil worried that Mary Bridgette, who was Neil's age, might have difficulty becoming pregnant at that stage in her life, but what Neil was really thinking was that he had no right to assume that Aleda would want to have children in her forties.

"It's important to me, too," Neil said, looking a little bashful, "that she be attractive. You know …"

"Sexy, you mean?" Both men laughed and Father Greg wondered if perhaps this was the problem. Perhaps Mary Bridgette was nice-looking but not appealing in a sexual way to Neil. But Neil was thinking of a long, passionate kiss on the beach at sunset. His heart had been stirred, he knew that, but more than his heart had been stirred.

Father Greg stood up. "I think we need a Scotch. That always helps the thinking process, especially when talking about women." When the men both cradled a drink in their hands, he turned to his friend and parishioner. "You should do what makes you happy, Neil. Marriage is a sacrament to us Catholics and marriage is forever, or at least it's meant to be. Forever is a long time. There are always ups and downs in marriage, you can count on that, so you might as well start out right. Marry someone you're crazy about."

Neil stared at the priest, then took a gulp of Scotch, a broad grin lighting his face. "Wonderful advice, Father. Fantastic suggestion."

"Hey, my friend, not a problem. It was my pleasure to give you some counsel. And if you need the services of a priest, I'm happy to perform the marriage." He swirled the Scotch in his glass.

"Did I mention … yes, this is very important to me, too … that my wife would have to be a person of faith, because the Christian faith is very important in my life. I would definitely want that in a wife."

"Yes, yes, I understand," Father Greg nodded. "And, I must say, it's wonderful that you've chosen a nice Catholic girl."

32
Levi

Roy's worrying had increased as his eyesight diminished. His favourite activities — gardening, woodworking, roaming the countryside looking for new day lilies — depended on his eyesight. What would life be like if he could not look forward to these things? What would it be like to live in darkness? How could he bring himself to ask others for help? It was the time of life when things should have been easier for him. Perhaps that is why, later in the day, he found the business with the boy, Levi, so upsetting.

From the time the Jacobi family had moved into the parsonage, he had dropped in daily — sometimes to see if there was anything Leah needed from the store, but mainly to see if there were any small ways in which he could help. Her weariness from the care of so many children was as evident as the lines of worry on her face.

He had gone up to Aleda's house to check on her flower beds, but when he arrived, walking through the grass alley between the church and the parsonage, he heard screams and cries.

He rushed around the corner and saw that the red-haired twins, Judah and Issachar, were holding pieces of broken wood in their hands, howling and shouting at Levi. Leah had hurried to the back porch, the baby on her hip, and was trying to calm the shrieking children. Levi, using his bare feet, continued to kick at a wooden structure that the twins were trying to defend.

Roy was known far and wide around Milburn Corners for his calm mild manner, but suddenly he flushed with anger. Glancing first at Leah, then at the screaming twins, he turned to Levi, grabbed him and lifted him away from the broken wood.

Startled, the boy dangled in the air, his legs kicking, trying to put his feet on the ground, until everyone heard a ripping sound. The back of Levi's shirt tore away from the collar and Roy lowered the child.

When he pieced together the story, Roy discovered that all three boys loved building things with wood, but, Leah explained, Levi had a bad habit of smashing the twins' creations, just as they were about to finish their project.

"Oh my," Roy said, gazing around the garden which had once been neat and tidy. Now the day lilies around the composter were trampled flat on the ground. Branches of the butterfly bush in the corner that should be fanning out elegant plumes of purple had been snapped off, presumably for the boys' building projects. The remaining jagged twigs poked up toward the sky. Aleda's favourite wooden cottage chair had been turned on its side to create a fort, and was that a broken slat in the curved back?

Roy wondered how Leah handled these difficult situations, but when he watched her wiping the nose of the baby, he could see that her forehead was lined, her eyes rimmed with red, her face weary. The woman was clearly overwhelmed having to look after six young children while her husband spent hours at the hospital with Simeon.

Turning around, he knelt in front of the sullen boy and put his hands on the child's shoulders. "Son," he said, turning Levi toward his property next door. "Do you see that shed?"

The boy looked up but didn't say anything.

"Do you know what's going to happen tomorrow?"

Levi refused to look at him, but Roy could see that he was listening.

"Tomorrow, at eight o'clock in the morning, I am going to come and pick you up. We're going to walk over to that shed and we are going to learn how to make real things out of wood with real tools. Then you'll come home for lunch with your family. You and I are going to bring a box of wood pieces for your brothers so they don't need to use the plants in this yard. Then I'm going to pick you up again at one o'clock and, in the afternoon, we're going to learn how to care for a garden. I'll return you home at five o'clock for supper with your family."

Roy stood up and walked away, back through the grass alley between the church and the house, wondering where he might buy a new shirt for a boy.

Levi and Roy were screwing together the pieces of a birdhouse when a police cruiser stopped at the end of Roy's driveway. Roy looked up from the open door of his workshop. "We meet again," he said to Neil, extending his hand, trying to push away his reservations about the police officer. He remembered the time when Constable Brennan had helped them through the devasting time of a teen suicide in their village. "I have to admit, it's always unnerving when a law-abiding citizen sees a police car pull up."

Neil smiled. "Hey, no worries. I see you have a new helper."

"Levi." Roy said.

Ah yes, Neil thought, the boy who got lost in the middle of the family. "Whatcha making, Levi?" he called over, but if the boy heard he paid no attention. He was busy with his project. Neil nodded his head toward the cruiser, indicating to Roy that he would like a private word. The two men strolled down the driveway, then leaned side by side against the police car.

Neil, his arms crossed over his chest, glanced sideways and felt a stab of envy as he remembered the way Aleda spoke so fondly of her wonderful neighbour. She once told him that she didn't know what she would do without Roy in her life. "He has been as good to me as my own father. So wise and always there to help, even when I don't ask," she had said.

Roy stood with his hands in the pockets of his overalls, jiggling the nails and screws he had been using. He glanced sideways at the man who seemed to have won Aleda's affection. He felt an uneasiness in his stomach, like the ache of loss. Was this man worthy of her? Would he whisk her away from them? Could he be trusted?

Neil cleared his throat and asked, "You happen to know when Aleda will be home?" He didn't tell Roy that he had her cell phone number but didn't want to bother her on her vacation.

"Wednesday, I believe," Roy said. He didn't want to tell Neil that she had called him the day before and they had a long chat.

Silence grew between the two men, turning from seconds into minutes. Finally, Roy said, "I reckon we'll have to help the family move out on Tuesday."

Neil said, "I'm off by three and could help after that." The two men stood in silence again.

"The place is okay? The place they're moving to?" Roy wanted to know.

Neil shrugged. "Standard housing. The social worker was lucky to find a three-bedroom unit, but still … with all those kids, it'll be tight." His voice trailed off and he shuffled his feet. "I really would like to talk to Aleda about …" but before Neil could continue, they heard a scream from the shed. Both men snapped upright and rushed toward Levi who was standing by the workbench, clenching a screwdriver, his face red.

"What on earth is wrong?" Roy called out. "You hurt yourself?"

"No!" the boy shouted, slamming his fist on top of the bird house. "It won't fit together!"

Before Roy could respond, Neil stepped forward, put his hand on Levi's shoulder and said to him, "Sit down." He pointed to a bench. The boy looked up, suddenly confused and frightened, then obeyed, sinking onto the seat. Neil settled beside him and hunched over, his hands folded, looking down at his black police boots.

"Do you know that it's wrong to lose your temper like that and scare a man who is being good and kind to you?" When Levi didn't answer, Neil said in a stronger voice, "Do you know that was wrong?"

The boy muttered, "Yes, sir."

"Will you do it again, lad?"

"No," Levi replied, shaking his head.

Neil sighed and said, "Well then, you can't be held to blame. Your father is not here to guide you and your mother has a lot of responsibilities with the little ones." Then he added, "I think you would make a fine altar boy for St. Mary's Church. I wonder if your parents would agree to that?"

An altar boy? Roy wondered if he had heard correctly. How could this police officer have the audacity to suggest such a thing? Had it not been him who took the child under his wing, patiently teaching him the skills of woodworking, tutoring him in the care of a garden? He had grown fond of Levi. Would Constable Brennan steal the child's affection and allegiance?

And yet ... gazing over to the bench where the small child and the large man sat looking down, Roy admitted to himself that the scene before him did not seem treacherous. What he saw was a confused and frightened young boy who needed guidance and care until he found the right path. He saw a muscular, tall police officer who did not seem stern or harsh. In fact, Roy thought, his face showed tenderness and compassion. Was it possible that there was room for both of them — Roy and Neil — in the boy's life?

33
Contentment

WHEN THE TIME ARRIVED TO LEAVE REST-A-WHILE, SHE FOUND THAT SHE WAS EAGER to get home. Her vacation had restored her body and soul; she felt strong, ready to face the year ahead.

As she sped along, she wondered how she might hold on to this tranquil spirit that had formed within her, the contentment she experienced after a rigorous hike, the excitement she enjoyed after a stimulating read, the pleasure derived from eating Norwegian flatbread sandwiches that were as beautiful as they were delicious. If only she could find some symbol that would capture this holiday feeling. In the year ahead, during times of turmoil or difficulty, she could summon this symbol. By associating it with her vacation, she reasoned, she could restore and calm herself. What image expressed tranquility, peace and, most of all, inner strength? Try as she might, she could not conjure up a mystical image. Then she remembered the last walk she had with Miss Madeira.

Throughout the time that their vacations overlapped at Rest-a-while Lodge, Miss Madeira had not shown any interest in Aleda's personal life. She hadn't engaged in the usual niceties of conversation, asking where she lived or inquiring about her occupation. Instead, she seemed to use Aleda as a human sounding board, thinking through her newspaper articles for the year ahead.

She might have labelled Miss Madeira self-centred or just plain anti-social, but she had rather enjoyed the privacy she experienced as she half listened to the daily lectures while they strode briskly up hills and around the curving road that twisted by the rocky lakeside.

On the last day, as they marched along, Miss Madeira expounded on a series she would do on the religious significance of foods. Like many people who had grown up in a Christian environment but turned against it, she had a curiosity about other religions. She planned to write an article on the meals prepared for Eid, the feast that Muslims enjoyed at the end of Ramadan after a long month of sunrise-to-sunset fasting. She would take a global perspective, she explained, because Islam was practised worldwide. She would analyze the nutritional value of laasida and tagines from Morocco, sheer khurma from India and lapis laget from Indonesia. She most certainly would include a recipe for bolani, the flatbread prepared in Afghanistan, because even the simplest of Canadians could prepare it, she declared.

Then, she pronounced, there would be newspaper columns on the food of Passover, a difficult season for practising Jewish people since yeast was banned. Miss Madeira explained to her bemused walking companion that Passover was a holiday that focused on the flight of the Jews from Egypt, and that was why, in their haste to leave, there had been no time to allow bread to rise.

It had taken a couple of weeks of training, but by now Aleda was able to walk in stride with Miss Madeira. She could even utter several sentences in a row without gasping. "Then surely you will also focus on some of the foods that have religious significance to Christians."

"Nonsense!" Miss Madeira barked. It seemed to Aleda that the woman increased the length of her stride.

"But why not?" she ventured. "Pancakes for Shrove Tuesday, you know. Gotta use up all that rich fat before the penitential season of Lent. Or pretzels. They were baked to look like folded arms to remind people to pray." Miss Madeira marched along, looking neither left nor right. If she was listening, she gave no indication. "Then there's baklava. You've eaten baklava, I'm sure? Did you know that a perfect baklava is supposed to have thirty-three layers of phyllo pastry, one for each year of Jesus' life?"

Miss Madeira stopped abruptly. Aleda, not noticing for a few steps, swung around and looked back at her quizzically. For a moment, neither woman spoke, until Miss Madeira demanded, "I've been wondering … Aleda Vastag … what kind of a name is that? What's your ethnic origin?"

"Um … Hungarian," she stammered. "I was born in Canada, but my parents came here when they were in their twenties."

Miss Madeira gave a little shrug and resumed walking. Aleda hurried to catch up. They walked in silence for some time until Miss Madeira asked, "What kind of food do Hungarians favour?"

Aleda began in a hesitant voice, unaccustomed to having a conversation with the woman. "Well," she began, thinking back over the many meals that her mother had prepared for their family, "I would say that Hungarians think soup is quintessential food. A meal is not a true meal unless it starts with soup. Soup stimulates the appetite and sets the stage for what is to follow." Aleda reflected for a bit, then added, "Pickled gherkins. Hungarians love them, and onions. Hungarians love their cabbage dishes and salami and smoked sausage."

Before she could continue running through her memory bank of childhood meals, Miss Madeira asked, "But just tell me this. If there is one food — one food," she emphasized raising her index finger, "that you would say is absolutely basic to the Hungarian diet, what is it?"

They walked along in silence. Finally, Aleda said, "Bread. I would say bread."

"Bread," Miss Madeira repeated in a flat tone that indicated that she had been hoping for something more exotic.

"Yes, bread," Aleda confirmed. "Crusty fresh bread. There are so many Hungarian dishes with sauces. In a family meal, it's quite polite to sop up those delicious juices with bread. Hungarians love drippings on their bread, too."

"Drippings?" Miss Madeira scoffed without breaking her stride.

"Yes, you know, the grease drippings from roast pork or bacon or beef. Sometimes we sprinkle a little salt and paprika on the bread and drippings."

"It sounds disgusting."

"Not at all," Aleda countered, for she suddenly felt defensive, remembering how her opinionated walking partner enjoyed her morning bacon. "And when you're writing about foods that are important to Christian traditions," Aleda declared, "you will surely include a mention of the Hungarian Easter loaf. Bread dough is divided into three rolls — the Trinity, you see — and braided, then shaped into a circle, the symbol of eternity. When it is baked and coated with butter and salt, we put coloured Easter eggs into the centre. Oh, it is a thing of beauty, and no self-respecting Hungarian would celebrate Easter without a glazed ham and a braided Easter bread."

They had arrived back at Rest-a-while Lodge and the women parted, Aleda moving toward a shower and Miss Madeira to the porch to order a cold drink. As Aleda stood in the shower, removing the skim of salty moisture from her skin, she suddenly realized that, despite pontificating about the virtues of bread and the beauty of the braided Easter loaf, she herself had never once made a loaf of Hungarian bread.

As she reviewed that last hike with Miss Madeira, Aleda concluded that she would take on a new challenge: she would learn to make her own bread. She realized, with a start, that the date of the hike had been August 20th, the date when Hungarians celebrated a festival called "Day of the New Bread." That day, she knew, was really St. Stephen's Day, the oldest holy day in Hungary, a day to celebrate that Stephen was crowned King of the Magyars on Christmas Day, 1000 A.D. She had heard her parents reminisce about this joyous festival. In the aftermath of World War II, when the Soviet Union imposed new political, social and economic systems on Hungary, the communists realized that this day was so precious, so old and so much a part of the fabric of Hungarian life, that they didn't dare to abolish it. Instead, they allowed St. Stephen's Day to be renamed "The Day of the New Bread."

Day of the new bread. The phrase rolled around in her head as she drove along. Despite its dubious beginning in a time of political turmoil, she found the phrase appealing. She had found the symbol for which she was searching! Bread — with belly-filling goodness and fragrance, with life-giving significance, a symbol of rising, the body of Christ. There was hope and anticipation in the phrase "day of the new bread," a looking to the future, an optimism connected to both her heritage and her faith. From now on, she would do her best to make her own bread, and when life got too busy and there was simply not enough time, she would still celebrate the day of the new bread every time she broke off part of a loaf bought from Ethel's corner store.

As she rolled along toward Milburn Corners, she remembered, too, her last conversation with Jørgen Jenssen. Throughout her time at Rest-a-while, she had struggled with whether or not she was prepared, as her friend Regina Davis has suggested, to try to keep Neil in her life when it seemed obvious to her that he was struggling with a decision to return to Ireland and marry another woman. The relationship she had formed with him seemed, from this distance, tenuous and uncertain, as if they barely knew each other. Yet something also felt right about their connection.

On her last night, lost in thought, Aleda sat on the small beach watching shadows fall over Lake Rousseau, listening to the plaintive call of loons across the lake. When she turned back toward the lodge, she met Jørgen Jenssen sauntering up the path.

"I hope you enjoyed your time with us, Aleda" he said.

"Oh, Mr. Jenssen, I simply can't find enough words to describe how wonderful these weeks have been!" Aleda enthused.

"Good, good." They walked along in silence and when they reached the steps leading into the veranda, he turned to her and said, "You know, over the years we've seen a lot of people come and go from this lodge, and our hope has always been that people found what they needed while they were here. I can't help but sense that you've been struggling with a big decision and I'm not sure that you've been able to resolve it."

She smiled and lightly touched his arm. "You and Mrs. Jenssen have been extraordinarily wonderful hosts, more than hosts really. You've been an inspiration to me. The contentment I see in your marriage … the way you work together to help everyone feel comfortable … it's been a true inspiration. But you're quite right! I've been struggling with a big decision. But you can rest assured. Tonight, as I sat by the lake, I came to a firm conclusion. For better or for worse, I know exactly what I want to do."

When she arrived home, she swept open the front porch door, threw her bag inside, then stopped, her head tilted to one side, noticing the combination of smells — disinfectant and lemon cleaning oil.

The previous day, when she telephoned from the lodge, Roy told her that the Jacobi family had moved into their new temporary townhouse in Owen Sound and that women from the Ladies Guild were going to tidy the parsonage for her return.

She shook her head, smiling, and headed to the kitchen. Roy had written a note and set it on a cluster of letters and bills. The red blinking light on her kitchen telephone told her that there were messages that needed attention and, for once, she was eager to listen to them. Martin, she learned, would walk down from his farm with Tracker, but not until she was settled. "And by the way," he added, "there is one little complication. Nothing serious, but I wanted to give you a heads up." What's that about? she wondered, concerned once again for her horse's health. Laura had left a message wondering if Aleda was still up for their usual Friday night dinner, as it was Martin's last night before returning to Guelph. The final message was from Burt Robertson. Dorrie, he explained, had returned home, and he hoped Aleda would pop up to the farm for a visit.

She turned toward the kitchen calendar and noticed that it was still set to July, still blank. How could I ever have thought that nothing would happen this summer? she mused, shaking her head. Now, I need to make myself a sandwich, brew a pot of tea and sort through the bills.

Still smiling, she opened the refrigerator and peered inside. Gone. Everything was gone. Totally emptied out. All the half jars of pickles and olives, the bottle of ketchup with its sticky lid, the plastic tub of margarine, the tin of tomato juice, even the box of baking soda, ripped open to absorb odours.

She shook her head. Nothing could disturb her contentment, not even the necessity of returning to Owen Sound to do some evening grocery shopping.

34
Full Day

THE DAY AFTER SHE GOT HOME, SHE KNEW THAT IT WAS TIME TO MAKE A LIST. In addition to getting Tracker home, she wanted to drop into the Richardson farm to see Dorrie. She planned to pop in to Owen Sound and see Simeon at the hospital, too. It would be a busy day, but Aleda felt full of energy and ready for the challenge. She glanced at her watch. It was early by city standards, but not to farmers. Dorrie and Burt had probably been up for hours.

When she pulled into the farmyard, she was surprised to find them sitting on the side porch gazing down into a cardboard box. They looked up as Aleda approached and Burt waved her forward. "Come and meet our new baby," he said, grinning.

Dorrie stood up and Aleda reached out with a hug. "It's wonderful to see you home, Dorrie. Totally wonderful." The women turned to look down into the box. There, lying quietly on an old blanket, was Pokey the puppy, the runt from Buddy's litter.

"I got him for Dorrie, a companion." Burt glanced sideways at his wife, then told Aleda that the puppy had been with them for two days. "Dorrie is mixing dog replacement milk in puppy chow and feeding the puppy three times a day to get him used to being weaned." Dorrie still hadn't spoken and Aleda, too, glanced sideways at the silent woman. "You must have women-things to talk about," Burt said, rising from his chair. "I'll get on with my chores."

Finally, Dorrie spoke, but in a hesitant voice, not her usual strong and confident tone. Aleda wondered if she was still on some type of medication. "It'll be good for me, I think," she said, staring down at the contented puppy. "Something to look after until I get used to being back."

Aleda nodded and murmured, "So true." After a time of silence, she asked, "How are you feeling? Do you feel stronger now?"

Dorrie nodded a little. "I think so." Another long silence followed. "It's just that I'm scared."

"Scared?" It was not what Aleda expected to hear. She thought Dorrie might say that the drugs made her thoughts foggy or that she felt numb and lethargic, but she had not considered that Dorrie would describe herself as scared.

"I'm afraid to go out now," she confided. "People will be awkward with me and that will make me feel bad all over again."

Aleda nodded, realizing that this was probably true. She turned to Dorrie, who was watching the sleeping puppy. "Do you have a notebook? And a pen?"

Dorrie looked up in surprise. She nodded, then rose to fetch a small black book from a cupboard.

"It's a little thing I used to do when I had to face a difficult challenge. I made myself twenty-four squares," Aleda said, drawing a chart in the notebook and showing the diagram to the puzzled woman. "You said that you are scared about meeting people. I can guarantee that by the time you've met and talked with twenty-four people — other than Burt — your fear will have vanished. Every time you talk to someone, put a check in one of these boxes. Trust me, Dorrie," Aleda said with a flourish, "when your twenty-four boxes are all checked, your fear will be gone."

Dorrie held the little chart in front of her, studying it. "But why twenty-four?" she asked.

Aleda looked as puzzled as Dorrie had been a moment before. "I don't know," she admitted with a shrug. "Maybe because I was twenty-four years old when I invented this little game; I was facing a big challenge at the time. I can't explain it. I just know that I've used it many times … and it works. Now then," she said gently, "why don't you check off the first box? You've had a visit with me. Do I have your permission to send Rose around tomorrow for your next visit?"

On her way home from the farm, Aleda pulled her van up in front of the village store. She wanted to take along a treat when she went to visit Simeon in the hospital. What might appeal to a ten-year-old boy undergoing cancer treatment?

Aleda gazed around the store. An old-fashioned gold-edged cash register sat on a long table that might have been used for measuring bolts of fabric in former times but now displayed the baked goods prepared daily by Grace. Silver trays were laden with bran muffins infused with brown sugar and molasses and golden raisins, nut-brown apple pies fragrant with cinnamon and nutmeg, lattice-covered cherry pies — and Grace's famous butter tarts, shining with glaze and rich with maple syrup, pecans, walnuts and raisins. Mmm … the last I heard Grace and Ethel were not speaking to each other, she thought.

The store smelled of years gone by; the enduring scent of flour and soap seemed pressed into the warp of the wooden floor. Unlike modern stores with multiple aisles of goods, Ethel's store was set up in a u-shape. Aleda had asked about that once and Ethel had responded, "Oh, it's simple enough. In the old days, this part," she said gesturing to the centre of the store, "was where the pot-bellied stove sat. They needed the space in the middle for people. That's where everyone shared a bit of a gossip and got caught up on the news. There were five or six stools there around the stove and they were nearly always occupied."

"Makes sense," Aleda had responded. As she looked around the store now, she thought that, with the exception of the missing stove, little seemed to have changed.

Ethel hurried out from the back room. "Wonderful to have you back, Aleda. How was the vacation?" Giving Aleda no time to respond, she hurried on, "My, you certainly missed out on something here in our little village."

"I did?"

Ethel laughed. "There was quite a little stir while you were away. There's some talk of holding a fall festival here in Milburn Corners."

"A festival? Whose idea was that?"

"That's the odd thing," Ethel declared. "Nobody seems to know. The idea just arose and people kept talking about it.

"Very strange," Aleda agreed. "So, what was decided?"

"Nothing definite. Someone suggested a butter tart festival, with a big competition for the best tart. But then someone told us that their cousin lives up in Midland and they already had a butter tart festival there and we'd better come up with something more original." Ethel shook her head. "Then someone suggested that we plan something with the children and teens in this village. We've been lucky, you know. We have some of the best teenagers in the municipality. They deserve a little recognition. Everybody's saying that."

"No kidding," Aleda muttered, turning her head to hide the tears that pooled in her eyes.

Ethel seemed not to have noticed. She continued to stack Aleda's groceries into a paper bag. "One good thing came out of all this," she laughed. "It got us all talking again, especially me and Grace. So even if the festival never happens, something good happened. I love those butter tarts and muffins and pies of Grace's as much as she loves making them."

Aleda nodded and murmured, "Good. I'm glad to hear it," thinking that, perhaps, many small problems, like the problem with Connie, sort themselves out, given some time.

"I'm wondering something," Aleda said, turning toward the table laden with baked goods. "Do children like butter tarts?"

"Far as I know, everybody loves butter tarts."

When Aleda rounded the corner into Simeon's hospital room, a square white box nestled under her arm, she found an empty bed. She pressed her hand to her chest, wondering if something had gone terribly wrong, waiting a moment for her heart to stop thumping. She spun around and hurried toward the nurse's station, but as she passed the waiting room, she noticed two sets of men's shoes — a pair of large black boots and, two chairs over, a pair of steel-toed work boots. Between them dangled a pair of bare feet. When she peeked in, she saw Neil and Jacob with Simeon between them, all eating orange popsicles.

"Hey! Want a bite?" Neil's face lit up with a smile. Aleda smiled back, then perched on the edge of an empty chair across from them, slipping her box of butter tarts back into her tote bag. At the moment, it seemed, a popsicle would take precedence over a butter tart. The boy looked less pale and the bruises had disappeared from his legs. Although he still seemed thin and frail, Aleda could see that he was responding well to treatment. She watched streaks of orange droplets running down the child's arm, wondering why the men didn't seem to notice.

Jacob nodded at her. "I was hoping for a chance to thank you for letting us stay in your house and for arranging the car. It was really good of you, what with Simeon being sick." Aleda smiled, but before she had time to respond he added, "It's given all of us a bit of time to think about things. Both Leah and I are hoping that we can stay on here in Owen Sound until we get the old church more comfortable."

"Ah," Aleda responded simply, wondering if she should say that it seemed a wise and good decision. She smiled at Simeon, but her eyes kept wandering to the dripping popsicle which by now was leaving orange dots on his white hospital gown.

Jacob glanced over to Neil, tipped his head sideways and said to Aleda, "This Constable Brennan has been a man of his word. He visits Simeon every day and makes sure that Levi gets out to Milburn Corners. My boy sure loves working with Roy. They're building a dog house, did you know?"

"I didn't know that," Aleda murmured, thinking that it must surely please Jacob that the son who had been such a challenge was now showing a keen interest in woodworking, like his father. But before she could continue, Jacob abruptly changed the subject.

"We've been going to the Catholic Church up on the hill, did you know?"

Aleda gaped at him, then looked at Neil, who lifted one shoulder in a shrug. "There have been some changes while you were away," he said.

When she turned back to Jacob, he said, "At first it seemed a bit strange to us, but after a couple of weeks, we all like it. It's quiet and mysterious. The priest has been kind and he's helping Levi learn the ropes of becoming an altar boy."

Aleda gasped. "Well, I'm speechless!" Her head swung between Jacob and Neil.

"Constable Brennan picks us up," Jacob continued. "It takes two trips to get us all there. The kids love that ride. They've never been in a convertible before."

She turned again to stare at Neil, who was sliding the last bit of popsicle into his mouth. "You had a good time in the Muskokas?" he asked.

"Very relaxing. The time went quickly."

"It seemed to go quickly here, too. We were busy." He glanced at Simeon and Jacob sitting next to him. "But there was also time to think and make decisions. Isn't that right, Jacob?" He nodded in agreement, his mouth also full of orange popsicle.

"I took a little vacation myself," Neil added.

Aleda tilted her head. "Really."

"Nothing like a good, hard two-day paddle in a kayak to clear your head."

"Kayaking."

"I've been a bit confused about the future," he said. "But out there on the bay, it became perfectly clear to me that I can no longer go back to Ireland. I belong here now. Everything I need for the future is right here in Canada."

"Really," Aleda responded, not trusting her voice to say anything more. She rose and turned toward the door.

"Where are you going?" Neil called out.

"At the moment, I'm off to find some wet paper towels," she called over her shoulder.

35
Puppies

The following day, Aleda prepared for her dinner date with Laura and Martin.

"Our summer has taken us in different directions, it seems," Laura commented when they had gathered in the arbour behind her house. "Sadly, Martin returns to Guelph on the weekend."

"Ah, the last supper," Aleda murmured. "We'll miss you Martin." She frowned a little, remembering how Laura had, earlier in the summer, suggested inviting Connie to their dinners. When neither she nor Martin showed much enthusiasm for the idea, it hadn't happened. It would certainly have changed the dynamics of their friendly Friday night dinners. It was wise not to invite her, considering how much grief she caused at the church and in the community, Aleda mused with a tinge of bitterness. Thank goodness that's over, she thought.

"But surely the two of you will continue getting together until I'm back again next spring?" Martin said.

"For sure. You can count on that, but it's true, we will miss you," Laura repeated. Martin looked both pleased and embarrassed to be the focus of so much affection.

To deflect the attention away from himself, he said, "There's something I need to tell you, Aleda ... about Tracker."

Her head jerked up. "Is there still infection in his hoof?"

"No, nothing like that. It cleared up quickly. You'll be getting a bill from Dr. Patel," he grinned.

"Then what?" she demanded.

"Well ..." he began. He seemed hesitant to reveal the whole story too quickly. "In the days when Tracker was a bit under the weather, I'd been letting the puppies out to play and explore. They began to venture farther and farther and that's how I noticed that there was something wrong with Tracker. You know how horses tend to snooze on their feet, but I saw that Tracker was lying down on his side quite a lot during the day. One night, when Buddy had rounded up the puppies, I discovered that the pup Coberta wasn't there. I looked all over and finally checked the barn. The pup was nestled on Tracker's neck and I had to use my considerable charms to get her to return to the house. The next day, when I let the puppies out, Coberta disappeared again. This time I went straight to the barn. Tracker was in a much better mood; the medication prescribed by Dr. Patel had kicked in. Sure enough, there was Coberta standing in front of Tracker, and that old horse was using her long tongue to groom the pup. Since then, they've been inseparable."

"What!" Aleda exploded. "Are you suggesting ...?"

Martin shrugged. "Look at it this way, Aleda. She's given Tracker a new lease on life and, on the bright side, since they seem inseparable, she'll be an outdoor dog." There was a pause in the conversation as she stared at Martin. "Think you could persuade Roy to build a nice insulated doghouse to fit inside the church shed?"

Later, as she crawled into bed, she felt good that the puppy adoption problem was close to being fully resolved. Only one challenge remained for Martin. He told them that Callum, the boy who owned Buddy, had wanted to keep the last puppy, Clifford, so Buddy would not be lonely.

"But," Martin had argued, "it costs a lot of money to feed a dog, maybe fifty dollars a month. If you had two dogs, how much would that be?" The boy had quickly concluded that feeding two dogs would cost a hundred dollars every month, and that *was* a lot of money. "That's when I reminded him," Martin told the women, "that Buddy would never be lonely, because she had Callum, and he was the best friend a dog could have." Martin shrugged. "If I can't find a home for Clifford around Milburn Corners, I'll take him home with me. I've grown quite attached to all the dogs, in fact."

As an act of good faith and concern, he told them, Dr. Patel had agreed to spay Buddy without charging. It all seemed to have worked out. In the morning, she thought sleepily, I'll pay a visit to Roy's workshop and see what he thinks about a doghouse.

It was the first thing she did on Saturday morning. She could hear the whine of a band saw as she approached the shed. She poked her head inside and there was Levi, using a square of sandpaper to smooth out the underside of a piece of curved wood. Roy, at the work table, wearing a paper mask, had just completed what looked like a rounded door. Aleda stood looking in, reluctant to interrupt their work, but when Roy spotted her, he smiled and called out, "Come in. Come in."

"This is certainly a beehive of activity," Aleda said, looking from Levi to Roy, both of whom seemed content to be working together on a project. She spotted a name painted in large bold letters on the side of a small house. Clifford's house.

"Clifford …?" she stuttered, gesturing toward the doghouse.

"Levi here has been wanting a dog, a pet of his very own. His dad returned my car yesterday, so we're off to Martin's farm in a few minutes to see what we can work out." She glanced from the boy to the man and raised her eyebrows. "We thought we'd get a start on a house. This dog will have to have a house no matter where he lives."

"But, surely …" she began, remembering that there were already eight children in the family and that the family was temporarily housed in a three-bedroom townhouse in Owen Sound.

"I think that Levi will take very good care of a pet," Roy said. Aleda nodded hesitantly, and then as if Roy could read the objections forming in her mind, he said, "There may be a bit of a problem until they get that church-house fixed up before winter, so Constable Brennan and Levi worked something out. They decided to help each other with the dog." The boy was looking up at Roy, nodding and eager. "Sometimes Levi will have the dog, and when he can't, the dog will be with Constable Brennan. We talked it over with his parents," Roy told her. "Seems they think it's a good idea, a companion for Levi and the barking would warn them against wild animals. The Constable donated all the materials and paint for the dog house."

Turning to set his hammer and nails on the workbench, Roy said to the waiting boy, "Come on, son. Let's git on up to the farm and see what we can work out with Martin."

She hurried home to get ready for an afternoon excursion to Lion's Head. Neil wanted her to see his new cottage and to show her the renovations to the kitchen and bathroom that were completed while she was away. She ran up the stairs and changed her clothes, but as she was dabbing on some makeup the telephone rang.

"Aleda, so glad you're home."

"Robert! Nice to hear from you. I'm so grateful to you for looking after things at the church while I was away," she gushed.

"It was a pleasure to help you. Don't hesitate to ask anytime, and do take your time getting settled in. That was always Patrice's advice to me, and it is good counsel. It takes time to ease out of vacation mode and back into work."

"Shall do my best. Things turned out okay for you in the end? After that commotion with Connie, I mean?"

There was a brief pause at the other end of the line. "I'm not sure that things are completely settled yet, Aleda. But I'm sure Roy will bring you up to speed when he has a moment." Robert hesitated, then added, "You all set for worship tomorrow, then?"

After thanking Robert again, she stared down at the phone, wondering if she should call Roy. No, she decided. In a few minutes she would be off on a pleasurable jaunt in a red Mustang. She wanted to leave behind her unease about the Connie situation. Besides, she knew, when Roy was ready, he would tell her everything she needed to know. He had always done that in the past and she knew that she could count on him now.

36
Neil's Cottage

IT WAS A GOLDEN END-OF-AUGUST SATURDAY, A DAY CREATED FOR HAPPINESS, BUT, AS she waited for Neil to arrive, the troubles with Connie nagged at her mind. Perhaps she should call Roy, after all. She wandered into her office, picked up a copy of her Sunday sermon, then set it down, fretting about whether it would be possible to set aside her worries for the afternoon.

Since Neil had dropped his small — but important to her — revelation that he was no longer considering a return to Ireland, she had felt a flutter of hope. Was there reason to expect that they might share a future together? Careful now, Aleda, she cautioned herself. She didn't want to have unrealistic hopes. Still, it seemed a good sign that he had called and invited her to see his cottage.

When he arrived to pick her up, he asked, "You okay, Aleda? You look worried or tired." She shrugged, assuring him that she was fine.

As they sped along, the top of the convertible down, she was grateful for the transition, needing the time to pull herself out of the funk that had descended on her since Robert's call. She had hoped that the troubles with Connie had blown over while she was away, but obviously that hadn't happened. Neil, sensing her preoccupation, smiled across at her and suggested a stop at a coffee shop, but she insisted that they keep going.

After the red Mustang crawled up the laneway to the white cottage, Neil turned off the car engine, pulled a house key from his pocket, handed it to her and said, "Be my guest."

She smiled at him, her worries and anxieties about Connie and the troubles at the church fading. She flung open the car door, jumped out and gazed at the cottage. "First impressions are very important," she announced.

"You approve?"

"I definitely approve." He came over and stood beside her. They surveyed the small cottage with its white brick base and steep peaked roof. The front entrance was a double French door, which had been painted navy blue, and the fascia under the peaked roof had an elevated medallion also painted blue to match the doors. To the left of the main part of the cottage was an identical but smaller structure. "How cute is that!" she exclaimed.

"The living area," Neil said, pointing to the larger half, "and the kitchen," directing her attention to the smaller part.

She hurried to the double doors. When they stepped inside, she gasped. "Oh, Neil! I've never seen anything so …"

He laughed. "I'll give you the grand tour," he said, beaming. There were three rooms downstairs: a living area with a large fireplace, the kitchen and a bathroom. "I bought it furnished," he admitted. "The owners moved south. This was their summer home. They were relieved that I wanted the furniture, and I was happy to get it."

She noticed that, while the floors and even the ceilings were lined with wood, the previous owners had painted the walls pale yellow and used a great deal of white through the cottage, giving the small space a sense of light and openness. Neil showed her the renovated kitchen and the upgraded bath, then led her up the stairs to see two bedrooms, a spacious one over the living room and a compact one over the kitchen. "Imagine waking up in the morning and the first thing you see it that," Neil said, his Irish accent strong. He pointed out the deep windows of the master bedroom to the grey-blue expanse of Georgian Bay.

"I love it," she said as they walked back down the stairs. "There are two areas that I especially love," she added.

"Such as?"

"This one," she said, pointing to a pine table and two chairs that sat in front of the kitchen window overlooking the bay, "and this one," she proclaimed, pointing to the soft white sofa which faced the fireplace. She sank down into the couch, patting the seat beside her. "It's a bit like sinking into a giant marshmallow."

He dropped down beside her, leaning back. "I wish it weren't such a warm day," he said. "I'd love to be sitting here in front of a roaring fire."

"That day will come." They sat in silence, turning their heads one way, then the other, gazing at the framed photos of wildflowers on the walls, admiring the blue ceramic mugs hanging from hooks in the open cupboards, looking at the yellow cushions piled onto a stuffed easy chair.

"You remember that day I visited you at Boiler Beach? When I stayed overnight?"

Aleda stiffened. "Of course."

"That was the start of it really. The start of thinking through what I really wanted. After I crawled into that bunk bed at Boiler Beach, I started to think about the few weeks before, when I bought this place. It was such a thrill to sign my name on the ownership papers of this cottage. A dream come true, really. I remember that it was a hot night, that night at Boiler Beach, but I started to imagine myself on a cold, winter night roasting marshmallows in this fireplace, snug and safe, while snow swirled in from Georgian Bay."

Aleda stared up at him. "Really."

"I was imagining a woman I loved sharing this time and space with me. I had almost drifted off to sleep when my eyes popped open. I realized then and there that the woman I imagined beside me was not Mary Bridgette. She would find this place cold and desolate and lonely. The woman I imagined sharing this space with me was curled up across from me on the next bunk bed."

"But ..." she stammered, feeling a blush rise into her cheeks, "the next morning we had that conversation at breakfast. You pointed out to me that we have too many differences to overcome." She heard the bitterness in her own voice.

"I did." He nodded solemnly. "I did say that, and the differences have not gone away. But what I forgot, Aleda, are the many things we have in common, the things that will keep us together."

He turned away from her, staring into the empty fireplace, but when he turned again to look at her, he could see that she was frowning a little. He couldn't tell whether she was upset with him or thinking deeply about something.

"I've been remembering too," she said. "I've been thinking about something that my friend, Regina Davis, said to me, about going to battle for something I wanted. And I'm also remembering that time ..." She stopped talking for a moment, thinking that she might begin to cry "... that time when you knelt in front of Simeon's cot and made a solemn promise to look after him. I still remember what you said." She looked up into his face. "You said, 'I am a man of honour, a man of my word. If you give me permission to take the child to a hospital to get help, I give you my solemn word that I will do everything in my power to help him become strong again. I will treat him as if he were my own family. You can count on me.'"

"That's what I said? I said all that?"

"That and more, I believe," she smiled. "So, I have a question to ask."

"What's that, Aleda?"

"Neil Brennan, man of honour, man of your word, will you give me your solemn word that you and I will work together to make a happy life together? Will you marry me?"

They were preparing to leave when Neil said, "I can't help but think that there is something wrong, Aleda. You've been so happy and relaxed all afternoon, but the minute I suggested we leave, you got that worried expression on your face."

"Can't pull anything over on you," she joked, but then, suddenly serious, she added, "There's a problem at the church, but I'm afraid I can't talk about it. Not at this time, anyway. You warned me though … about Connie."

"Okay. I understand."

"I suppose … really, when I think of it, you and I will always have parts of our lives that we can't share with each other. Confidentiality is just part of my work and yours."

He had been gathering up the remains of their lunch and wiping clean the mugs they had used. He turned to her and drew her toward him. As they stood in the kitchen, their arms wrapped around each other, he kissed the top of her head, then lifted her chin and looked into her eyes. "We'll make this work, Aleda. I know we will."

37

Laura Visits Roy

On Sunday, Roy was despondent. He knew that he needed to speak to Aleda about Connie's complaint, but it worried him that he did not have a clear plan about how to proceed. When, on Sunday morning, Aleda announced the scheduled meeting with the elders for Tuesday night, he sighed in relief. Perhaps the other elders would have an idea of what to do.

After church, he was standing at the kitchen stove, stirring a pot of chicken noodle soup, when the phone rang.

"Laura! This is a surprise." Other than chatting from time to time at the mailbox, they had had little interaction since she moved back into Milburn Corners and settled into her parent's former home.

"Are you busy after lunch?" she inquired. Laura sounded different somehow — hushed, breathless, worried. "I have something that I'd like to talk over."

Laura and Roy sat together on a long bench in the garden. "Aleda told me about your garden rooms," she said, "but honestly, I had no idea that they were so beautiful. You've done an amazing job."

Roy dipped his head in acknowledgement. "It's one of the best things in my life," he told her. "I love getting outside, making order and creating bands of colour. That's how I think of them. Like a rainbow."

For a few minutes they talked about plants and shrubs, but then Laura turned to face him. "You must wonder why I've come."

"I am wondering."

"I'm sure you know that Aleda, Martin and I have become good friends over the past few months. We get together for dinner every Friday night, or as often as we can manage."

"Aleda did mention that."

"At the beginning of the summer, I met Connie," Laura gestured diagonally toward the house across from the corner store. "She seemed friendly and young. I thought maybe she could be invited to our Friday night dinners, so I suggested it to Aleda and Martin. But they didn't pick up on it, so I let it drop. Now I'm glad I didn't insist. I hear from the village gossip that there has been some tension around Connie at the church."

"That's true," Roy admitted.

"I'm sorry if that will cause trouble for Aleda. I really am. She's one of the best friends I've ever had and I don't want this to lead to some hurtful experiences."

"I'm afraid it is a little late for that. Things have already gone too far."

Laura's head swung around and she stared at Roy. "What do you mean?"

Roy explained about the letter of complaint that Connie had submitted, but didn't give many details. "I don't want to say too much," he added. "I want things to stay confidential."

"That's what I've come about, really," Laura said, her voice tight, her breathing shallow. "I have something confidential to tell you. It was always a tension when I was teaching. When do you stay silent and when do you tell? The bottom line for us at school was always this: will someone be terribly hurt if I stay silent?"

Roy gazed over at her. Something was deeply troubling her, but he sat and waited.

"A couple of weeks ago, when we usually get together, Aleda was still up at her lodge and Martin had gone into Guelph for the weekend. I thought, what the heck, why don't I invite Connie up for dinner? She was eager to come. I think she finds village life a little quiet and lonely. We found we had quite a lot in common, although I'm considerably older than her. We both hate to cook," Laura laughed, "and we both have — in my case, had — challenging careers. She grew up in a small town north of Toronto and as a teen some of her social life gravitated toward the city, so we had a lot of shared experiences — going to the Toronto Film Festival and the Exhibition and the ROM. We're both Blue Jays fans, too. Then, somehow, we got talking about our families."

Laura took a deep breath and Roy glanced over at her. She was staring into the pool at the swimming koi and gold fish. "At first it was the normal stuff … sibling rivalry and so on, but then we got talking about our fathers. I confess that I told her of the difficulties I had with my father, how respected and honoured and loved he was as the community doctor, but at home he had been moody and volatile at times. It created such a problem for me that I went into therapy while I was at University."

Laura paused and rubbed her hands together in an absent-minded way. "That's when she told me everything. She virtually exploded. 'Ha!' she said. 'Talk about volatile.' What she told the church people here in Milburn Corners was true — her father was a pastor in a small independent church and, although I'm not a religious person, it sounded to me as if it was a very conservative and traditional church. No lipstick, no dancing, no women working outside the homes. Men were definitely the head of the household and ruled the roost. Connie internalized many of the beliefs and standards of her father," Laura said. "She really does seem to believe in a literal interpretation of the Bible and that women should not be leaders in any way in the church. But this is where things got weird."

Roy shifted on the bench to look at Laura as she continued. "She told me that her father was a disciplinarian and that he took Connie or one of her three brothers out to the back kitchen and beat them almost every night." Laura shuddered and Roy shook his head in disbelief.

"The mother never tried to stop him?" Roy inquired. "Teachers never noticed bruises?"

"Apparently, they attended a small private school run by the same church and the teachers were allowed to use corporal punishment too, although she said it was never as harsh as they received at home. This went on for years and years, all through her childhood and early teens, but it seemed to get worse as the kids got older. One day, when her oldest brother was fifteen and the father started to beat him for some misdemeanour, the brother fought back, knocked his father down and punched out his two front teeth."

"Oh, my," Roy breathed, wondering where this story would lead.

"Her brother ran away, Connie said, and for days they tiptoed around the house, avoiding their father as much as possible. Then the police were at the door. They took her father in for questioning and next thing you know he was behind bars, awaiting trial. The police interviewed all the children separately, and the wife. Connie never found out what her mother said, but the stories told by each of the four children were so identical and so believable that her father was charged with abuse causing bodily harm and was sentenced to time in the old Don Jail in Toronto. I'm not sure how long the sentence was. She didn't tell me that."

"That's a horrible story," Roy said. "One that would leave a person scarred in more ways than one."

"You haven't heard the worst part yet," Laura said. Roy stared at her, his mouth open. "At the trial, the prosecutor pushed and pushed. He tried to get at the reason why a pastor of a church would behave in such a despicable way. He finally got the man to confess what the children had told the police, what they had come to understand as they got older. Their father only beat them at bedtime. It seems that he couldn't get an erection without violence. He used the beatings in order to become sexually aroused."

With the exception of two birds chirping in the lilac tree and the sound of the splashing waterfall, there was silence in Roy's garden, and when Laura looked over at him, he had a look of profound sorrow on his face. "I don't understand such evil," he said finally.

Laura shrugged a little. "I'm not a religious person, but I suppose there is the real possibility of evil in every religion. People are people," she said. "I hope you don't mind that I told you. I felt I had to, because it seems as if Connie really has a personal vendetta against Aleda and Robert. I really don't totally understand this, but there is a seething anger under her gentle demeanor. I want you to keep this confidential, Roy, but I thought that perhaps it might help in working things through."

Roy nodded and stirred. "Certainly not the most pleasant news I've ever heard," he said. "And I'm not sure how to proceed with the letter of complaint, but it does help a little to understand that someone who has been hurt so badly might want to hurt others."

When Laura stood up to leave, Roy also rose. They walked slowly through the path between the garage and Roy's house. They stood together for a moment, staring at a white English climbing rose that clung to a trellis at the back door. "There's always hope," Roy said at last, staring at the rose. "I thought last year that this rose was a goner. But I gave it a little fertilizer, a little water, some mulch and a bit of sweet talk. Look at it now." He reached out to caress a bloom. "There's a chance for everything to grow and start again."

Laura nodded and waited, wondering what was going through Roy's mind.

"We all need redeeming," he declared.

Laura sighed. "Sorry, Roy. I'm not really a religious person. I told you that."

"You don't have to be a particular kind of religious person to see that a fresh start is always a gift."

38
Green Peas

As Aleda was about to settle down in her office on Monday morning, she heard a knock on the front door.

"What a wonderful surprise!" she exclaimed sincerely when she saw Dorrie there. It had been a few days since she had seen Dorrie and it was, Aleda believed, brave of her to venture off the farm.

"Can you use some fresh green peas? Burt planted a second crop and we have far more than we need."

"Come in. Of course! I'll gladly accept. I haven't shelled peas in years," she said, looking down at the mound of green pods in Dorrie's basket.

"I could give you a hand, if you like," she offered.

"Oh!" Aleda exclaimed. "Thank you!" She waved her into the porch. "Come, sit down and I'll get some bowls."

For an hour, both women sat side by side in the screened front porch performing the methodical task of shelling peas: snap, open, push the peas out, discard the shell.

"Have you ever wondered how factories do this? Shell peas, then sell them back to us so cheaply, two or three dollars a bag?" Aleda asked.

Dorrie smiled. "Yes, how do they do that?"

"And where *are* these mysterious pea-processing factories? I'm forty-two years old and I've never seen one." It seemed to Aleda that their side-by-side conversation, focusing on the peas instead of each other, was comforting to Dorrie. She looked more relaxed, even smiled a little from time to time.

When the basket was empty and they had a few cups of fresh green peas rolling around in the bottom of their bowls, Dorrie stood, saying that she needed to get home to the puppy. At the door she smiled and said, "I'll be able to put another check in my little book. I'm up to twelve now. Halfway there.

People have been so good to me, dropping in and bringing me cinnamon buns and butter tarts. Martin came over yesterday with a new collar for the puppy, and Roy brought up a bouquet of gladiolas."

"Wonderful! That's simply wonderful," Aleda replied, thinking of a conversation she had with Rose. They had bumped into each other outside the store.

"I'm just back from visiting Dorrie," Rose told her. "She seems so much happier and that frisky pup seems to delight her."

"I'm glad that you're taking time to do that, Rose. Dorrie was worried that it would be difficult for her to connect again with people in the community. The more congenial visits she experiences, I believe, the more she will feel ready to fully enter community life again."

Rose nodded, her face solemn. "We're trying to make amends," she said.

Aleda looked at her in surprise.

"We've been talking a bit," Rose confided. "The women from the Guild and even some of the men in the village. That business with Grace's underwear and my roses and the painted bench. We're all feeling a bit ashamed of ourselves. We jumped to conclusions about the teenagers, pointing a finger when we had no proof whatsoever. It blinded us, kept us from recognizing that one of our own was suffering shock and needed help."

Aleda nodded. "I understand perfectly. It happens," she murmured, remembering that even she had fallen into the trap of wondering if Roy had painted the bench orange as a belligerent attestation to his Protestant loyalties. "We all live and learn. Now all we can do is learn from our mistakes. Thank goodness we believe in a God of infinite forgiveness."

"So true, so true," Rose replied.

Church people — including Roy — accepted the fact that each new year started on the first day of January, and they also understood that the liturgical year started with the season of Advent in late November or early December. The "functional" church year, on the other hand — the time of meetings, Sunday school, Women's Guild and special events — followed the school year from September through June. For this reason, it had been a long-standing custom for the elders of Milburn Community Church to hold an official meeting in the last week of August. It was a way to prepare themselves and the church for the year that lay ahead.

Like him, Aleda would be preparing for the elder's meeting on Tuesday night. Roy knew he could no longer put off having a serious conversation with Aleda about Connie's letter. It would have to be discussed at the meeting, so he owed it to Aleda to show it to her first.

Throughout the morning, he kept watch on Aleda's house. When he saw Dorrie's car pull away and turn up the hill toward her farm, he tugged on his rubber boots and started up the knoll. The thought of telling Aleda about Connie's letter filled him with anxiety and uncertainty, but he knew he had to do it. It was clear that Connie had done her homework. He could see that she had followed the appropriate procedure for filing a complaint against a minister within the denomination.

Earlier, when he had shown the letter to Rose, she said, "This could be very hurtful, not only to Aleda but to our church and community, too." He nodded in agreement. Certain phrases from the letter stuck in his mind: "women are unsuited to ministry since there is no biblical precedent; if Jesus had intended for women to be in leadership in the church, he would have had female disciples."

There was also the paragraph about Robert being "excessively libertarian" and leading people astray. But perhaps the most surprising and upsetting paragraph was the accusation that Aleda interfered in the Jacobi case. It was, Connie claimed, an issue that belonged with the Child and Family Services and the police. The minister, she had written, had been meddlesome, intervening with the family, even interfering with the housing process by offering the parsonage for the family, something that had not even been discussed through proper channels.

Rose had asked, "If Aleda doesn't yet know about this letter and if it will just stir up hurt and anger, is it not possible for those of us who are elders to have a private meeting and deal with it?"

"Oh, no!" Roy was adamant. "Aleda chairs our meetings, so it's quite impossible to have a private get-together. That's just not the way things work. Besides, it's not a good thing to have a secret, especially one kept from a minister who we love and respect."

Rose nodded, pursed her lips and slid her reading glasses into a case. Roy was right, of course. It was not wise or good to keep secrets from Aleda. On the other hand, Rose reflected on her secret love affair that only Aleda, Laura and Martin knew about. Was telling the truth sometimes more harmful than keeping a secret?

After Rose left, Roy turned back to his desk and pulled out the church's *Book of Forms*. He flipped to the index, looking for "complaints," and studied the recommended process. Connie had somehow found out how to do this properly. It was only when he read Section 331 that he felt a glimmer of hope. It clearly stated that he must pass along the complaint to the presbytery for study and action *unless* the minister, elders and the complainant could meet and find a resolution of the matter.

Section 331 had seemed like a gift, offering a way forward. Could he bring Connie and Aleda together with the other elders? Could they persuade Connie to withdraw her complaint? Was that even possible? Connie seemed to be a very determined young woman.

Aleda heard a knock on the front porch door.

"Roy! What's up?"

"I need a word before the meeting tomorrow night, Aleda."

"Sure. Come on in. I've been kinda expecting you."

Seated at the kitchen table, Roy folded his hands and rested them against the edge of the table. "This bit of trouble with Connie ..." he began, "it's been on my mind and I'd like to get it settled."

"Oh, me too! Believe me, I hate something like this brewing in our church life." They sat in silence. Aleda waited, knowing that when he was ready, Roy would tell her what was on his mind.

"She's written a letter of complaint, you see."

Aleda felt her stomach clench. "A letter? I knew that she had conversations with people about her concerns, but writing a letter seems to formalize things." She was silent for a moment. "What's in the letter, Roy?"

"I've made a copy. Don't want any surprises for you in front of the other elders."

"Oh, Roy," she moaned, "I just wish this would go away."

Roy leaned forward. "Listen to me, Aleda. Now you just listen to me very carefully. We have to receive this letter tomorrow night, but I have a plan about how to deal with this situation. Yes, I have a plan."

39

Meetings

THE MEETING WITH THE ELDERS WAS NOT SCHEDULED UNTIL EIGHT THIRTY — LATE BY city standards, normal for farming communities, where cows had to be milked and straw had to be baled before the dew fell.

It was a difficult meeting for everyone. Aleda felt attacked and defensive as Connie's complaints were read. When Roy suggested to the other elders his tentative plan for resolving the tension, they were silent and perplexed. Finally, someone said, "Well, I'm sorry this is disturbing our peaceful church and upsetting our minister, but I have a summer crop to get off and that is demanding all my attention these days."

"Understand completely," Roy murmured.

In the end, Roy had suggested that they arrange a meeting as quickly as possible with Connie, himself and Aleda. When he asked the elders to appoint a representative from their group, all eyes turned to Rose.

Aleda had a restless, almost sleepless night. She hated conflict. Well, who likes it? she bemoaned. Maybe there are a few people who enjoy a good fight, but she believed most people would prefer a peaceful and smooth existence.

What on earth has happened to my questing for happiness? she demanded of herself. What happened to that moment of realizing that the little yellow flowers on Boiler Beach always lean toward the light? What happened to my resolve to make the bread of happiness, the bread of the new day?

Aleda had felt an unshakable unease ever since Robert's phone call on Saturday. How could she experience any peace of mind while this tension about Connie was hanging over her head?

When Thursday arrived, the day of their scheduled meeting with Connie, they were all nervous, in their own way. Rose, Roy and Aleda arrived early and waited together until Connie walked in. She came into the church hall meeting room, her back tall and straight, nodded to each person and sat down in the chair which Roy offered.

"Thank you for agreeing to come. It's important to have conversations about the things that are bothering us," he said.

"I haven't anything more to add," Connie said. "I believe I expressed my concerns and expectations clearly in my letter."

"You did," Roy nodded. "Now, if I may ... since we're all believers, I'd like to start with a word of prayer." Roy folded his hands on the edge of the table, bowed his head and prayed for wisdom and discernment. When the prayer was over, he straightened the note paper in front of him and laid his pen diagonally across the pad. He didn't intend to take notes, he told Aleda and Rose before Connie arrived, but he thought it made him look more official to have the note pad.

"As you know, Connie, I am an elder here at Milburn Community Church and act as the clerk of session. Rose, here, is also an elder and she has been chosen by the rest of the elders to represent them at this meeting. Aleda is here, of course, because the matters in the letter concern her — directly or indirectly. I invite all of you to speak openly and respectfully to each other."

Connie glanced at Aleda but seemed to show no malice in the look. She merely nodded.

Roy cleared his throat. "I am going to ask you to withdraw this letter, Connie, but I'd like to speak to the three points you made in your letter. The first point. You say that you'd like your letter passed on to the presbytery level for consideration and action, but your first objection is to the ordination of women. You don't name Aleda directly, but since you name our church, I'm assuming that you have both a general and a specific objection to women in ministry."

"I certainly do. I explained that clearly in writing."

"You did. The problem is ... we went down that path in our denomination decades ago. There was much debate across the country, and then it was decided that women would and should be ordained as ministers of Word and Sacrament. I'm afraid that the presbytery will simply not even consider an appeal about the ordination of women. Do you know," Roy said leaning slightly toward Connie, "that a student minister will not be accepted in our denomination if he does not agree with ordaining women? No one at the presbytery will agree with you on this point."

"Grace does. She told me so herself." Connie's head lifted and her chin jutted forward.

"Yes … well …" Roy couldn't say what he was thinking. Grace might have some local clout because of her tasty bran muffins and butter tarts, but at the presbytery level she had zero influence.

"Your second point, the claim against Robert being too liberal." All three women focused on Roy as he continued in his unruffled manner. "The thing is, Connie, no one at the presbytery would understand that at all. Robert is minister emeritus at one of the biggest churches in our country. He's been a fine churchman, a model minister. He was elected as the Moderator of our General Assembly and he is loved and respected. He's not considered liberal in our denomination at all. Besides," Roy added, "you say in the letter that you are new to our village and also to our church. That makes you, in our terminology, an adherent, not an official member. The presbytery is apt to dismiss your complaint on —"

"This will not stop me from asking to have the letter sent on," Connie interrupted, maintaining her composure. "If I were a member of a political party — the Conservative party, for instance," she argued, "and I saw something wrong in the Liberal party, I would have every right to protest and object, even though I'm not a card-carrying member of that party. Wrong is wrong and needs to be named."

"But surely, Connie," Roy continued in his reasonable voice, "on your third point, if you consider that Aleda interfered in the Jacobi case, you should take this concern to the head of Bruce Grey Child and Family Services and not the presbytery."

Aleda spoke for the first time. "Connie, I want to assure you that I had no intention of interfering with the Jacobi family. I was merely trying to help out in a difficult situation." What she was thinking, but couldn't say, was that she had helped out on the personal invitation of a police officer and assisted mainly because Neil thought that Phillip from the Child and Family Services was both inexperienced and ineffectual.

"I've chosen to send the letter to the presbytery. I believe that's the best route," Connie insisted stubbornly.

Roy glanced over at Aleda. She was looking down, biting her bottom lip. Rose also looked uneasy. All three understood that things were not going well.

Later, Roy told Aleda and Rose that it was at that moment that he said a silent prayer. "Forgive me, God, for this little white lie I'm about to tell. You know very well that I have no cousins."

"Connie," Roy said, his voice soft and low, "I want to ask you again to withdraw your letter. I'm asking you to lodge your complaint about interference in the Jacobi case with your supervisor at Child and Family Services. I have a cousin, you see. Lives in Toronto. He's quite the guy. Intense, that's the best way to describe him. He's an expert on prisons, especially old historic prisons. Not only does he know about the actual buildings, but he has researched the histories of hundreds of the inmates who spent time there." Roy paused and rearranged the pen lying on top of the note pad. Aleda stared at him, then flashed a look toward Connie. If it was possible, it seemed that Connie had straightened her back even more, leaning out from the wooden chair.

"He was telling me about the Don Jail," Roy said, but before he could continue, Connie slapped her hands on the table. As all heads swung toward her, she seemed to shrink in front of their eyes. Her back curved and her head drooped forward, her shoulders slumping, her hair falling across her pale face.

"Then you know," she said. "You know about my father."

"I do," Roy said truthfully while Aleda and Rose stared at him, frowning. They had no idea what was going on.

"And you know why I'm here ... working in the Bruce Grey office. You know that I'm on probation. Oh, there was no problem with getting a Master of Social Work," she said, bitterness in her voice, "but I've had anger management problems all along the way. This is my last chance, they told me. Make it work or I lose my job. There's no way I can take this grievance to my boss. He would have zero tolerance for this. You knew this all along, didn't you?" she demanded of Aleda, Rose and Roy, her voice rising. All three shook their heads.

"I honestly did not know that," Roy said quietly. "I hope that you are getting —" but Connie interrupted him again.

"Oh yes, therapy. You can bet your bottom dollar that a social work agency has a good benefits package. Now, if you'll excuse me, I'd like that letter back." She extended her hand toward Roy and he slowly reached into his hip pocket and pulled out the letter. She ripped it sharply in two, then across the other way. She set the torn letter pieces in the middle of the table, stood up very erectly and strode out of the room.

"Should we go after ..."

"I think she needs a little time and space."

40
Bread

Aleda, at first, opted to keep her copy of the letter. It would, she told Rose and Roy, keep her humble. But later, when she returned to the attic to retrieve the winter clothes she had packed away to make room for the Jacobi family, she found it lying on top of her treasures. I've been humbled enough, she told herself.

Taking the letter downstairs to the kitchen, she picked up the packet of matches that she used to light her dinner candle and burned the letter in the kitchen sink. She looked out the kitchen window where she could glimpse the corner of Roy's garden. "Kudos, Roy. Thanks again, faithful friend."

Her mother's brown mixing bowl sat on the kitchen counter. She had left it there the previous night, when she remembered the promise that she had made to herself on vacation. Before returning to her office, she would start her bread.

She moved to the cupboard and set ingredients on the counter. She dissolved yeast in a little warm sugar water. She measured flour, then melted some butter in warm milk and mixed everything together. She began the slow rhythmic task of kneading and turning, sprinkling flour on the counter.

Throughout the morning, she left her office, from time to time, to peek under the tea towel that covered the mysterious lump. By late morning she had baked two crusty nut-brown loaves, which sat on the kitchen counter, shimmering with a buttery glaze. A flood of well-being flowed through her and, for a moment, she thought that she might cry, so moved was she by the fragrance and appearance of the bread and her new resolve to lean toward happiness, even when things were not going well. The image of the tiny yellow flowers on Boiler Beach flashed through her mind.

Fresh bread seemed such a gift; it was a pity to enjoy it alone. She felt a sudden urge to share a loaf of bread, and she knew exactly where she would go.

She arrived in his driveway with the still-warm loaf wrapped in a clean tea towel and tucked under her arm. "Roy! Roy!" she called as she wandered down the path between his workshop and the house. She spotted him sitting in one of the "rooms" of his garden — the blue room, the room that reminded her of Lake Huron with its variations of azure, indigo, cornflower, even a robin's egg blue and a grey Prussian-blue that often appeared on rainy windy days.

When he heard her calling, he rose to his feet and declared, "What a nice surprise, Aleda!"

He led her over to the blue flower bed and they stood side by side as he told her the names of some of the flowers. She realized that she had a lot to learn about flowers, and was reminded of Neil's interest in wildflowers and how he had named them for her at Boiler Beach. How is it, she wondered, as she gazed at the swath of blue, that the two men who are so important in my life share a love of flowers? Beauty, she concluded. Beauty and mystery. They both appreciate beauty and mystery. And what can be more mysterious than a plant that seems dead in winter but pokes its head above ground to promise beauty in the spring?

Roy was pleased to receive her gift of warm bread. "You made this yourself? Aren't you the clever one!"

"Really, it wasn't so difficult," she laughed. "The yeast did all the work."

They sat on the blue bench in silence, content to enjoy the beauty of his garden, the serenity of the day.

"I can't help but think of the fall now. Do you, Roy? It's been a wonderful summer, but it always seems that autumn starts when school begins in September."

"I know what you mean. Things seem to change in September." He was silent for a moment, then added, "I don't know why I said that … that things seem to change in September. Things change all the time. This garden is always changing. Our lives …" he paused, thinking of Levi, his eyesight, the troubles with Connie. "Even our ideas. They're always changing, too." Was this the time to tell Aleda that he no longer saw a need for the Orange Lodge to continue? That he had come to realize something simple but important … that Protestants and Roman Catholics were different but both important and valued expressions of the Christian faith?

"There's no doubt about it," she nodded in agreement. "Change is the one constant we can count on." Was this the time to tell him of her intention to get married? Was this the time to tell Roy about her struggle to define happiness and how she had become convinced that Neil Brennan was an important element in a happy future for her?

"Roy," she said, summoning all her courage, "there's something I need to ask you."

"What's on your mind?"

"Well, you see ..." She felt suddenly unsure about how to proceed. She swallowed and started again. "Well, you see, I've been hanging out with ... well, dating really ..." Her voice cracked.

"With that nice Constable Brennan, you mean?"

She laughed. "Nothing escapes your attention, Roy." They lapsed into silence. "It's just that I have a question."

"Well, I'm waiting to hear it."

"Okay, then. Do you think ... would it be overlooked ... how would people around here respond to ..."

"To what?" he asked.

All right, she thought grimly. He's going to make me say it. "If I got married," she blurted in a rush. He looked at her, nodding, until she demanded, "What do you think, Roy? Would it be acceptable? Him being a Catholic and me ..." Her voice trailed off and still Roy did not speak. She waited, knowing that with Roy there was no other approach but to wait.

He gazed into the pond, his hands folded, his brow creased. He tilted his head and seemed intent in following the path of the fish. "Well, Aleda," he said at last, "I reckon it's your own business. You have a lot of common sense and we would trust your judgement on a serious thing like marriage. We've all seen that constable of yours in action. Catholic or Anglican or Presbyterian, it doesn't much matter. We all recognize a good man when we see one. You need to do what you think is right, Aleda, and what will make you happy."

She stole a look at him, then dabbed at her eyes, determined not to break down beside the stoic, faithful man who had been so good to her.

"You've been a good minister to us," he continued. "More than good. You've been very involved in our lives. You care about what goes on around here. We all know that about you. We want as much happiness for you as you want for us."

They sat in silence for a few moments. "I'll always think of you as our minister," Roy confessed, "but to tell you the truth, Aleda, I think of you more like a daughter. Me and the wife never had children, which was a great sorrow in our life, but I think I've managed to help out a lot of young folks along the way."

"Oh, you have, you have," she enthused. "I can think of Dwayne and now Levi …"

He nodded. "I'm getting on in years, but there's one more thing I'd like to do. It would make me the happiest man on earth."

She looked at him intently. "What, Roy? What would make you happy?"

He looked a little self-conscious and uncertain. "I know you're a modern woman and you don't need any giving away, but it would make me so happy if I could act as your father and walk you down the aisle to your new husband."

Forget the decorum, Aleda decided in an instant. Tears rolled down her cheeks and she began to sob.

"Did I say something wrong, Aleda?" he asked in alarm.

"What you said was perfect, Roy, absolutely perfect," she assured him between sniffles.

Aleda had spent the summer contemplating, and sometimes brooding over, the meaning of happiness. She still didn't have the complete answer. Perhaps she never would. But she did understand that somehow happiness was tied up with love and laughter, with courage and compassion and commitment. Happiness crept up on you in times of transformation and wafted into the spaces of life when God's presence seemed touchable. In all these moments, she had felt truly blessed. Perhaps, after all, it was enough.

She reached across the loaf of still-warm bread and squeezed Roy's hand. "What are we waiting for?" she demanded. "You got a sharp knife and some butter?"

Aleda's Bread

Prep and kneading time: 15 minutes
Rising time: about 1 ½ hours, then on the second rise, about 1 hour
Needed: large mixing bowl, small pot, 2 greased 8" x 4" (1.5 L) bread pans; mixer with a dough hook (optional)
Cooking time: 30 minutes in 400° oven
Makes: 2 loaves

1 tsp	sugar	5 mL
1 cup	warm water	250 mL
1 tbsp	active dry yeast	15 mL
1 cup	milk	250 mL
2 tbsp	sugar	30 mL
2 tbsp	butter	30 mL
1 tsp	salt	5 mL
5 cups	all-purpose flour (approx.)	1.25 L
	1 egg yolk	
1 tbsp	water	15 mL

1. In large bowl, dissolve sugar in warm water. Sprinkle yeast on top and set aside.
2. Over medium heat, mix milk, sugar, butter and salt. Stir until sugar is dissolved and butter is melted.
3. Stir the sugar-yeast water, add to the warm milk mixture, then beat in 3 cups flour. (If using a mixer, let the mixer do this.)
4. Turn dough onto lightly floured surface and knead for 10 minutes until smooth and elastic, adding additional flour when the dough becomes sticky.
5. Clean the large bowl and grease it. Set the dough in the bowl and turn it around to grease the surface. Cover with a clean tea towel and let rise in a draft-free place for about 1 ½ hours or until doubled in size.
6. Turn out dough on counter, punch down and divide in two with a sharp knife. Shape into two loaves and set each in a greased bread pan. Cover and let rise until doubled in size (about 1 hour).
7. Whisk egg yolk with water and brush on loaves. Bake for 30 minutes in 400° oven.

For a shiny top, brush baked bread with melted butter or margarine.

Grace's Butter Tarts

Prep time: 25-30 minutes
Needed: bowl for mixing pastry, pastry blender, muffin tin, measuring cup, small bowl or measuring cup for filling
Baking time: 15-20 minutes in 375° oven or until golden brown
Makes: 12 tarts

Pastry

1 ½ cups	flour	375 mL
¼ tsp	salt	1 mL
¼ cup	cold butter	50 mL
¼ cup	shortening	50 mL
	1 egg yolk	
1 tsp	vinegar	5 mL
	ice water	

Filling

½ cup	brown sugar	125 mL
½ cup	corn syrup	125 mL
	1 egg	
2 tbsp	soft butter	30 mL
1 tsp	vanilla	5 mL
1 tsp	vinegar	5 mL
	Pinch salt	

About ¼ cup of some or all of these: raisins, walnuts or pecans, shredded coconut

1. To make the pastry, combine flour with salt.
2. Using a pastry blender, cut in the butter and shortening until the mixture looks like small peas.
3. Using a measuring cup, beat together egg yolk and vinegar, then fill to the ⅓ cup line with ice water. Stir and add to the flour mixture, gathering up into a ball of dough.
4. Chill, if possible, for up to an hour.
5. Roll out pastry on lightly floured surface and use a 4-inch (10 cm) cookie cutter to cut out 12 circles. Press gently into muffin tins.
6. To make the filling, beat together all the filling ingredients listed above.
7. In the bottom of each pastry shell, add a pinch of raisins, nuts and/or coconut as desired.
8. Pour filling into tart shells until three-quarters full.
9. Bake for 15-20 minutes in a 375° oven or until puffed and golden brown.

About the author:

Dorothy Brown Henderson lives in Exeter, Ontario, with her husband, John. Henderson has enjoyed a variety of careers: music teacher, mental health worker, writer, Christian educator, and most recently, minister of Caven Presbyterian Church in Exeter, Ontario.

Henderson holds an ARCT in piano (University of Toronto), a BA in Religious Studies (University of Waterloo), an MA in Religion and Culture (Wilfred Laurier University), and a MA in Religious Education (University of Toronto) as well as a three-year diploma in Christian Education from Ewart College (Toronto). In 2006, Henderson received the *Educator of the Year* award from the Association of Presbyterian Church Educators.

Now retired, Henderson enjoys spending time with her three grown children and their spouses, and her three grandchildren, especially at the family cottage on Lake Huron. She also enjoys writing, reading, cooking, running community culinary camps for children, growing an ever-increasing garden, saving seeds, and community activities.

Besides *Happy Are Those*, Henderson is also the author of *The Season for Strawberries* (2017) and a cookbook *Loving it Local: Preparing Delicious Fresh Local Food* (2014).

55045577R00116

Made in the USA
Middletown, DE
14 July 2019